Tootsie Barron was born in North Jersey, Jersey City, and she now calls South Jersey (just outside of "The Queen," Atlantic City) her home. She has two grown-up children and is widowed. Since her beloved papillon, Wiseguy, crossed over the rainbow bridge, she lives in a world of mostly silence and her words. When she needs a break from them, she closes her eyes and remembers everything good. "As always, I wish you all that Heaven allows."

This book is dedicated to

Dr. Monte E. Barron O.D., the man I will love, "In Foreverland."

Tootsie Barron

S UGAR P APER

Sugar Paper

Copyright © 2023 by Tootsie Barron. All rights reserved.

No part of this publication may be reproduced, stored in a retrieval system or transmitted in any way by any means, electronic, mechanical, photocopy, recording or otherwise without the prior permission of the author except as provided by USA copyright law.

The opinions expressed by the author are not necessarily those of URLink Print and Media.

1603 Capitol Ave., Suite 310 Cheyenne, Wyoming USA 82001
1-888-980-6523 | admin@urlinkpublishing.com

URLink Print and Media is committed to excellence in the publishing industry.

Book design copyright © 2023 by URLink Print and Media. All rights reserved.

Published in the United States of America

Library of Congress Control Number: 2023914331
ISBN 978-1-68486-484-3 (Paperback)
ISBN 978-1-68486-487-4 (Hardback)
ISBN 978-1-68486-490-4 (Digital)

19.07.23

The US Review of Books

by Jordana Landsman

"'Don't you ever put me in harm's way again. Remember, I too have a godfather.'"

Uncle is always there for Kiki. As doting godfather to her child and a nearly omniscient, problem-solving presence when her no-good husband gets into scrapes, Uncle is always one step ahead, a trusted fixer and protector who treats Kiki (his "princess") like a precious commodity and an infallible superheroine. If Kiki wonders why she is worthy of such timeless devotion, she is patient and compliant. She allows the course of her life to be set and guided in a 1960s environment of gamblers, bookmakers, and organized crime that connects two Jewish and Catholic friends across generations, ultimately empowering Kiki in ways she and her male-dominated society never expected.

There is a mystery here, a suspenseful story whose ending is dangled in a tantalizing fashion. Likewise, history is told through the lens of American war, sports, ethnic subcultures, and crime. At the core, however, this is a character story of individuals and their choices to love and protect their own while defining their own paths of loyalty and earning, even if that places them outside the law. In this sense, the characterizations read as both fresh and familiar.

Kiki's tough talk and willingness to step up to perform as asked, contrasted with her subordinate place in a male-dominated culture, are reminiscent of other familiar organized crime matriarchs and daughters, from HBO's Carmella and

Meadow Soprano to the movie *The Kitchen* and even back to Mario Puzo's 1965 epic maternal powerhouse, Lucia Santa, in *The Fortunate Pilgrim*. Uncle likewise evokes the vision, power, and connections of such Jewish figures in history as Meyer Lansky and Bugsy Siegel. All told, the foundation of Uncle's love and guidance propel Kiki toward a future bright with shattered glass ceilings and a road that she, not her patriarchy, defines on her own terms.

Hollywood Book Reviews

by Philip Zozzaro

Kiki Fontana receives a phone call hinting of a raid on the family business. She is alarmed, but knows the tip carries credibility. Her husband and father-in law are rounded up in a raid, but Kiki remains resolute in protecting her small family. Her husband, Bobby, is smart but has become increasingly involved in his family's business. Kiki is no babe in the woods, she learns that the Fontanas are involved in illegal activities, the depths and risks of which becomes clear over time.

    Dysfunction is the norm when it comes to the rest of the Fontana brood. Kiki's family background possesses a warmth and closeness, whereas the Fontana house engages in regular histrionics. The Fontana men tend not to value the women in their lives. Kiki speaks her mind and stands her ground when it comes to herself or her son. Her marriage to Bobby is fraying at the edges, as Bobby has been placing Kiki in increasingly precarious situations. A breaking point is fast approaching.

    Kiki is not alone in her concern over the criminal enterprises the Fontanas have been flaunting. Kiki's father and uncles have taken notice and are concerned. Her Father and Uncles view Kiki as their Princess to be protected. Bobby Fontana Jr. may not be the Prince she or they thought he was. The arrests of Bobby and his father, the demise of a possible witness to their rackets, and Bobby's burgeoning gambling habit may just force their hand in speaking up.

Sugar Paper by author Tootsie Barron unites the themes of family, loyalty and crime in a compelling manner. The turbulence of the 1960's and the continued instability of the 1970s form a backdrop with the unsettled domestic world of Kiki Fontana. Kiki shines as the strength of her immediate family, raising her son Bobby III, while her ne'er-do-well husband Bobby schemes and steps out on her. Kiki's strength of character is reinforced by her blood relations, a tight knit brood that values loyalty, honor and family. The Fontanas, however, seem to lack a cohesive honor. The shadow of organized crime looms over the domestic situation of Bobby and Kiki. Kiki distinguishes herself as not being a spoiled Mafia Princess, but as a free-spirited woman who will do what is needed as the situation presents. Barron's book presents a heroine in Kiki worthy of regard and respect.

Sugar Paper is a story done well, and will appeal to a wide audience of crime/fiction fans, bringing creative twists and turns, which makes this book definitely worth reading.

Chapter 1

I received an urgent call from Uncle in the middle of June. "Kiki, I need you to do exactly what I say. Pack up enough clothes and whatever else Bobby III will need for two days. Take him over to my place, where Aunt Esther and our staff will take care of him. You are going to be busy for the next few days.

"Then, get to the store as quickly as possible. It is being raided by the police as we speak. Father and son are both going to be arrested later today. Call Rose, and give her a heads up. More than likely, you'll be on your own. But don't worry, I'm doing what needs to be done. I have arranged for two lawyers to meet you at the Hudson County Jail when you arrive there later today.

"Do what you have to do. And, Kiki, one more thing, keep your father in the dark. As you know, he hasn't been feeling very well for the past three months. I'll take care of everything."

By the time I arrived at the store, a large box truck was parked in the lot, and rack after rack of merchandise was being wheeled out of the store. The front door was blocked by a uniformed officer. I approached him, identified myself, then he stepped aside so I could enter. The warehouse was swarming with more officers, and detectives as well.

As I made my way to the back of the building, I recognized a man who was being interrogated. He had been introduced to me as Tommy Glue Stick. Then, to my horror, right before my eyes, the left pocket of his pants went up in flames. He started slapping the pocket with his hand, but the flames didn't go out. Tommy began to frantically unbuckle his belt as he clearly had no choice but to take his pants off.

So I ran past everyone and grabbed a large towel from the bathroom. Before Tommy could cover up, I saw that the top of his leg was badly burned. I yelled to Bobby J, who was also being interrogated nearby, "Find Tommy a pair of pants to put on! Anything will do."

Officer Russo was coming toward me. He worked out of the local precinct, and his Captain was a close friend of Uncle's.

"Officer Russo, I'm glad you're here. You see, I need some help. Who is in charge here today?"

He pointed and said, "That's Detective Brady."

"Officer Russo, please go to him and ask him to release Tommy so he can get some medical help for his burns.

"To my dismay, I know that Big D and Bobby J will probably be arrested in connection with today's raid. I'll deal with that later. But right now, this place is in the depths of pure chaos with everything going on. The saleswomen are being traumatized. You and I both know they just work here. I'd like for all of them to be cut loose immediately. As Louise is the bookkeeper, I understand that she will need to stay. But I know Uncle will be most grateful if everyone else would be allowed to leave. Please see if you can make that happen."

Bobby J was able to find a pair of pants for Tommy, who had been given permission to leave. Then I went over to speak to Big D privately.

"Big D, I tried to make it sound as if the situation wasn't too serious, but Rose fell apart anyway. I asked Mario to look after his mother until this blows over. He packed a bag immediately and is already on his way to your house, to calm her down and help out with the children. In the meantime, Uncle assured me that two lawyers will be waiting for both you and Bobby J at the jail. I'll follow right behind when you leave here."

The search was wrapped up an hour and a half later. The box truck, filled to capacity with confiscated merchandise, pulled out; then the police officers started driving away. Next, detectives escorted my father-in-law and husband out in handcuffs. I got in my car and headed to the jail, leaving only Louise and Evelyn behind to lock up the store.

When I arrived at the jail, Big D and Bobby J were being processed. While I was waiting, two professional-looking gentlemen approached me and introduced themselves as lawyers sent in by Uncle. Al DeMaio would be representing Big D, and Irv Glassman was on board to take care of Bobby J. They went on to say that they had already registered themselves as their attorneys of record.

Al said, "Mrs. Fontana, we are being paid handsomely to tell your father-in-law and husband exactly what to say and what not to say. They are going to be arraigned at ten o'clock tomorrow morning. Milton gave us a blank check to use when the bail is set, but he doesn't think we'll have a need for it. However, if bail is required, it shouldn't be too high since this is a first arrest for both of them, and it's a non-violent crime."

"Thank you, gentlemen, I'll be waiting at the courthouse tomorrow morning before the arraignment."

Three hours passed before I was allowed to visit with Big D and Bobby J. I couldn't believe my eyes when they were brought in, they both looked so downtrodden.

As shocking as their appearance was to me, I was determined to keep my eye on the ball. "I know you've already met with the two lawyers Uncle sent here. He assures me they are both at the top of their game. Please take their advice as Gospel and trust them. I will return in the morning and stay until bail is set so that upon your release, I'll bring you back to the store. Big D, when I get home, I'll call Rose first thing and assure her that both of you are just fine, that you will positively make bail in the morning, and that I'll be your ride back to the store. Don't worry, sleep tight, this will all work out."

"Kiki, thank you for being here for us, and for keeping Rose informed. Please be sure to extend my heartfelt gratitude to your uncle for all his help, we are most grateful."

"Bobby J, might you be the least bit interested in the whereabouts of your son since I've been running around sticking like glue to both of you guys all day?"

"Kiki, I've got a lot on my mind."

"Just in case your conscience kicks in, Bobby III is being cared for at Uncle's penthouse until you both make bail. He's in very good hands there, and if I didn't know that for a fact, I assure you, I wouldn't be here managing the fallout from today's events."

I asked Big D what would Rose be expected to do with four children still in school if he got convicted and sent to jail? "Bobby J, I have a two-year-old. What am I supposed to do if you have to go away? Any ideas?"

"Kiki, Rose has never been anything other than a housewife; you know that. What could she possibly do to help out?"

"My point exactly, she'll be up the creek without a paddle for sure. Without the family patriarch and her oldest son in the picture, her circumstances become fraught with uncertainties, as do mine. Who do you think is going to pick up the slack for your combined abandoned responsibilities? Mario is only nineteen and can't be expected to run the store by himself. And is my family supposed to take care of me and Bobby III for the foreseeable future? Have either one of you ever given that a single thought? Did you guys have a Plan B?"

Big D answered, "I honestly do not have any idea. We were not prepared for this."

I slowly shook my head back and forth and said, "I'll see you both in the morning. But before I leave, here's an idea. Perhaps the two of you can put your heads together tonight and come up with a plan that would benefit both of your families should the worst-case scenario become a reality."

When I left the jail, I went straight to Uncle's penthouse to visit with my son. There was a parking garage underneath, and the penthouse apartment came with not one, but two assigned parking spaces, which was quite a luxury at the time. However, Uncle paid a monthly fee for two additional spaces so that he could accommodate any guests or business associates who might visit. The Journal Square neighborhood was considered the "high-rent" district, so parking spaces were practically as valuable as gold. Therefore, every time I visited Uncle, I was grateful that I never had to search for one on the street.

Since I was a child, I had always loved this building. I could remember going there to visit Uncle and Aunt Esther, thinking that while the entire apartment was lovely, it was the view that was truly spectacular. Back in the 1950s, Uncle had purchased two top-floor adjoining units and had converted them into a single apartment.

Even though Uncle and Aunt Esther didn't have any children for me to play with, that didn't stop me from exploring. But I always returned to my favorite spot. I loved standing in front of the windows in the vast living room, which afforded me a magnificent view of the Manhattan skyline.

After today's events, a visit with my godfather was exactly the tonic I needed as I was determined to stay optimistic.

"Good evening Aunt Esther and Uncle. Standing by these two Fontana men is beginning to feel like a full-time job. I have to arrive at the courthouse before ten o'clock tomorrow morning. I'd sure like to spend some time with my son before I go home. Thank you for taking such good care of Bobby III."

By this time, my little boy had heard my voice and came running into the living room. "Hi, Mom! Come look at what Aunt Esther and Uncle Milt bought me."

He took my hand and led me into one of the guest bedrooms. I couldn't believe my eyes when I stepped inside. It had been completely furnished and decorated as a little boy's room. One wall was complete with shelves that contained children's books and stuffed animals. There were assorted toys and games scattered around the room.

Aunt Esther said, "Kiki, your son is two and a half years old now, and Milt and I are not getting any younger. With your permission, we would like for Bobby III to start spending more time over here with us. We want to be a bigger part of his life as he grows up, just as we were when you were a child."

"I am honored and blessed that you have made a place for him in your home. I know that one day, my only child will be a better man because of the time you both spend with him now. Aunt Esther, Uncle, how can I ever repay you?"

"You already have, now enjoy some relaxing playtime with your best boy. When you are finished, please join me in the kitchen, I need to speak to you privately. A fresh pot of coffee is being brewed for us as we speak."

When I entered the kitchen, Uncle was already seated at the table drinking a cup of coffee. After the maid poured a cup for me and laid down a dinner plate, she discreetly exited, leaving us in private as Uncle had requested.

"I understand you were 'privileged' to see the bizarre turn of events where Tommy Glue Stick set his pants on fire. Tommy is a bookmaker. He was probably there to settle up with Bobby J, and just happened to be in the wrong place at the wrong time. Tommy got his nickname, "Glue Stick," because he wears a toupee, and a very bad one at that. Everyone in that business knows he hides his betting slips under it for safety whenever he thinks that the law is sniffing around. The rest of the time, he keeps his work in his pocket, right next to his cigarette lighter. You see, he writes his work on 'flash paper,' which is purchased from magic shops in New York City. It is expensive to buy because once it is lit, flash paper becomes impossible to put out. Only when it is reduced to ashes completely will it finally burn out. Flash paper is one of the best ways to eliminate evidence, and that is why it is a preference of many bookies.

"There is another way, I'll tell you about it in the near future, but not now. My guess is that once the store was unexpectedly raided, Tommy didn't have time to hide his work in his usual spot; he is well known to the police as a bookmaker, so he only had one recourse. He had to set the flash paper on fire. Otherwise, he probably would have been busted along with Big D and Bobby J. and a man like Tommy would rather roast his nuts than take another pinch. Please pardon my coarse language, Kiki.

"I still have a lot of work to do, but by tomorrow, I will be in possession of a complete list of the inventory that was removed from the store today. Since my father worked his entire life in the Garment District in New York City, I still have a lot of connections there. I will be able to obtain matching paid receipts for most of the merchandise that was confiscated.

"The two lawyers will then petition the court to release the merchandise that is backed up with bona fide paid receipts. At the very least, those goods can never be introduced as evidence when this goes to trial. I have instructed the lawyers to invoke their respective clients' right to a speedy trial, as they will both be pleading 'not guilty.'

"Now, go home and get a good night's sleep. Don't worry, it will all work out."

When the judge entered the courtroom, everyone stood up. After we all sat back down, the bailiff read the docket number and the charges. The two defense lawyers each entered "not guilty" pleas and asked that their clients be released on their own recognizance. The prosecutor argued that because of the large volume of allegedly stolen merchandise found in their possession, bail was warranted in this case. The judge quickly made a decision that the defendants would be released on their own recognizance due to the fact that this was a first offense for both of them, they were accused of committing a non-violent crime, and their family-owned business created strong ties to the community, thus posing a low flight-risk. When the judge swung the gavel down, I sighed with relief.

After the paperwork was completed an hour later, both Sr. and Jr. were brought into the waiting room. Now that I saw them close-up, it was obvious they were sleep-deprived, but looked like a great weight had been lifted. Both men were eager to return to the store where hot showers and a change of clothes awaited them. When we arrived, Evelyn was waiting for Big D with open arms.

But I have digressed, it is now time for me to go back and start at the very beginning. I met Bobby Fontana in the fall of 1963. One night, about five months later, he got down on one knee, held out a black velvet box, and asked me to marry him. As the clock struck midnight, we became officially engaged.

This is my story, Kiki Cipo Fontana. It is my journey of how I went from A to Z to become "The most stand up lady" in the state of New Jersey and "The Legend" in the world of bookmaking. This world is owned by the most powerful mobsters in the country and run entirely by men.

Fasten your seatbelt because this ride is about to get bumpy.

Chapter 2

My name is Kiki, which is a nickname for Catarina. Yesterday I married Robert Francis Fontana, Jr., everyone calls him Bobby.

We were married in St. Patrick's Church, where I had been a parishioner my entire life.

I was born and raised in the Bergen-Lafayette section of Jersey City. My family had recently moved into the Greenville section where Bobby grew up and lived. When I was born, Jersey City had four major sections: Bergen-Lafayette, Greenville, The Heights, and Downtown.

Greenville is in the southernmost section of Jersey City, located north of the city line with Bayonne whose central core is primarily residential.

In view of the fact that all four sections are quite large, with a total population of over 300,000 people at that time, each had its own public high school. I graduated from the one in my neighborhood called Lincoln High School, but Bobby didn't attend the high school in Greenville. He attended Stevens Academy, which was a private school located in Hoboken, New Jersey.

Bobby is three and a half years older than me. By the time I met him, he was working full time in the family business, Fontana and Sons. Later I learned that he had two extraordinary opportunities practically laid down at his feet before his graduation from Stevens and had already turned the first one down.

Upon his graduation from the academy, he could have entered Stevens Institute of Technology, which was also located in Hoboken.

Before Bobby graduated from Stevens Academy, he had also been scouted by the Philadelphia Phillies baseball franchise. He was offered a contract to play for their minor league team. He had been a phenomenal short-stop and made the All-State team. Besides that, he was an exceptional hitter, averaging over .450 all four years he played varsity.

Bobby had already made the decision to forego college, but he did sign the contract with the Phillies. Then fate stepped in and changed the course of his life forever.

One wall in the warehouse of his father's business was stacked to the ceiling with pallets containing merchandise. No one knows how it happened, but one of them came crashing down from the top and hit Big D on his right side. The weight from the pallet dislocated his shoulder and broke his arm in several places. Lady Luck was shining down on him that day because the pallet missed striking his head by mere inches, or he probably would have been killed.

Big D had enough competent help in the store so that wasn't the immediate problem. In view of the fact that his family lived in the suburbs, he wouldn't be able to drive into work every day for the next three to four months. Now, that presented a problem.

Bobby's father also owned a two-family home in Jersey City, which had a studio apartment in the attic. Bobby moved into that apartment right after he started driving, so he didn't have to commute back and forth to Hoboken from the suburbs while he was still going to school. Now, he would have to move back into the family home so he could drive Big D to and from work every day until his arm healed.

After Bobby graduated, he started to spend all day in the business, and became involved in the many aspects of it. He enjoyed working with the inventory, but he soon realized that dealing with customers one-to-one was more his speed. As it turned out, he was a born salesman who just happened to have an adding machine built into his head.

Right before Labor Day, Big D was nearing a full recovery. Bobby had already made up his mind to join the family business and take his place at his father's side. He realized how much he loved working there, and Big D welcomed him with open arms. It was always his intention to one day have all of his sons working in the business.

By the time I met Bobby, he was fully entrenched in the family business, running it side by side with his father, but he had one last offer still to come his way in the near future.

I spent most of my courtship to Bobby at the bowling alley as he bowled in leagues Monday through Thursday nights. He had his picture up on the wall with only six other men who had ever achieved the level of play necessary to enter into "The Elite 700 Club."

To enter, a bowler had to bowl three consecutive games in league play for a total of 700 or more points. Bobby had two perfect 300 games documented in league play.

After the league play was over, some of the best bowlers stayed behind. Since they were now sufficiently warmed up, the real bowling began. That's when they started bowling for "pots." Big money was being waged on these match-ups.

I became one of the official scorekeepers for the league, and continued the task as the "pot" bowling was being played, which usually lasted three to four hours. Of course, I didn't keep the scores from the lanes on which Bobby played.

Bobby played cards on Friday nights, but Sundays were always family day, and that meant going to his father's home for dinner.

Every Saturday, we went out to dinner with the same three couples. He met the three men at the bowling alley years before. They were at least ten years older than us, thus making me the baby in the group.

These three men who bowled with Bobby also played cards with him, but they were not "pot" bowlers. They went straight home after the league play. All three couples attended our wedding.

At that time, I was still working for the Introcasso's Insurance Agency at Journal Square. Mr. Introcasso, who was one of my father's oldest and dearest friends, approached my father prior to my graduation and told him that he wanted me to work for him. That was that. As always, I did what my father wanted.

I ran the front-end of the agency. My responsibilities included answering the phones, doing all the correspondence – in and out – and all of the billing. I guess it was the billing, mostly the entries of the payments, I enjoyed the most. Bobby insisted on driving me to work every morning and he was never late picking me up at exactly five o'clock. As the boss's son, he could come and go as he pleased.

Seven months before the wedding, Bobby's father informed his first-floor tenants that we would be taking the apartment once we got married. They vacated in a timely fashion, which gave us sufficient time to completely renovate it.

Even before Bobby and I became engaged, we drove out to Saddle Brook every Sunday to have dinner at Big D's home. That was an Italian tradition.

The first Sunday I ever went up there was also the first weekend I started dating Bobby. Big D was waiting for our arrival and greeted us at the front door. We proceeded into the kitchen where I was introduced to Rose, Bobby's mother. She appeared to be a lovely woman, but seemed to be a bit overwhelmed. I was about to find out why.

All of a sudden, I was being bombarded by screeching and screaming, which sounded as if it were coming from all directions. I was about to meet five of Bobby's six siblings. Only the oldest daughter was not home. She was second in age to Bobby.

Big D asked where she was. Rose said she had no idea, she stayed out all night, and never phoned to say where she was.

Every Sunday Big D drove over to Paterson and headed straight to his favorite bakery. He bought all the "goodies," as the family called them. I helped Rose arrange everything onto the kitchen table.

The coffee was made. Everyone could just come in and help themselves. Within a few minutes, the kitchen was swarming with all the kids. They ran around the table grabbing whatever they wanted, knocking over some of the beautiful display in the process.

The gravy was already cooking on the stove, and the kitchen smelled delicious. I asked Rose if there was anything I could do to help. I've been around kitchens my entire life. My mother and father owned Cipo's Restaurant in our old neighborhood. Before that, my father had always owned a tavern because he loved being a bartender.

After I helped Rose set the dining room table, Bobby took me downstairs to see the finished basement. When I got to the bottom of the stairs, I couldn't believe my eyes, it was a very large room and right in the center of it stood an exquisite oval bar which had twenty bar stools around it. It was fully stocked with liquor, and also had a beer tap that was connected to a keg.

In front of the bar was a wooden dance floor. It had a beautiful strobe light which hung above it.

Bobby turned the strobe light on and asked me to dance with him. Then he walked over to a corner of the room and turned on a magnificent Wurlitzer jukebox. It was filled with doowopper records.

After we finished several dances, Bobby turned the jukebox off and showed me around the rest of the room. Let's see, one wall housed a shuffleboard game, a skee ball machine, and two pinball machines. There were three slot machines lined up on another wall in three different denominations; quarters, dimes, and nickels. Most people don't see that every day. As I kept walking around, I came upon a finely detailed old player piano.

I kept going around the room, and there it was, the granddaddy of them all. I was staring at a stage right in front of me. Velvet curtains were hanging behind it with lettering that spelled out "Bobby Fontana and the Gigolo's." An organ was standing in the back, and a full set of drums was set up next to it.

Apparently, Big D had his own band before World War II broke out. After he joined the army, he continued performing during his tour of duty. When he returned from the service, big band music was still at the height of its popularity. Big D was busy supporting his family, but still found time to play occasionally by picking up a gig here and there.

By the time we went back upstairs, dinner was just about ready. Everyone was called to the table. Then the children appeared. They were so loud, and then two of them started arguing at the table.

About halfway through dinner, Jeanette showed up. She didn't say a word to anyone. Rose asked to speak to her privately in the kitchen. Even though the dining room was far enough away from the kitchen not to be within earshot, it was perfectly clear that a big argument was going on between the two of them. Suddenly, Jeanette came over to the table and gave me a dirty look before she stormed out and headed for her car. Then she peeled out of the driveway.

That first Sunday was one of the most laborious I ever had to get through. I couldn't wait to go home to peace and quiet.

I wasn't sure if I had been inside of an arcade, a nightclub, or a casino. Then again, it could have been a combination of all three. I did know that house was filled with unruly, disrespectful children. I wasn't the least bit impressed with what I had witnessed. The Fontana family was definitely dysfunctional.

Years later, when I finally told Uncle about my introduction to the Fontana family at that first Sunday dinner in their home, he told me something that shocked me. He said he knew exactly what went on inside that house, and he also knew everything about the people who inhabited it. I will forever remember his next words. He said, "I wish you would have cut Bobby loose that very night, but Hemmy would never have allowed it."

Chapter 3

Seven months after the honeymoon, we received the joyous news that had been confirmed. I was two months pregnant with our first child, due on or about the twentieth of December. I couldn't think of a better Christmas present for both sides of our families.

When they were told, both sets of soon-to-be first-time grandparents were over the moon with the anticipation of the birth of their first mutual grandchild.

Bobby seemed to be excited at the prospect of becoming a first-time father. You know what they say about "Murphy's Law." A little over a month later, one of the top-rated professional bowlers came knocking on our door with an offer to sponsor him on the Pro Bowlers Tour.

Of course, Bobby turned the offer down, after all, he couldn't be expected to travel all over the country on the bowling circuit while waiting to become a first-time father.

In the meantime, my mother, who was as much of an expert seamstress as she was an accomplished chef, began to make the see-through lace overlay for the bassinet. Mother would have ample time to add the appropriate color and fabric to go underneath the outer lace layer after the baby was born while I was still in the hospital.

Rose, on the other hand, was busy buying everything and anything in sight to fill up the bassinet and much more.

There was a complication after the delivery, so I had to undergo a hysterectomy. When I awoke, the doctor told me about the surgery and informed me that I would never be able to have another child. Mixed in with all of the joy of having a beautiful, healthy baby boy that day, my heart was broken.

Bobby took off as soon as our son was born. No one knew where he went. He had no way of knowing about my surgery. Later that afternoon he returned with a beautiful bouquet of roses. I told him what had happened and then gave him the bad news. He said he was sorry, but showed no other emotion. I guessed he was holding a lot inside. That couldn't have been an easy thing for him to hear, that your first child would be your last child, at least the last one with me.

When I brought the baby home on Wednesday, I was greeted by a house full of people. Both sets of grandparents were there as well as five of Bobby's siblings.

I went into my bedroom first to see what the bassinet looked like. My mother had gotten right on it as soon as she returned from the hospital. A blue layer of fabric needed to be added under the lace, and the result was gorgeous. Next, I went into the baby's room. It was so cute. All the stuffed animals, which were scattered around the room, were chosen by Bobby's siblings, who had now become young aunts and uncles.

My mother prepared the food, and after we had all eaten, the conversation turned to what the baby's name would be. Bobby spoke right up and said, "Why, Thomas of course." Nobody had ever bothered to bring the subject up the entire nine months of my pregnancy. It was automatically assumed it would be Thomas, since Italian tradition dictates that the first-born son be named after the father's father.

I know it appears like the Fontana's didn't follow their own tradition since Big D is Bobby Sr., and Bobby is a Jr., but they did in fact follow the tradition. Bobby would have had an older brother whose name was Thomas, but sadly, he was stillborn.

So, I jumped right in and said, "Absolutely not, my son will be named Robert Francis III. To alleviate some of the confusion, he will be known as Bobby III. I'm sure I've earned the right to choose the name considering what I went through after he was born. It's non-negotiable."

Big D said, "Kiki, why would you, of all people, break with tradition?"

"I can tell that Bobby hasn't told you and Rose the whole story. First things first. I'm going to start calling Bobby, Bobby J and the baby, Bobby III, which should keep the confusion at bay.

"Now, Big D, I'll answer your question. After Bobby III was born, you went back to the store, Rose went back home to take care of the kids, and Bobby J took off. Soon after, a problem arose and I was taken into surgery. The doctor called the store to speak to Bobby J. Evelyn answered and told him he wasn't there. My mother and father stayed at the hospital. While I was sedated, they received the sad news that I can never have another child. I hope that explains why I chose to name the baby after his father. I mean no disrespect and I hope you can understand. It wasn't up to my mother or father to tell you. Bobby J should have done that himself."

I asked Bobby J why he hadn't told his parents. He didn't answer. He seemed to have retreated inside himself. It would be many years before I found out where he went that day. When I did find out, it didn't surprise me since it didn't matter anymore. By that time, it was already water under the bridge.

Then Big D took me aside and asked to speak to me privately. He said, "Kiki, I know Rose has spoiled our four sons. Bobby J, as the oldest, is the most spoiled. I'm hoping that fatherhood will force him to change his ways. Rose and I both agree that you are the best thing that ever happened to him. I'm asking you to be patient with him. I know he holds a lot inside, but please give him some time to grow up."

"Big D, you know how much I love and respect you. He does what he wants, when he wants, and nobody gets to tell him what he should do. Besides that, I now know that he partakes big time in some kind of gambling. I don't know exactly what he's up to, but I promise you this, if he ever does anything that would hurt or endanger my son, I will make him pay. Even if it takes me the rest of my life."

The conversation was over. We returned to the dining room and joined the others. I was confident that I had finally stood my ground. I alone named my son, and I knew I would keep my promise if it ever came down to it.

The next day, I started to make arrangements for Bobby III's Baptism. The first call I made was to Father Grady at St. Patrick's Church.

Then I called my cousin Donna and gave her the date. She was expecting a phone call from me to formally ask her to be Bobby III's godmother.

Big D stepped up and suggested that after the Baptism, we have the party at an Italian restaurant called "The Gondola" in Bloomfield. He knew one of the owners and offered to call him and make all the arrangements.

I was fine with that as I knew there was no way I would allow my mother and father to open up their restaurant for the special occasion of their grandson's Baptism.

A few weeks later, Bobby J called me and asked that I pack up the baby, diapers, and enough food to last for several hours, and get to the store as quickly as possible because he needed me to help him take care of some business.

I brought the baby into the store at about eleven-thirty. Bobby J approached me and said, "I need you to accompany my brother Mario to this address in Newark. He will drive the van." He handed over a piece of paper with an address on it. Then he continued, "Mario is driving on a learner's permit, so he needs a licensed driver to go with him."

"What are we supposed to do when we arrive there?"

"Mario will turn over the keys and the van to whoever comes out to greet you. Then the plan is in place for you and Mario to have lunch. While you two are eating, the van will be loaded with merchandise. Mario will get the keys back and then you will bring the van back here."

"Please check in on Bobby III. Make sure the ladies don't spoil him too much."

"I'll have my father do that as I'll be taking care of something very important elsewhere."

"Bobby J, is it anything serious? I'm just wondering why you aren't driving the van yourself. I figure you must have a very good reason."

"I have someone I must go see. I'll see you later this afternoon."

Mario was clearly my favorite of the Fontana siblings. I asked him, "Why aren't you in school today? You know the reason the Christening has been delayed is that Christmas fell two weeks after Bobby III was born."

"I took the day off. I'm not really into school. In fact, I don't like it at all. Now that I'm past sixteen, I'm thinking about quitting school to start working at the store."

"Please give that some more thought. Don't rush into that decision since you only have eighteen months left to go. It's important to have a diploma, even if you do plan to join the family business. Maybe someday, you might realize that the business is not the right fit for you."

"Kiki, I can talk my mother into anything. She's so preoccupied with taking care of the other kids, she wouldn't even notice if one of us started doing something else."

"Mario, that's so very sad. But what about Big D? Doesn't he have any say about your future?"

"Kiki, get your head out of the sand. You know who and what he is. I can't believe that you would pretend not to know that."

"I'm just trying to keep this dysfunctional family together to the best of my ability for the sake of my son."

We arrived on time at the address we were given. The building was a restaurant that appeared to be closed.

After we parked in the rear of the building, I knocked on the back door. A man opened it up, and escorted us into the dining room. A second man arrived, seemingly out of nowhere. He said to Mario, "I'll take the keys to the van now. It will be loaded with merchandise and then returned to you. In the meantime, the chef will cook something while the two of you wait here."

The restaurant was definitely closed. We were the only two people in there, yet a chef cooked for us.

After we finished eating, and the table was cleared, the man who had let us in very abruptly reappeared and brought us a deck of cards to occupy our time as we waited. Then he disappeared again. We never laid eyed on the chef again. The other two men came and went like ghosts, but I suspected that at least one of them was watching us at all times.

"Mario, I have a bad feeling about this, we've been here since about one o'clock. It's now past four o'clock. Something very bad is going down here, and you and I are stuck right in the middle of it. I'm going to get to the bottom of this when one of the ghosts shows up again. Let's get the keys to the van and beat it out of here."

"Kiki, I don't like these guys either. We don't have any idea where they took the van. Let's ask my father to find out what's going on."

"Right on, brother-in-law. I'm asking to use the telephone pronto.

"Hello? Is anyone there? I need to use the phone. I have to check on my son, he's an infant." Mr. Back Door Man materialized out of nowhere and said, "No calls will be allowed." I said, "Excuse me? Are you saying I can't make a call to inquire about my son?" Now I knew for sure that we were in fact being watched all along.

"Not a single phone call can be made," Back Door Man said. "This deal is going sour. Nobody wants to back down. Two godfathers from two different areas are now involved. That's all I can say."

I was beginning to get the picture, as young and naïve as I was at the time, so I decided to give it one more try.

"Since we're not negotiators, why can't I call and just ask about my son?"

"The call would have to go to the business and that is not an option at this time."

"I'm beginning to get the feeling we are being held hostage here, and I don't like it one bit. Am I correct about this?"

"I'd prefer it if you would think of yourselves as our guests for the foreseeable future."

Then Back Door Man disappeared once more.

"Mario, if we ever get out of here, your father and brother better have a damn good reason for this insanity that we have been subjected to on this day. Someone had better answer for this when the time is right."

Around seven-thirty, both men reappeared. Mario was handed back the keys to the van, and the only words that were spoken were, "Now you can leave."

We were out of there faster than smoke through a keyhole. As we left, I took a good, long look at the name of the restaurant we had been held hostage in. It was called "La Piazza."

When we pulled into the Fontana and Sons parking lot, Mario finally spoke and said, "Kiki, I wonder what kind of merchandise was being fought over."

"Mario, I bet the beef had nothing to do with any kind of merchandise."

I suggested he stay upstairs in the attic apartment for the entire weekend. After all, it had been a very long, trying day for both of us. He agreed and entered through the side door. I gave him a hug and said goodnight.

When I entered my apartment and checked on Bobby III, he was sound asleep. I had been away from him for almost an entire day. I didn't get to kiss him goodnight. I was not a happy camper.

Then I walked up to Bobby J and got right in his face. "How could you put Mario and me in such a dangerous situation?"

"You were never in any real danger."

"Are you kidding me? You don't think these kinds of men deal in danger? I've got news for you. They probably live for it. I wasn't even allowed to make a phone call to check in on the baby. It's quite evident that restaurant is just a front for other things. Let me take a wild guess. These guys are running a gambling operation and you probably owe them money. That's why they wouldn't release the van or us until an arrangement was worked out. I'll also guess that the person you said you had to go see was your godfather. I'm sure he had to straighten things out for you once more.

"Someday, you will be asked to pay your tab. You will be called upon to do something really bad at some point. And on that day, you will have no choice but to make a deal with the devil. Don't ever say you weren't warned. Here's one more thing. Don't you ever put me in harm's way again. Remember, I too have a godfather."

Chapter 4

Big D called me and asked if he could come over because he had something important to discuss with me. I told him sure.

After Big D checked in on his grandson, I poured the coffee and we sat down at the kitchen table. He shocked me by saying, "Jeanette is threatening to boycott the Christening because she feels that since her brother won't be having any more children, and since you don't have any siblings, she should have been asked to be the baby's godmother. How can we fix this problem?"

"Almost every Sunday since that first date, Jeanette is rarely present. On the rare occasions when she finally does show up, it's always the same scenario. She starts a fight with one of her siblings, and it's all downhill from there. Then, before she storms out again, she always manages to say something disrespectful to Rose.

"Big D, you must be aware that protocol dictates the person who served as the maid of honor should be asked to be godmother to the first child. I cannot change that tradition, nor do I want to. My cousin Donna will arrive on Saturday morning, and she will be godmother to Bobby III.

"Let me be blunt and completely clear. Your daughter Jeanette has some gall to think that I would ever ask her, with all her rudeness, to be godmother to my only child. Quite frankly, I don't want her around my son too often. Your family can continue to tolerate her brand of disrespect if they want to, but I will not allow myself to be bullied or blackmailed in any way, shape, or form. Big D, most respectfully, I'm asking you to step up and take a leadership role in your family. It's time to say 'enough', and finally put your daughter in her place."

He just sighed, shook his head, and kissed his grandson on the forehead, said goodbye, and then he left.

Before Bobby J left for work on Friday morning, he made an odd request. "Can you make sure you are here around noon time to accept a furniture delivery? It's a table, and I want it placed in the middle of the room in the basement."

We had a finished basement complete with a kitchen.

It took two very large delivery men to carry the table down to the basement. When they uncrated it, I couldn't believe what I was seeing. There it was, to my amazement, a handsome, professional card table made of solid wood.

After I gave it a very good dusting, I thought to myself, *what is Bobby J up to this time?*

The first thing Bobby J did when he came home that night was head straight down to the basement for an inspection of his new purchase.

"I've made an investment that should make us a nice piece of change every Friday night. It will take about three weeks to round up the kind of players we want for this game."

I picked right up on the word "we." That could only mean one thing. There had to be a Heavy D involved somewhere in the background of this new endeavor.

"I am going to run a high stakes poker game here. I'll be cutting every pot. You will have to serve the players for the length of the games."

"And how long do these games usually last?"

"At least through the night and into the next day, maybe longer if the money is going back and forth. I really can't be sure, but I've heard they could last up to three days. I have to do this. I have a very important partner."

"I bet you do."

"We have to take a chance and do these things while we're still young. I'm sure you can do your part, and contribute. We can do this together."

"For your information Bobby J, I think I have contributed more than my fair share."

"You just have to make them simple sandwiches, nothing messy, as the game never stops. They have to be able to pick up a sandwich with one hand and play cards with the other. They won't even take a bathroom break until they are dealt cards that they have to fold, and get out of the hand. These guys dislike being out of the action, they are that serious.

"You will have to set up a smaller bar and have a variety of sodas available. At various times, they will stop drinking the hard stuff.

"They won't be drinking anything too fancy. Oh, and you will have to set up the coffee urn. They probably will want dessert with the coffee. Maybe danish and donuts, nothing too sticky. Remember, they only have one hand available to use."

"Let's see Bobby J. It takes about forty-five minutes to feed, change and put the baby back down. I'm going to guess it will take another forty-five minutes to serve the players. That leaves me maybe two and a half hours of rest before I have to be up for Bobby III again."

"At least you can sleep in between. I can't leave the table at all. I have to keep adding up each chip thrown into the pot. The cut must be taken after the last wager has been made, but before the hand is called."

"Well, Bobby J, one thing is for sure, that affinity for adding numbers in your head that you were blessed with will sure come in handy on Friday nights."

"That's precisely why I was given the task of running the game in the first place."

Finally, the day of the Christening arrived. It was sunny, but bitterly cold. Everyone had to really bundle up. Bobby III looked angelic in his white Christening outfit. It was such a shame I had to cover it up with so many layers of outerwear and blankets.

The Baptism was to start promptly at two o'clock. The rest of the guests would meet us at the Church.

When Father Grady got to the part where he asks, "Robert Francis Fontana III, will you be Baptized?" and poured the blessed water from the font over his head, my baby boy was such a little trooper. He never even cried; he just stirred a little.

When the Baptism was over, we all headed over to "The Gondola" restaurant.

As everyone started taking their seats, I surveyed the room. The floral arrangements were lovely, as was the hanging banner that read "HAPPY CHRISTENING DAY ROBERT FRANCIS FONTANA III." The cake was on display on a separate table for everyone to view.

Before the party ended, Uncle took me aside and asked me to join him and Aunt Esther at his table. "I want to have the same latitude with your son that I've always had with you, so I can watch over your child as well. Hemmy wants this for you. Please don't ask me why at this time. But one day, I will tell you all you need to know, I promise."

"Uncle, I would be honored if you would take on that responsibility. A child will always need good men in his or her life to guide them. I, for one am truly blessed to have two of them, my father and my godfather in mine."

"I will always be there for you."

Then I looked around as I realized the party was coming to the end.

It seemed like I had just recovered from all of the preparations and excitement that surrounded Bobby III's christening when it became time for me to declare, "Let the card games begin!"

By seven o'clock, I had everything ready for the game. The bar was all set up and the refrigerator was stocked with an assortment of sodas.

As for making the sandwiches, I had selected various meats, cheeses, and breads. I kept the condiments to a minimum, just mustard and mayonnaise. I hoped my choices would suffice.

The coffee urn was ready to go. All I had to do was plug it in. The game was scheduled to begin at eight o'clock sharp. The dessert table was set up next to the coffee urn with some cookies, donuts, and Danish.

At seven forty-five, the doorbell rang at the side door. The first player to arrive introduced himself as John. Then Sam, Lee, Colin, Pauly, and lastly Dennis arrived. Bobby J then appeared, seemingly out of nowhere. That's the way he usually does it. He brought a bottle of Harvey's Bristol Crème with him and placed it on the bar.

I noticed a carousel filled with poker chips in the middle of the table with six decks of unopened cards scattered around it.

Bobby J went to work exchanging money for chips, and began to shuffle the cards. I played my part by walking around and asking each man what he wanted to drink.

Right then and there, I had to memorize what each one of them drank so I wouldn't have to repeat it. I asked if they wanted any sandwiches, someone answered, "Not at this time, but probably in about an hour." I assured them I would be back. Then I left and went upstairs to our apartment.

This was my very first encounter with a poker game, let alone such a high stakes one, and it was turning out to be the polar opposite of what I expected.

Conversation was not prohibited, but it was on lockdown, temporarily off the grid once the game started. Basically, the only words I ever heard were, "I raise," "I fold," or "I'm in."

I refilled all of their drinks and made the sandwiches. The only sound I heard was the clinking of the chips hitting each other as they were thrown into the pot.

When I completed my duties as the hostess, I addressed the players saying, "Gentlemen, I will return in several hours."

I certainly hoped it would be a profitable venture, since I saw piles of chips being thrown into the pot.

Around two o'clock in the morning, Bobby III's crying awakened me, right on schedule. After I was finished taking care of the baby, I went back downstairs once again. I noticed that only two players were still drinking. This check-in was certainly easy enough. I told them I would return at about six o'clock in the morning.

By this time, I was starting to get tired and fell asleep until Bobby III let me know he was hungry. After I took care of him, I went back downstairs, but this time, I figured that since the game had now passed the ten-hour mark, the players would probably be getting hungry again.

They were all very hungry, so I started making sandwiches all over again. Surprisingly, the men didn't look the worse for wear yet. If anything, Bobby J appeared to be the most tired.

It became a routine. I went back downstairs at ten o'clock and when I went back at two o'clock in the afternoon there were only two players left, Lee and Dennis. It was anyone's guess why they were still playing.

At four o'clock, I heard the side door slam. Shortly after that, I saw both players emerge from the alleyway, as I looked out of the front window. The game was finally over. Bobby J left right behind them without ever coming upstairs or saying a word to me. I guess he went to deliver his partner's take of the money that had been collected from all those pots.

Now, I had the task of cleaning the entire poker room. I couldn't believe the amount of cigarette butts overflowing from the ashtrays.

The weekly poker games took place in our basement for almost a year. The longest game dragged on for two and a half days straight.

I can confirm unequivocally I never once complained. I'll always be able to say that after serving the players, and staying up for days at a time, I absolutely did "my part" as Bobby J called it.

There's one more thing I'll always remember about the poker games. I very quickly learned the denominations of the chips, so every time I served a player while they were making their wagers, I made sure to take an extra look at the pot.

I can say, without a doubt, those pots represented thousands of dollars. As a lowly woman in a man's world, I was never privy to the knowledge of what the initial buy-in was, if there was one, or what the final cut of each game was. But I'm quite sure based on what I witnessed it had to have been an enormous amount of money.

After all was said and done, when the weekly games came to an end, I had to ask myself, "What ever happened to all that money?" I will swear that I was never offered or ever saw one thin dime of that money.

Chapter 5

A few months after that first poker game, I would mark my first Mother's Day.

Big D came up with an idea that would put both sides of the family together. He suggested that we go back to the premier champagne brunch in West Orange just as we had done the previous year because we all had such a wonderful time. Of course, Uncle and Aunt Esther would be joining us.

After giving it some thought, I decided that it might be too chaotic for the baby. The place gets filled to the maximum and extremely noisy.

When I voiced my concern to Big D, he concurred with me and suggested we go back to "The Gondola" restaurant. My mother wanted to come over and spend some time with her grandson before we left.

My father, Uncle and Aunt Esther would meet up at my house later. We would then all leave together in two cars. My in-laws would meet us at the restaurant.

When I arose for Bobby III's six o'clock feeding and went into his room, I switched on the lamp. It didn't come on. I assumed the lightbulb blew out. I quickly opened the blinds, which immediately let some light in. The baby was wide awake in his crib.

Each morning as I entered Bobby III's room, I marveled as I looked down at this sweet little boy. As soon as he saw my face, he smiled from ear to ear. He looked all around as if he already knew this world was exactly where he would take his place and make his mark one day.

As I was changing Bobby III, he sneezed several times. I was hoping he wasn't coming down with something. I checked him for a fever. Thankfully he didn't have one.

Suddenly, it occurred to me that there seemed to be a chill in the room.

I dressed the baby as quickly as possible and went straight to the kitchen to heat up his formula and feed him his breakfast before I would have to start getting ready for Mass.

When I got to the kitchen, I flipped the light switch on, but that light didn't come on either. The kitchen did have a window in it, so I opened the blinds. Then I reached into the refrigerator, and that light was also out. I took out one of the baby's bottles which contained the formula I made for him every day. I had to put the bottle in a pot of water and heat it on the stove. When I turned on the gas stove, to my horror, it was out as well. We had no gas, no electricity, and no heat. I quickly opened all the blinds and curtains to let in as much light as possible.

Then I went in and awakened Bobby J. I explained the problem and asked him to go down to the basement to check out the fuse box.

I couldn't give Bobby III his bottle since it had to be at least room temperature, but I was able to feed him cereal and fruit.

As much as I loved coffee, my mother loved it even more. If Bobby J didn't fix the problem, I would be totally humiliated that my mother couldn't enjoy a cup of coffee on Mother's Day in my home.

Bobby J came up from the basement as I was getting ready for Mass. He informed me that some of the fuses were blown out. I was getting the feeling that I wouldn't have a speedy resolution to the problem any time soon.

When I returned home from Mass, mother never said a word about the gas and electric being out. She continued in her enjoyment of spending time with her grandson. I usually drove over to the restaurant with the baby twice a week so my mother and father could spend a half hour or so with him.

I had been home for about ten minutes when Bobby J told me he couldn't find any fuses anywhere. The house was beginning to feel chillier with each passing hour.

Aunt Esther, Uncle, and my father arrived at two o'clock on the dot. Uncle was a successful business man. When he was in New Jersey, he resided in a penthouse apartment in the upscale St. James Apartments, which was located in the Journal Square section. It was a perfect location because of its proximity to New York City, where he maintained offices for his business. The main reason he never left Jersey City completely, was because of my father. They had been best friends since childhood. Uncle also had offices in Las Vegas and in his mansion in Palm Beach, Florida.

I'm not sure if it was my father, Aunt Esther, or Uncle who entered Bobby III's room first. I had him dressed in a spiffy new outfit. It had a black velvet jacket, and a red bow tie. He was already quite the little gentleman to escort his mother on her first Mother's Day celebration.

If any one of them noticed that there wasn't a single light on in the house, no one ever mentioned or questioned it.

We were taken into the same room that the Christening party had been held in. The entire Fontana family were already present when we arrived at 'The Gondola.'

After the dinner was over, my mother asked me to go to the ladies' room with her. I knew she wanted to speak to me privately. "Your father and I don't know why the gas and electricity isn't working in your house, and quite frankly, we don't care. You know we never interfere, but what I'm about to say is not a request. Our grandson cannot stay in a home with no lights, and especially no heat. How can you expect to take care of your son in a cold house while stumbling around in the dark? Let's get out of here as quickly as possible, there should still be enough light outside when we return to your house. You will be able to pack anything necessary for the three of you to spend the night at our house. This comes directly from your father." Mother held up her hand and said, "You will stay at our house until the problem is resolved, enough said."

I walked over to my mother and gave her a big hug. "Thank you both for being the best of parents. I'm so sorry that I wasn't able to give you a cup of coffee this morning, on your Mother's Day. I will make this promise to you. No matter what I have to do, or how hard I might have to work, some day, I will make it up to both of you. When I give my word, my reputation will precede me like a parade. I don't know how just yet, but I guarantee it."

When mother and I returned to the table, Uncle took me aside. "I'd like to come over tomorrow to visit with our special boy. I think it's about time for me to tell you a true story. Do not return home before noontime. And Kiki, when you do return home, and get Bobby III settled in, do me a favor, go into the kitchen and perk a pot of coffee.

"Kiki, make the best of the rest of your first Mother's Day. Trust me, tomorrow will be a much brighter day."

Everyone remarked that a good time was had by all. After some hasty good-byes, everyone went their separate ways. My mother and father came back home with us so I could pack. We did spend the night at my parents' home.

I didn't get much sleep that night, I kept going over the day's events. The thing that seemed so inexplicable to me was the fact that Uncle always seemed to know everything about anything before anyone else. I had a very strong feeling that Uncle was the first person to become aware of the problem with the gas and electric. He wasn't buying into the "blown fuse story," and neither was I.

Growing up, I always knew Uncle was brilliant, and, he probably was the sharpest man I would ever meet. I had no idea who this man really was, or the magnitude of his business dealings.

I had a feeling that I would be enlightened tomorrow.

Uncle arrived at the gas and electric building at nine o'clock sharp the next morning.

He walked up to one of the windows and introduced himself to Miss Lynch. He told her he wanted to pay a bill, and gave her my address.

While she was looking up the information, Uncle took out a $100 bill and folded it in half.

Before she could say a word, Uncle pushed the bill toward her. "You don't have to tell me what I already know. The service has been turned off. You see this money? It is your tip for expediting the return of power to that house. Take the money. It is a small token of my appreciation for a few extra minutes of your time. You see, a baby resides there.

"I'm going to pay the back bill, and put $500 up front into this account for any future payments in case this account ever goes in the arrears again. If that money ever gets used up, please contact me at this address or phone number. Here is my business card. That's all you ever have to do.

"By the way, there is one more thing. When a man named Robert Fontana, Jr. comes in to pay the bill, take his money as if I had never been here and add it to this account. I insist it must be handled this way. Miss Lynch, thank you so much for all your help, and please see to it that the service is restored before noontime today."

Miss Lynch looked down at the business card in her hand and answered, "Mr. Kaye, I'll see to it personally."

Standing at a mere five-foot seven-inches tall, Uncle is not a big man, but what he lacks in stature, he more than makes up for in his presence. He is a very imposing man, if not downright intimidating. Uncle is always dressed, in equal measure, impeccably and expensively, and as such, he is the epitome of elegance. Uncle is a very pleasant looking man. At first glance, he is quite formidable. When he walks into a room, he commands it, and one automatically knows he is a successful businessman. And that's probably before you even notice the four-carat diamond pinkie ring he wears on his right hand.

His business cards read, "Milton Kaye-Business Consultant." But he never mentions, and no one knows, what that business is. It would be many years before Uncle would tell me about his part in the "Fuse Box Fiasco," as I started calling it after I was finally told the truth.

I returned home at eleven forty-five the next morning. The power had been restored.

Uncle rang the doorbell at twelve-thirty p.m. He went to the playpen and picked Bobby III up to give him a hug. Today was going to be the day he would introduce Kiki to her father's past, and tell her how the two of them met as young boys growing up in the same neighborhood.

"I know for a fact that your father, has never told anyone this story, not even your mother. Never underestimate him. You have no idea how far his arms can reach out. There are reasons why he chooses to stay in the background. I can't tell you anymore about that at this time.

"Hemmy and I grew up a few blocks from each other on Center Street here in Jersey City, located behind the McGinley Square area. I was always a pale, scrawny kid, but I was also the snappiest dresser in the neighborhood because my father, Abe, worked in the garment district in New York City.

"Think of our neighborhood as a big square with three long blocks on each side. I never had a problem in the area until that one particular day. The only time you might see someone from a different section is if you were walking through the neighborhood going someplace else.

"I was coming down my stoop as Hemmy came walking through. At the same time, two Irish hooligans came across the street and started challenging me in a threatening way. 'Go back inside Jew-boy, if you know what's good for you.'

"Your father took offense and said, 'Whoa, there's no need to talk like that. We all live in this same area.'

"One of the hooligans said, 'Mind your own business. What are you, a Jew-lover?'

"Before they could make a move toward me, your father punched the talker in the nose, broke it, and then hit the other one in the eye. As they ran away, one was holding his bleeding nose, and the other was covering his black eye.

"Then I said to him, 'Thanks for your help, but they will come back to teach me a lesson for the beatings they took today. By the way, I'm Milton Kaye."

"I'm Hemmy Cipo. I've seen you around, and don't worry, they won't come back. I'll take some of my Italian friends with me. We will have a talk with them and work it out."

"Where did you ever learn to fight like that? You have the fastest hands I've ever seen."

"I love to box. Someday, I'm going to be a professional boxer. I'll have to pray that I will be able to box good enough so no one will ever be able to hurt my face too badly because I know if that ever happened, it would break my mother's heart. You see, I'm an only child, and my mother is a widow. I guess you could call me a mama's boy."

"Hemmy, do you know that everyone says you are the most handsome boy in the neighborhood? That's probably why your mother doesn't want you to get that face of yours hurt. How old are you?"

"I'm ten and a half."

"Well, I'm twelve and a half, Hemmy, and I'm also an only child. Do you want to be friends?"

"Sure, Milt, why not?"

"Think of me as an older brother from this day forward. You know, the teachers at school told my parents I have a genius IQ. Between your fast hands and my brains, I think that we will do big things together."

That was the day we became the life-long friends we are to this day. When I was seventeen, I started running a craps game in the Italian part of the neighborhood. I would never have been given the green light to do that if not for your grandmother's connections. I am sure you know your grandmother's maiden name was Gallo, so even though she was widowed, she still had powerful relatives everywhere.

"We made pretty good money on those craps games. Your father's first love was still boxing, so I took him to a prize fight for his birthday that year. It was the second time a fight was named 'The Battle of the Century.' It took place on July 2nd, 1921. As you know, Hemmy's birthday is July 3rd.

"The fight was between Jack Dempsey and Irishman Georges Carpentier for the heavyweight championship. The fight promoter, George 'Tex' Richard, initially wanted the fight to be held in New York City, and even considered the Polo Grounds. But the then-governor, Nathan L. Miller, opposed prize fighting. Still, Richard wanted the venue for the fight to be close to New York City.

"There were three cities in the running, all of them located in New Jersey. They were Newark, Jersey City, and Atlantic City. Jersey City got the nod.

"The sight that was chosen for the fight was called, 'Boyles Thirty Acres,' located on Montgomery Street, an eight-sided arena was constructed costing three hundred and twenty-five thousand dollars. The official attendance for the fight was about eighty thousand people, but the stands were built for ninety-one thousand, and it was packed to capacity. The fight grossed $1,789,238, well over twice as much as any previous fight.

"In attendance was a list of high-profile people including: political figures Mayor Frank Hague of Jersey City and New Jersey Governor Edward Edwards; on top of that, two thousand women attended.

"The press corps came in from across the nation as well as from England, France, Spain, Japan, Canada, and South America.

"According to some experts, the two fighters were not in the same league. Dempsey was clearly the favorite. He was paid $100,000 more than Carpentier. The 'Battle of the Century' was also celebrated as the first sports event broadcast on the radio. Actually, the preliminary bout between Packey O'Gatty and Frankie Burns was transmitted first.

"Dempsey knocked Carpentier unconscious one minute and sixteen seconds into the fourth round.

"Three years later, when your father was eighteen, he started his amateur career under the name of 'Hemmy Ross.' He was never knocked out and won every bout.

"Right before his twenty-first birthday, as he was getting ready to go pro, he had a tough match and had his left eye severely damaged in that fight. He won it, but his eye was never the same.

"When he went home that night, his mother took one look at his eye and screamed, 'Enough! This ends now, or I'm going to disown you.' That one line coming from his mother's mouth permanently ended his boxing career. You know, to this day, he still watches all the fights on television.

"It's now 1927, and Prohibition is at its height. Hemmy had already been bartending on the side for a couple of years at a local speakeasy. He came to me one day and said he no longer wanted to work for someone else. He wanted to be the proprietor of his own speakeasy.

"The large majority of speakeasies were established and controlled by organized crime. In fact, it was Prohibition that motivated them to become more organized in the first place. They opened everything from plush nightclubs to smoky basement taverns.

"By that time, I was financing many of the shipments of booze coming in. Right before he had the grand opening, I toured the place. It was a tavern, but it was an upscale one. He called it, 'The Tioga Tavern.'

"It didn't take very long before The Tioga became one of the busiest and most profitable speakeasies around.

"Your father possessed a million-dollar personality. Besides that, he was movie-star handsome. Women came from all over to socialize with him, even if they came with another man. It was always Hemmy they wanted to be around. As much as he loved the ladies, he loved his widowed mother even more.

"During prohibition, I became more interested in real estate. So, during the day, I went around looking for buildings to buy. Then I started renting them out. I handled all of the collections myself. My high IQ was once more beginning to manifest itself in my new business venture.

"Almost every night before I went home, I stopped by Hemmy's place for a nightcap. He loved running that business, and he was very good at it. Hemmy also knew that Prohibition would end eventually, and he wanted to keep The Tioga Tavern, but as a legal business. With all of his connections and mine, Hemmy had no problem securing a legal liquor license.

"By this time, I had honed my business acumen, and was well on my way to becoming a wealthy man, hence I started to dress much snappier, right down to my first diamond pinky ring. Hemmy always worried about my flashy attire."

"Milt, you're asking for it. Some day you are going to get yourself in trouble. It's not safe to walk around like that. You are a married man. Think about your beloved Esther. I wish you would tone it down before you get mugged."

"Thanks, my friend, but I'll be fine. Don't worry about me."

"Kiki, I should have listened to your father. About two weeks later, I was exiting The Tioga late in the evening when I was grabbed by two thugs. They were both brandishing knives. I was jumped and dragged behind the building. Then they demanded I hand over my pinky ring and wallet. I had no problem handing over my wallet, however, giving up my ring without a fight, that was another story.

"Fate stepped in as I was, no doubt, seconds away from being stabbed. Hemmy came out the back door of the tavern with some trash at that exact moment. Then, with the speed of a jungle cat, he sprang into action. Before the thugs could raise their knives, he punched both of them in their faces so fast and so hard that they dropped their weapons and I scooped them up. Hemmy proceeded to knock them both out, but not before he gave them the beatings they so richly deserved.

"Kiki, in all the years that have passed, your father has never once said, 'I told you so.'

"Regardless, he saved my life, and even with all my financial success, I owe him more than any man could ever repay.

"But I'll let you in on a little secret. After the events of that night, I started carrying a pistol on me at all times, and I still do to this day."

Chapter 6

Once a month, I enjoyed cooking a dinner and entertaining my mother's younger brother, Uncle Vito, and his wife Aunt Mary, at my house.

They have two children of their own, but my cousins are now teenagers, and seldom tag along with their parents to visit relatives.

I had called Big D earlier in the day and told him I would be delivering his dinner at around six o'clock.

"Uncle Vito, how's the insurance business treating you these days?"

"Pretty darn good."

Aunt Mary had gone over to the playpen to pick up Bobby III, who had already pulled himself up and was reaching his arms toward her.

"Aunt Mary, what's been keeping you busy lately?"

"Your cousins are out of school for the summer, so I've been doing some shopping for them." Aunt Mary is a homemaker.

Uncle Vito said to her, "I sure hope you bought something pretty for yourself, Mary."

"You see Kiki, what a fantastic husband your uncle is to me."

"I sure do Aunt Mary, he's one of the great ones, and a wonderful uncle as well."

"Aunt Mary and Uncle Vito, may I impose upon you for about a half hour? I promised my father-in-law I would bring him his dinner tonight. Would you mind watching Bobby III while I deliver it?"

"It will be our pleasure to spend some time alone with Bobby III. Please give your father-in-law our best, and to Rose as well."

"Please answer the phone while I'm gone."

"Kiki, no problem. We will be enjoying this little guy's company. Take as much time as you need."

"Aunt Mary, would you please keep an eye on the stove?"

"Of course, go do what you have to do."

Then I packed up Big D's dinner, put it in a box and loaded it into the car. When I arrived and pulled into the parking lot, I noticed that only three cars were left there. I had expected to see a few more. The store should be open for at least another hour.

When I reached the front door, Evelyn came running out and almost knocked me over. She was crying hysterically as she ran toward her car.

"Don't go in there!" she yelled as she got into her car. She opened the windows as she turned her car around and said, "Do yourself a favor and go home. Do it now."

I had never seen Evelyn so upset. No way could I ever go home now, I had to find out what was going on in there, so I went in.

I could hear a woman screaming profanities at Big D. "You no good son of a bitch bastard! When you started banging me, you promised that you would stop seeing Evelyn. So what do I walk in on? You and Evelyn, all over each other back here!"

As I got closer, she continued her tirade. "I'm going to crucify you, you dirtbag!" Then I heard dishes and glasses being broken.

"What the hell is going on here?" Then I saw the woman who was acting like a lunatic and causing all the commotion. I recognized Janet; she was one of the other saleswomen who worked there.

"What's going on here? What kind of madness is this?"

Big D looked pale, and I noticed he was holding the right side of his chest under his shoulder. Then to my horror, I saw that he was bleeding profusely from a wound.

I ran, grabbed some towels from the bathroom, and started to apply pressure immediately. Now, I could see what appeared to be a stab wound. Very weakly, Big D said to me, "Kiki, don't call for an ambulance. If you do, this incident will make its way to the newspapers, causing a scandal, and then your mother-in-law will find out. You don't deserve to be dragged into this mess. You are a wonderful daughter-in-law, and I appreciate you."

"Big D. I'm a Gallo-Cipo-Fontana. I'm not leaving you here alone with this nutcase. Until tonight, I would never have thought of crossing this line, but now I must take my place. Janet, you bitch, you're fired.

"Your son is flawed, you know that Big D, but as long as my son carries the Fontana name, I can't stand by and watch any member of the Fontana family get hurt."

Big D didn't say a word to protest. Maybe it was the pain from the wound, or maybe it was the sight and sounds of the two police officers running through the warehouse toward us with their pistols drawn, shouting, "Everyone, hands in the air!" wacky Janet raised her hands up and started trembling all over.

"Officers, I'm Kiki Fontana, his daughter-in-law, he's been injured." At that same moment, the phone started ringing. "Officers, may I please answer the phone? My aunt and uncle are babysitting my six-month old son. It might be important."

When I answered the phone, Uncle was on the other end. "Kiki, do exactly as I say. Tell Officers Flynn and Russo that a doctor will arrive on the scene within five minutes to take care of your father-in-law. Do not call for an ambulance. When I am finished speaking with you, put Officer Russo on the phone. His captain wants to speak to him. Janet will not be questioned or charged with any crime. There will never be a written report or an investigation of any kind made concerning this incident.

"Now, you can put Officer Russo on the phone. When he is finished talking to his captain, both officers will leave. Then I will give you the rest of the instructions."

I held out the phone for Officer Russo, and just as Uncle said, after a quick conversation with his captain, both officers left without saying another word.

I took the phone back and told Uncle that the doctor just walked in, and had passed the officers on their way out.

"Good, now go and lock the front door. Your father-in-law will be in good hands with this doctor, he is one of the best. He will be stitched up, given a shot of antibiotics for infection, and he'll be fine. The doctor will locate the ice pick, put it in his black bag, and dispose of it after he leaves.

"Big D will spend the night with his son Mario in the upstairs studio apartment. He will call Rose and tell her that he had to stay for a large, late-night delivery. When the doctor finishes patching up your father-in-law, drive him to your house and make sure you enter through the side door. Take him up to Mario's apartment. Mario is out for the evening, so as soon as your aunt and uncle leave, tape a note to his door telling him that his father is staying the night and he is not to be disturbed.

"Then, come in through the front door as if nothing happened at the store. When Bobby J comes home from bowling, don't tell him anything. Let your father-in-law tell his boys whatever he wants them to know tomorrow. Don't worry about a thing. I made it all go away, it never happened."

No one ever spoke of the events of that night again.

The two officers never wrote out a report, the story never saw the light of day in the newspapers, and Rose never heard a word about the incident.

Then I asked myself, what about all the unanswered questions involving Uncle? How did he find out about the stabbing of Big D in the first place? Lastly, and most importantly, what was he doing standing next to the captain at the police station when he called the store that night?

As always, there would be more questions than answers with Uncle.

The next six months passed so quietly that life in the Fontana family was beginning to seem, comparatively, almost mundane. Now, the time had come for me to begin planning Bobby III's first birthday party.

Once more, the poker game would be halted at midnight on Saturday to allow for Bobby III's party on Sunday that weekend. Of course, I had to invite Evelyn, since she was Big D's number one saleswoman, and still his girlfriend. She was always around. That's the way Big D wanted it. I guess they were lovey-dovey again, now that Janet was long gone. Poor Rose never suspected a thing.

Bobby III's birthday happened to fall on a Sunday.

Just when I thought everything was going smoothly, as it had been for a while, Bobby J lowered the boom. "Kiki, I'm entered into a big bowling tournament on Sunday. My mother will be coming along with me to be the scorekeeper."

"Bobby J, how could you sign up for a bowling tournament on December 11th? That is your only child's big day. That's the day he was born. It's impossible to forget that date."

"Kiki, I didn't realize it when I signed up for the bowling tournament."

"I'm sure you could cancel, if you really wanted to. We will be having our son's party here. You, as his father, and Rose, as his grandmother, should be here for that."

"Kiki, I can't cancel, it would throw off the entire schedule for the other bowlers. You can handle the party until we get back. You will have plenty of family with you to help out."

"Bobby J, that's not the point. Call it a cautionary notice if you will, but don't ever think for one moment that I'm going to put up with your shenanigans forever."

"Kiki, I promise, I will make it up to you and Bobby III one day."

"Look on the bright side Kiki, this is an elimination tournament; if I bowl poorly, we will be home early."

"No way Bobby J. I expect you to bring your "A" game with you and nothing less. Don't worry, I'll hold the fort down here."

Big D arrived at one o'clock with four of the siblings, so Rose and Bobby J could get on the road. Mario had only two flights of stairs to climb down. Once again, it was anyone's guess if Jeanette would show up. With so many young aunts and uncles eager to play with him, I knew Bobby III would be occupied for the rest of the day. They asked if they could take him out of the playpen.

"Sure." I said, "But keep him away from the Christmas tree."

Big D got right in there and moved all the dining room chairs into the living room. Then he went down to the basement and brought up a dozen folding chairs and scattered them around as well.

I needed to have clear access to the dining room table.

All the food was set up so everyone could walk around the table and help themselves, which turned out to be a great idea. All the dinnerware, silverware, glasses, and napkins were stacked on the dining room buffet.

Big D turned out to be a right-hand man to me that day, much like a Guy Friday. He helped my father tend the bar, carried in hot replacement trays as needed, and mingled with all the guests.

If any of the other guests thought it was a bit odd that Bobby J wasn't present at his son's first birthday party, they never uttered a word.

We started opening up Bobby III's gifts at about four-thirty p.m. The siblings, as I always called them, were just great to Bobby III. Each one of them had picked out and wrapped a present for him all on their own.

To my pleasant surprise, they were all on their best behavior in my house. Then I got another surprise an hour later when Jeanette arrived with Vincent. I welcomed them as warmly as everyone else.

Everything else was unwrapped within the hour. Then Big D insisted on carrying in the birthday cake. After all the guests had coffee and cake, it was time for me to get Bobby III bathed and ready for bed.

Uncle went in to kiss the baby goodnight, and then he took me aside. He showed me what he had decided to give Bobby III for his birthday. He opened up a bank account in my name and Bobby III's name for ten thousand dollars. It was to be used for his college education.

I knew he had something on his mind, he had more to say. I could feel it, as I have known this man my entire life. The memory of me riding on his shoulders around the room with him calling me his princess, assuring me that one day I would own the keys to a kingdom, would forever be etched in my mind.

I always believed in my heart, although he never said it, that Uncle never wanted me to marry Bobby J. Something told me that Uncle had many reasons not to like Bobby J, but he seemed to find it necessary to keep them to himself, at least, for the time-being.

Then he cut to the chase. "Kiki, this husband of yours should be here at his son's first birthday party. I had to get that off my chest. But that has nothing to do with what I'm about to say. Kiki, with your permission, I would like to keep this bankbook in a safety deposit box I keep in that bank. Every year, I will add another ten thousand dollars to it on Bobby III's birthday. I don't want Bobby J to know it exists. I'm determined to protect Bobby III's future."

"Uncle, I have never questioned your intentions before, not once, and I never will. I am so very grateful for what you and Aunt Esther have done for my son. Uncle, you are correct, Bobby J should have been here. A child can only ever have one first birthday. What he did today will always remain unforgiveable to me, and as a Gallo-Cipo, I will never forget it. I'd like to think it was a success even though Bobby J was a no-show."

"Kiki, you are as gracious a hostess as your mother and father are in Cipo's Restaurant. That's part of their success. This party was a big hit today because of you."

I thought I heard the guys talking about a football game. The game seemed to have grabbed Uncle's attention big time.

Bobby J finally returned at ten o'clock. I wasn't even that angry anymore. I was feeling more sadness than anything else. I was sad Bobby J had missed a milestone in his son's life. He would never have the memories that were made today.

I was never jealous or annoyed that my mother-in-law took my place keeping score at the bowling tournaments after I had the baby. It just shouldn't have been done on that particular day.

I put together a plate of food for Bobby J, and then I finally retired for the night. But I didn't fall asleep for a long time. For some inexplicable reason, my mind kept going back to all the weekends Bobby J had taken me to Greenwood Lake when we were dating, and the many hours I used to spend at the bowling alley.

Maybe those memories, and my vivid recollection of Bobby J's extraordinary natural ability when it came to sports, were conjured up because he had done so well in today's tournament. I knew that whatever money he had earned in the tournament that day was probably destined to end up in the hands of his bookies. And that last image did not make for an effective sleeping pill.

Chapter 7

In 1967, Valentine's Day fell on a Tuesday. Apparently, Big D arrived at the store early that morning, presumably between seven and seven thirty a.m. to organize a big Valentine's Day sale.

The night before, the saleswomen had dressed and arranged eight mannequins in full length leather coats which were trimmed in mink collars and cuffs. Each coat had a beautiful red rose pressed through the button holes in honor of Valentine's Day.

No one knows if Big D intentionally left the front door open for Evelyn to arrive right behind him.

I do know he was shaving in the bathroom at the back of the store when the loud bell which was attached to the front door started ringing.

He didn't see anything amiss at first glance. Then he heard a loud sound that seemed to be coming from about the middle of the warehouse, so he yelled, "Who goes there?"

There he was, a young man with an arm full of the leather coats, sprinting toward the front door. Big D yelled, "You bastard! Drop those coats right now!" By the time Big D made it out the front door, the young man was halfway up the block. Then he called my house.

"Kiki."

"Good morning Big D."

"Wake up Bobby J right away. Tell him to get dressed and get to the store as fast as he can. We just got robbed. I'm waiting for the police to arrive."

"Bobby J, wake up!" I said as I shook his arm.

He said, "What time is it?"

"It's a little after eight o'clock. Big D just called. He wants you to get to the store as soon as possible."

"Why so early?"

"Well guess what, spoiled owner's son that you are? You know, the one that comes in whenever he wants, and does whatever he wants? The jig is up for now. I'd put a move on it because the store was just robbed. If I were you, I'd high-tail it over there pronto, because I've never heard Big D sound so angry."

I never saw Bobby J jump out of bed so fast, brush his teeth, skip a shower in favor of splashing water on his face, get dressed, and just about knock me over as he ran out the front door in about five minutes flat.

Big D described the entire incident, and then pointed the police in the direction the punk ran toward. They assured him they would start canvasing the neighborhood and report back to him as soon as they had any pertinent information.

Big D went around the entire warehouse and determined that five of the leather coats had been snatched off the mannequins.

Later that day, Big D spread the word through the neighborhood, to be on the lookout for the punk who had robbed him.

He dispatched Bobby J and Mario to question all of the other shopkeepers in the neighborhood. Big D instructed his sons to cross over the Bayonne line, and continue the same line of questioning there.

By the time the store opened at nine o'clock, the police were long gone, and the five mannequins were redressed in other coats as if nothing had ever happened. The three remaining leather coats were sold that day, and the overall business was better than usual.

The same officer who was present after "the stabbing," called Big D at two o'clock that afternoon. Big D asked him for a favor. He asked if he would enter through the back door. He wanted any information to be kept private. Around that same time, I was receiving an urgent phone call from Uncle.

"Kiki, I'm calling from my office in Las Vegas. I'm gathering vital information as we speak. I will be catching the red eye back to Newark tomorrow evening. I'm returning because I must speak to you alone on Thursday morning. It's very important."

"Uncle, do you know the store was robbed this morning?"

"Of course, I do. That's precisely why I'm coming back on the red eye."

Officer Flynn arrived a half hour later and entered through the back door. Big D asked where his partner was.

He said, "My partner, Russo, received an anonymous tip about a possible suspect and is following up on it. The tip led to a young man named Jethro Thompson with a home address in Bayonne. I'm going to meet him there now. I'll get back to you."

Later that night, Bobby J told me that Rose had put her two cents in on this situation, she suggested they give the young man a break. Big D told Officer Flynn that he didn't care if all the coats were not recovered, he only cared that the thief make a full restitution for them. And once arrested, he and Bobby J would be visiting the thief at the jail. If they could work out a bona fide deal, then they might think about dropping the charges against him.

The two officers staked out the suspect's home and waited for him to return. He lived on Avenue C in Bayonne. He drove up, and when he stepped outside of the car, Officers Flynn and Russo grabbed him, threw him up against the car, and then they handcuffed him. There were leather coats clearly visible on the backseat, along with the wilted roses. "Hey punk, are you Jethro Thompson?" asked Officer Flynn.

"Who's askin', and what do you want?"

"Five coats just like these were reported stolen earlier this morning from the Fontana and Sons store which is located not too far from here."

"I ain't sayin' a word, I know my rights."

"Oh, I see, Jethro," said Officer Flynn, "you already know something about that fairly new law called the 'Miranda Rights.' Rest assured, you will certainly be read your Miranda Rights before you are booked."

"For now, let's go upstairs to your apartment. I think we should have a look-see, so move it. Is anyone home?"

"I think my mother is up there. Ma, are you home?"

"Yes, Jethro, I'm here."

"Mrs. Thompson, I'm Officer Flynn, and this is Officer Russo, we caught your son Jethro in possession of four of five coats that were allegedly stolen this morning. Have you seen the fifth one? Perhaps Jethro gifted it to you for Valentine's Day. If we recover all of the coats, maybe the people who own the store will have a change of heart and drop the charge."

"Officers, I don't have the other coat. Jethro, what are they talking about? My boy is a good boy."

Officer Russo had enough. "I know he's got a rap sheet as long as my arm. He's a junkie and a thief, many times over. But he'll have his day in court once more. Mrs. Thompson, instead of bending our ears by extoling his virtues, perhaps you should consider retaining a lawyer for him."

Officer Flynn called Big D after Jethro was arrested and told him that he had to come to the police station that evening and make the identification of the coats that had been recovered.

Uncle called me Thursday morning to tell me he was back. When he arrived, he seemed a bit more intense than usual. Of course, he went straight to the playpen. He picked up Bobby III and hugged him ever so tightly.

We went into the kitchen and had coffee.

"Kiki, late yesterday afternoon, a man showed up at the jail with credentials and a business card that read 'James Sparks, Attorney at Law,' presumably to represent Jethro. He spent about forty-five minutes with him.

"An hour after he left, both Senior and Junior visited with the alleged thief. Based on the log-in book, I know they were both there for over an hour. I had a strong feeling I should go straight to the jail. You know how I always say, 'money talks,' so I had no problem getting in. I'm so glad I followed my hunch.

"The thing is Kiki, sometime around midnight, Jethro Thompson hung himself in his cell. He left a rambling suicide note for his mother. That suicide note will never see the light of day. I paid a lot of money to take possession of it. I can't tell you why I had to remove the note, at least, not now.

"My people were put on this situation as soon as I received a phone call about the robbery two days ago. Kiki, once again, there are more questions than answers. For now, I positively know there isn't a lawyer in the tristate area named James Sparks.

"Other things are going to start happening by tomorrow, and you must be prepared. The warden at the Hudson County Jail is on the warpath. Anytime a suicide occurs at any jail, red flags go up. It's a very good bet that the alias James Sparks has already been removed from the log-in book. There will be a cover-up at the jail. It will be as if James Sparks, or whoever the imposter was, never existed. Someone at the other end will have to take the heat, whether it be the Fontanas, or the imposter, if he is ever found.

"You know Kiki, I was able to make that other incident go away entirely because I handled it before any charges were pressed. This is different. There will be some serious repercussions. You see, when the jail personnel look bad, so does the rest of law enforcement.

"More than likely, the police will never be able to find the imposter, so their next course of action will entail coming down hard on the Fontanas in search of answers. Make no mistake Kiki, they will be coming after you as well. The men that will come here most probably will be high-ranking detectives, and they will be coming with an attitude.

"They are working on Big D and Bobby J as we speak, both are being interrogated at headquarters. That's why you didn't hear about the hanging before I walked in here. I'm sure the detectives will be here sometime tomorrow morning. Now, we must get started. Kiki, it is imperative that you do exactly what I am about to teach you today. I know I am being vague, but that's all I can tell you. Listen, and learn.

"Sadly, Kiki, my heartbreak is that I wish I could tell you that you will only have to utilize this information one time, and your heartbreak will come when you realize that's never going to be the case. This lesson I'm about to give you must be ingrained in your brain for the rest of your life.

"Kiki, I know you can't understand the veil of secrecy surrounding some of our discussions. All I can tell you now is that's the way your father wants it."

"Uncle, what has my father got to do with this?"

"Everything. Let's begin. When you go into the arena tomorrow, you need to be able to fight back, you cannot be a bantam weight. I will make you into a heavyweight, because from this moment on, you're always going to be up against higher ranking, seasoned lawmen.

"For now, we will concentrate on the detectives. When they ring your doorbell, ask them to show you their identification first. Right from the start, they will know you are no dummy. Let them in and always be the lady that you are. Look them in the eyes every time you answer them. Never volunteer anything they haven't asked for and most importantly, never ever change one word of your story. They will try every trick in the book to bait and switch you into getting caught in a lie. They do this all day long for a living.

"Then they will bring out the biggest weapon in their arsenal, their ace card, intimidation, they will probably promise you that if they ever find out you lied to them, then you will be charged and sent to jail. This is done, and often is effective, because young mothers are so fearful of being separated from their children.

"Never change a word of your story, ever. Make that your mantra, and you will be well on your way to becoming someone very special.

"I've always said Hemmy is the most stand-up man I ever met. That term has always been used only for men, but I'm about to change that. Kiki, someday you will be known as the most stand-up lady in the state of New Jersey. Take my word for it, I will make it happen. You may not know what that means, or how important it is in certain circles, but when the time is right, you will come to realize the value in it. Now, repeat the mantra."

"I will never change one word of my story, ever."

"Kiki, in doing so, you will never give anyone up, and that's the most important component in being a stand-up person.

"One last thing. As of this moment, the Friday night card games are cancelled, permanently. Do not let any players in this house, no matter what Bobby J says. Tell him from now on, he will be watched by the law for the foreseeable future. I must go now Kiki."

I had work to do, so I got right on it and repeated the mantra over and over again.

When Bobby J came home that evening, he didn't say anything about being questioned by the detectives.

"Bobby J, Uncle assures me that detectives will be coming here tomorrow to question me, but don't worry, I'll handle it."

A look of shock registered on Bobby J's face, but he said nothing in reply, or for the rest of the evening.

I wasn't quite sure how I would summon up the amount of confidence it would take to rise to the occasion, but it was crucial that I did. Whatever came through my door the next day, I knew instinctively and unequivocally, I would be able to handle it because I had the best mentor in the state of New Jersey. Little did I know, I actually had the best teacher in the entire country.

Uncle, who I trusted unconditionally, had prepared me well. And with that thought, I was able to sleep like a baby.

At ten o'clock the next morning, the doorbell rang. Since Bobby III was now running all over the house, I placed him in the playpen on my way to answer the front door. Low and behold, the two middle-aged men standing there introduced themselves as Detectives Patrick Doheny and Perry Spiros, they asked to come in to speak with me.

I asked to see their identification. They seemed a little taken aback by that, but quickly hid their surprise and flashed their gold badges.

I then graciously invited them to enter and showed them into the living room. Then I said, "Gentlemen, before we get started, please give me a moment with my son."

I had placed the playpen between the living room and dining room. I went over to Bobby III and motioned for him to come over to me as I said, "Come to mother, sweet boy." As he stood, I lifted him up and told him, "Mother will be busy for a while, so I need you to be a good little boy and play with your toys." I did this for two reasons. First, I needed Bobby III to stay in one place where I could keep an eye on him. Second, and maybe even more importantly, I wanted these detectives to know that nothing came before my son, not even an unannounced visit from the law.

"Now gentlemen, how can I help you?"

Detective Doheny spoke first. "I suppose you've heard about the young man who committed suicide in the jail."

"Sadly, of course I've heard about it."

Detective Spiros asked, "Mrs. Fontana, what do you know about it?"

"Just that he committed suicide by hanging himself. What else is there to know? Isn't that bad enough?"

Detective Spiros replied, "Well, we know that both your father-in-law and husband visited with the alleged thief for a little over an hour on Wednesday afternoon. Mrs. Fontana, what do you know about their visit to the jail?"

"Well, I can't say how long the visit lasted. I only know that Bobby J said they were going to visit him."

"Why did they want to speak to the deceased?"

"Bobby J said they wanted to work out a payment plan as restitution for the one coat that was not recovered."

Detective Doheny said, "And you believe that story?"

"Of course, I do."

"Well Mrs. Fontana, as veteran detectives. We are not buying one word of that story. We don't believe in coincidence. So, I'm going to ask you again. What do you know about their visit to the jail?"

"And I'll answer you again. I wasn't there. But I do believe that my mother-in-law Rose encouraged them to cut the young man a break. Now, gentlemen, may I ask you a question? Isn't it true that most people who commit suicide leave behind a note? Did Mr. Thompson leave behind any such note? If he did, then it might explain the motivation for his tragic action."

Detective Spiros said, "Mrs. Fontana, we are not at liberty to discuss the details of an ongoing investigation, and it's our job to ask the questions."

They were being very coy.

"Understood gentlemen, ask away."

Detective Doheny said, "Mrs. Fontana, did your husband or father-in-law say anything about sending in another man. Possibly a lawyer, to speak to the alleged perpetrator?"

"No, neither one of them said anything to me about anyone else going there."

Detective Doheny continued, "Mrs. Fontana, we know who your family is. What are you doing with these Fontana people? Sooner or later, you are going to find out the hard way what the Fontana family is all about. Mrs. Fontana, if we ever discover you held out on us by covering up for your husband or father-in-law, we will come back here. I promise that you will be taken away from your son when we arrest you."

"Gentlemen, if you ever come back here again, I suggest you both bring frightening Halloween masks with you. But it will take a lot more than that to scare me. Now, if you don't have any more questions, I should get some chores done before lunchtime."

Begrudgingly, they thanked me for my time as I walked them to the front door and bid them a polite good-bye.

Wow, Uncle was right on the money. I knew the detectives had expected a naïve young wife and mother from a good family, who would be easy to overwhelm with some harsh questioning. What they got instead, thanks to Uncle's careful tutorage, was the new and improved Kiki Fontana, the one who would never be intimidated by anyone ever again.

The circumstances surrounding the suicide would forever remain a mystery, except for a select few. The note was never mentioned in the one newspaper article that talked about a suicide at the jail, nor did Mrs. Thompson ever hear a word about it. And just like that, all questions regarding the entire incident vanished completely, like a puff of smoke.

Chapter 8

I met a very nice young mother who lived up the block from me. She had a son, Peter, who was four months younger than Bobby III. We liked to go shopping together, and we enjoyed walking to the park with our sons.

Labor Day weekend had just passed. While the weather was still mild, Eileen and I decided to take the boys to the park. I told her I would be taking Bobby III to the store earlier to visit with his grandfather for a while. She agreed to meet me outside the store at twelve o'clock.

By eleven fifteen in the morning, Big D was having a good time with his grandson.

I don't think I was there but fifteen minutes, when four policemen stormed in with a search warrant. They approached Big D and told him they were going to search the premises for stolen electric typewriters.

After reading the search warrant, Big D said, "Go ahead."

Big D signaled me to follow him to the back. Just as I was about to join him, I was stopped by two policemen. It turned out that Officers Flynn and Russo were on the case once more.

They approached me and said, "Hello, Mrs. Fontana."

"Hello Officers, I'm going to say good-bye to my father-in-law and then I'd like to leave through the back door, if that's okay with you guys."

"Absolutely, Mrs. Fontana. Please say hello to your godfather for us."

"I will certainly tell him both of you treated me with the utmost respect and kindness. I'm sure he will pass that information along to your captain."

Big D had a brown paper bag in his hands. "Kiki, this bag contains three guns. I need you to smuggle it out of here in the stroller immediately. They cannot be found on these premises. Take them to your house and hide them."

"Big D, are these guns loaded? I will absolutely refuse to put that package in the same stroller with my son if even one of them is loaded."

"They are not loaded, now please, go and hide them well."

"Don't worry, I'll handle it. I hope there is no trouble for you today."

I walked around to the front and met up with Eileen. I told her to go on ahead to the park, and I would meet her there in about forty-five minutes as I had to run an errand for Big D.

I kept Bobby III strapped in the stroller and told him I would be right back.

The first thing I did was grab the rubber gloves I use for heavy duty cleaning. Then I grabbed a thick cleaning rag. I had never held a gun in my life. I wiped each gun down, in order to remove any fingerprints from them. There were a few things I knew how to do well, and one of them was how to clean something until it gleamed.

I brought the guns down into the kitchen in the basement. It occurred to me that everyone who lived in this house had access to the basement. I thought to myself, *that's a whole lot of people coming and going to that area, making it difficult, if not impossible, for the law to pin ownership of the guns on any one particular person.* So it was a no-brainer to stash the guns downstairs.

The phone started ringing. I figured with everything going down at the store, it could be important, so I answered it.

"Kiki, have you taken care of the package?" Uncle asked.

"Yes, I have."

"Good, I'm on standby just in case lawyers are needed."

"Thank you, Uncle."

Uncle told me later that day he already knew I had smuggled the guns out in the stroller with Bobby III, and he wasn't too happy that Big D had put me in that position. However, he was impressed with the way I removed the fingerprints, and the place I had chosen to stash the guns.

The next day, Uncle paid me a visit. While we were enjoying a cup of coffee, he got right down to some points he thought were most important.

"What you did on the spur of the moment was exemplary. You moved fast on your feet without any hesitation. More than that, your mind was engaged. Now, remember Kiki, I'm here to remind you that the law is still watching father and son, off and on. The police will keep watching for a while longer."

Seven weeks later, Uncle stopped by to bring me the good news that he had it on good authority the police had closed the case on the suicide incident.

The following week, Bobby J came home five days before Thanksgiving and unceremoniously announced to me that he was going to Las Vegas with some of the guys. One of them had just been sprung from jail, so they were taking him out to celebrate his release.

"All of the guys are flying out together. Kiki, it's not just me, none of us will be home for Thanksgiving. It just worked out that way. I'm part of that crew, I have to go. I know I've never flown before, but fear of flying or not, I have no choice. You will be fine."

"Let me ask you this. Why did you ever get married in the first place? You're not suited for marriage and fatherhood."

"Kiki, you just don't get it. I've been bailed out many times, so sometimes, I'll have to do what I'm told to do."

"Ah, remember when I told you that someday you would have to pay the piper? Is that what this is all about?"

"It's something like that, but not quite. You'll never understand how it really works."

"Well, guess what Bobby J, you're wrong about that. I promise you this, by the time you return home, I'll know exactly how it all works."

"That's great Kiki, then you'll understand why I really don't have a choice."

On Thanksgiving morning, I called Rose and Big D to wish them a Happy Holiday, I sensed Big D was terribly disappointed that I wouldn't be joining his family that day.

In spite of all the overwhelming antics surrounding this dysfunctional Fontana family, I genuinely loved Big D and was sorry we wouldn't be together.

I finally realized that as much as I was beginning to find my voice, I had never once questioned my father or godfather. That was about to change. Today was the day I was going in search of answers.

It was my pleasure to serve the traditional Thanksgiving meal in my home. My mother would be bringing the antipasto and the lasagna.

When dinner was over, I asked my mother and Aunt Esther if they would look after Bobby III as I needed to speak to my father and godfather about something very important. They didn't interfere, and jumped at the chance to take over in getting their mutual prince ready for bed. What I didn't know then was that these two special ladies would become very prominent figures in his future.

I'm very sure my father and godfather knew I had something important to discuss with them when I asked that they join me in the living room.

"Dad, Uncle, tonight I seek the truth. It's time. Dad I want answers, we can all see clearly that Bobby J is not marriage material, or much of a father to Bobby III as he's never around. When Bobby J was courting me, you encouraged us to move forward with the relationship. And when he came to you and asked for my hand in marriage, you gave your blessing. Why?"

"Sometimes things have to be done a certain way. I don't want you to worry about a thing. In time, one of us will tell you the entire story. For now, your duty is to raise a good boy who will become an exceptional man one day."

"Just this one time, as Bobby J's father-in-law, I must defend him. When one of the higher end members of a crew gets released from jail, his peers are responsible for taking him away on a mini-vacation. It's called blowing off steam. And when the crew returns, that man is ready to get back to taking care of business. So whoever he is, it's a good bet that he's a high earner for his family."

"Kiki, as your godfather, I'm telling you not to take it personally that Bobby J is not here. Your father and I know why he does some of the things that don't seem quite right to you. Just continue to go with the flow, have patience, and now, no more questions."

I guess in hindsight, some major clues were dropped that night.

When Bobby J returned, it was already the height of the Christmas shopping season, and the store was extremely busy. Bobby J and I went out with the Saturday night gang on New Year's Eve, and we all had a great time ringing in the year 1968.

I was very surprised that Uncle spent the entire holiday season at his penthouse in Journal Square. He was always at his offices in Las Vegas during the Christmas holiday season. In the third week of January, I received an urgent phone call from Uncle.

"Kiki, Sr. and Jr. are being questioned by detectives at the store this very moment. In a day or two, they will be knocking on your door. Stay the course, and remember the mantra. I have a lot of work to do."

I approached Bobby J when he came home that night. "Uncle called me earlier and told me detectives were in the store questioning you and Big D. what's going on? And before you answer me, remember, I can't help fix it if I don't know what's broken."

"Do you remember when I introduced you to a man called Brownie?"

"Sure, I remember him, who could forget a name like Brownie? What's he got to do with the detectives?"

"It seems that his wife reported him to the police as a missing person. He hasn't been home for two days."

"So, why are the detectives questioning you and Big D?"

"Because his wife told them that the last time she saw Brownie, he said he was going to our store to take care of some business. He did make it to the store, picked up some money and merchandise, said he had other stops to make, and left."

"I believe you Bobby J. Enough said."

I received a phone call from Uncle at nine o'clock the next morning informing me that two detectives would be coming at eleven o'clock to question me. They arrived right on time.

"Gentlemen, may I see your identification?" they flashed their badges, and I said, "Thank you, please come in and have a seat in the living room. I'll be with you in a few minutes."

When I returned to the living room, I had Bobby III in tow with some of his toys. I sat him down on the living room floor.

"Okay gentlemen, let's get started before he gets tired of playing with his toys and starts running around."

"Mrs. Fontana, we want to know if your husband was home three nights ago, and at what time did he arrive?"

"Detectives, Bobby J comes home every night, and he usually arrives around ten o'clock."

"Are you sure about that? Maybe he went back out later?"

"No, soon after he came home, he went to bed."

"Do you know a man who goes by the name of Brownie Scarducci?"

"Yes, I've met him several times in the store while he was playing cards with Bobby J."

"Well, he has disappeared. Mrs. Fontana, Brownie is an alleged bookmaker, loan shark, and God only knows what else. Your husband is a known gambler. We are trying to connect the dots because Brownie's wife told us he was definitely going to the Fontana store and take care of some very important business. His wife insisted that he always came home every night."

"Just a minute, gentlemen. If you believe Mrs. Scarducci when she says her husband went home every night, then I have to insist that you believe me when I say the same thing about my husband."

"Mrs. Fontana, we are convinced that Brownie went to the store that night and he never left there alive. You damn well know your husband wasn't home at ten o'clock. We want the truth right now."

"Detectives, I've just about had enough. I told you Bobby J was home by ten o'clock. I'm sure you've already searched the store. By the way, it's not what you two believe or are convinced of that counts, all that counts is what you can prove. Did it ever occur to you, that just maybe, Brownie had other people to see that night after he left Fontana and Sons, and ran into foul play elsewhere?

"Gentlemen, if you wish to question me again, and you conduct yourselves properly, I will cooperate. The bottom line is this, Mrs. Scarducci isn't privy to any more information about her husband's business dealings than I am. She has no idea what her husband was actually doing that night. I stand by what I said, my husband was here that night. Maybe you should expand your search and look elsewhere."

Then I said good day as I walked them to the door.

A week later, my doorbell rang, and there they were, in all their glory, the FBI. They showed me their identification before I invited them to take a seat in the living room.

The first thing I noticed about the two agents was how impeccably dressed they were. Their pants had creases in them that would make a gunnery sergeant proud. They wore black shoes that were so highly polished, I was sure they could see their reflections in them. Most detectives start out as beat cops, work very hard, and come up the ranks to make the grade. These men were highly educated, and extremely intelligent. This would be my first encounter with them, so I was curious to see what approach they would use on me in their interrogation.

"Mrs. Fontana, we found Brownie Scarducci's car in the long-term parking lot yesterday at Newark Airport. Once a car is found at an airport, an assumption is made that the owner of the vehicle took a flight out of state. That's when missing person reports become our jurisdiction, which in turn, brought us to you."

"Understood, but if Brownie left the state, how can I help you? I'm not a travel agent."

"We don't think he went anywhere. We believe the car being left at the airport was staged to make it look like he left town. Mrs. Fontana, we know your husband is a degenerate gambler who just happens to have a godfather who is very fond of him, ergo, he bails him out every time he gets jammed up. We are thinking that, just maybe, your husband's godfather called in a favor. Then we think Brownie was taken for a ride and disappeared. You see, we have a neighborhood witness who positively places Brownie's car in the Fontana parking lot at nine-thirty on the evening in question. So we know he was in that store."

"Excuse me, gentlemen, is there a question looming on the horizon, sometime in my immediate future?"

"Yes, we have one for you. What time did your husband come home that night?"

"Just as I told the detectives last week, he was home at ten o'clock, and remained here for the rest of the night. We all know it's all about the timing. You have nothing on Bobby J, because I know he was here. And I assure you, I will never change my story. Isn't it possible Brownie concluded his business at the store, and then another car arrived, and he followed it somewhere else? Since you said you only had one question for me, I assume you are finished here."

The agents thanked me for my time and left.

In early March, Uncle told me he heard that Mrs. Scarducci spent five thousand dollars and hired some psychic to see if she could help in locating Brownie.

Neither the detectives nor the FBI ever returned to question me about that night. Mrs. Scarducci waited the obligatory seven years required by law before she could have her husband declared legally dead, and Brownie's name was never mentioned again.

Chapter 9

I was surprised to see Frankie Daily, my father's longtime bartender and friend, behind the bar at noontime. He usually didn't start his shift until three o'clock.

My mind wandered years back to the day my father sat me down, and regaled me with the tale of their first meeting during Prohibition when Uncle Frankie had walked into his speakeasy looking for a job.

"Frankie, how did you hear about my place?"

"Are you kidding me? Everyone knows about The Tioga, Hemmy Cipo's place. It's reputed to be one of the hottest joints in the entire city."

"What are your qualifications as a bartender?"

"Well, to start with, I'm Irish on my father's side, and Italian on my mother's, she's a DeCecco. So I sure know how to drink, but I can make 'em just as good as I drink 'em, if not better."

"Understand this Frankie, when we're making them, we're never drinking them."

"I've been told that you have the fastest hands around, and that you were an excellent boxer a few years ago. Give me a chance to prove to you what a hard-working, loyal employee I can be."

"Let me tell you what will be expected from any employee in my place. This business is all about the people. Every woman that walks through my door gets put on a pedestal, and stays there. A number of men come in by themselves so they're not drinking alone. Some of them just want someone to talk to, and it will be your duty to listen. Just serve the drinks, lend an ear, and always remain friendly. However, sometimes others don't want to talk at all, in fact, they won't say a word to anyone except to order drinks. That's the way they want it, so leave them alone and they will be just fine. Those are the basics; do you think you can handle this kind of work?"

"No problem, I know I'm the right man for the job Hemmy."

"Good. That's the kind of attitude I like. Now, come step behind the bar and show me what you've got."

As it turned out, Uncle Frankie was indeed the right fit for my father.

After the attack on Pearl Harbor, which took place in the early hours on December 7th, 1941, President Roosevelt declared war against Japan the next day. Every man between the ages of eighteen through sixty-five was required to register for the draft. All able-bodied men up to the age of forty-five were required to serve in the military in one capacity or another. My father, Uncle, and Uncle Frankie enlisted together right after the attack, like so many other men.

Uncle wanted to do his part for the war effort, but deep down, he feared that he would never be able to pass the physical, because when he was five or six years old, he came down with a severe case of strep throat. Then he got rheumatic fever, which is one of the complications associated with it.

Both bartenders were classified 1A, or fit for service. They became part of the infantry, and fought the Germans on the front line.

As usual, Uncle was correct, there was no possible way he could have ever passed the physical, and when the time came, he didn't. Since Uncle was left behind, he promised my father that he would keep the bar open and run it for him.

Not long after he returned home, a mutual friend introduced my father, still the elusive bachelor, to a lovely young woman named Angela, and for the first time in his life, he was thunder-struck. She became "a keeper," and they were married in April of 1945. Of course, Uncle stood up as his friend's best man.

Soon after Uncle Frankie returned home from overseas, he found his true love as well, and when the time came, he asked my father to stand up for him. My father called his cousins Gabriel and Salvatore and asked them to cover for him and Uncle Frankie on the Friday night and Saturday of the wedding festivities. They agreed without any hesitation; these two men looked up to their older cousin, and would do anything for him.

Until that Friday night, when the small bridal party gathered for dinner, my mother and Frankie's bride-to-be, Aunt Carrie, had never met each other. When the two women were introduced, their faces broke out into wide grins and they hugged each other. As it turned out, they weren't strangers at all, because they had worked together for several years in a manufacturing plant that supported the war effort.

The next day, my mother couldn't have been happier watching her old friend, who she had just been reunited with, marry into my father's and Uncle's circle.

As soon as Frankie saw me, he smiled and said, "Come over here and give us a hug!"

When he released me from his bear hug, I said, "What a nice surprise to see you! But where's my father?"

Uncle Frankie nodded toward the back, then walked away to refill a customer's glass.

I went into the kitchen and found my mother cooking. "Mom, where's Dad? He's not behind the bar where he should be."

"Kiki, as you know, he hasn't been feeling like himself lately."

"Should I be worried?"

"Of course not. He's simply having a few tests done today. I'm sure his doctors will have some answers when the results come in, and when I know something concrete, I'll let you know. So, where is my grandson? You always bring him with you when you visit us."

"Aunt Esther and Uncle wanted to spend some family time with him, so he spent the night at their penthouse. Well, I will let you get back to work and I'll return in a day or two with your grandson, and hopefully both of you will be here."

And indeed, when I returned to Cipo's two days later with Bobby III, my father was where he should be. As he greeted me with a hug, I could feel how much thinner he had become. "How are you feeling Dad? What did the doctors say about all the weight you've lost? Please tell your little girl what's going on."

"Kiki, slow down. You know I've had bleeding ulcers for many years. But I'm about to get them under control as I've just started taking a new medication. Now, let me get your mother, and then I want to hold my grandson."

I smiled because I knew what was coming next. My father had made it a tradition that every time I went into the restaurant during the lunch hour, he and my mother would pick up Bobby III, sit him on the bar, and, beaming with pride, would announce to all the customers, "Our grandson is buying a round of drinks for everyone here." My father would then go back behind the bar with my son, as Bobby III "helped" make the drinks while my mother and I watched in amusement. It was obvious that everyone got a kick out of this tradition, and I indulged them by intentionally scheduling my visits around lunch time.

The summer was nearly over, and I had attempted several times to corner Bobby J into telling me what "backup plan" he and his father had concocted that night in the jail cell, but the only response I could ever get out of him was, "Don't worry about it, things are under control." Uncle had essentially said the same thing to me on the night Big D and Bobby J were arrested.

The trial began on Monday, September 9th. Bobby III was being looked after at Uncle's penthouse. When I entered the courtroom with Big D and Bobby J, we found the defense attorneys already sitting at the table up front. Both lawyers had previously petitioned the court that their clients be tried together, and it had been granted in a pre-trial motion.

When the proceedings began, Al DeMaio addressed the Court first. He made a motion to dismiss the charges against his client on the grounds that since most of the confiscated merchandise had been legitimately accounted for, there wasn't enough evidence left to warrant spending the time and the money to proceed with a trial. Irv Glassman made the same motion for Bobby J. The prosecutor objected to both motions. Judge Harvey pondered the request for a few minutes and then ruled, "Both motions are denied. However, I will allow both defendants to change their pleas from not guilty to guilty, otherwise, we will proceed to trial." Both defense lawyers stood up, took their turn, and said, "The plea stays the same, we are ready to go to trial. May we please start jury selection?" The judge called for a brief recess so that the prospective jurors could be brought into the courtroom.

A short time later, the jury pool was brought in, and the selection process began. It took all day, but by the time the Court shut down at four o'clock, a jury which was acceptable to both the defense and the prosecution had been chosen.

At nine o'clock the next morning, the bailiff said, "All rise," and the trial continued. The prosecutor gave his opening statement, which didn't have too much gusto since most of the evidence originally collected had been deemed inadmissible thanks to Uncle's intervention. Then it was Al's and Irv's turn. They said similar things, and by the time they were finished speaking, as far as I could tell, the prosecution's case had been reduced from a mountain to a molehill.

The prosecutor called every policeman and detective that had been involved in the raid at the store. Each one of them testified to the same thing, that the search and subsequent investigation, which included reviewing the last three years' worth of invoices for the business, yielded forty-five cases of merchandise that were missing paid receipts. Neither defense attorney chose to cross-examine a single witness.

Detective Brady, who had headed up the investigation and was the prosecution's star witness, was called last. To my surprise, Al chose to cross-examine him.

"Detective Brady, how big would you say the Fontana and Sons store is?"

"I don't know the exact square footage."

"Well, you testified earlier that you and your team searched the entire building. Would you say that it's a medium-sized warehouse?"

"You could say that."

"How many cases of merchandise do you think it would take to fill that back stockroom?"

"I have no idea."

"How about taking a guess? Could it be two hundred cases? Five hundred? One thousand? Perhaps two thousand?"

"I really couldn't guess."

"Well, it might interest the jury to know that at any given time, including on the day my client was arrested, between the sales floor and the stockroom, there were approximately twenty-five hundred cases worth of merchandise, which is normally turned over in its entirety four times per year.

"So, Detective Brady, am I correct in stating that your testimony is as follows? That after an extensive search of my client's warehouse and financial records, your investigation uncovered forty-five cases of merchandise that didn't have paperwork tied to them? Are we really having this trial at the taxpayer's expense, and at the inconvenience of the citizens serving on this jury, for a paltry forty-five cases of goods?"

The prosecutor jumped up immediately and croaked out, "Objection, Your Honor!"

"Sustained. Mr. DeMaio, you know better than that."

"Understood, Your Honor. Thank you, Detective Brady. I have no further questions for this witness."

Irv declined his turn to cross-examine the witness. After the point Al had just made, at Detective Brady's expense, I couldn't imagine there was anything else to gain from further questioning.

The prosecutor, who was still a little shaken, stood, and in a meek manner, rested his case. Because of the late hour, the judge said, "The defense can call its first witness at nine o'clock tomorrow morning."

As Big D was still the sole owner of the business, that made Al the lead defense attorney. Al called Louis Silverman as the first witness for the defense.

"Mr. Silverman, would you please tell the Court the name and location of your business?"

"The name of my business is ABC Wholesale Clothing Distributors, which is located in New York City."

"Mr. Silverman, are you associated in any way with the proprietor of the Fontana ad Sons business located here in Jersey City? And if so, please tell the Court the nature of your business relationship."

"Certainly. I have been doing business with Robert Francis Fontana Sr. for about twenty-five years. He has always paid his bills promptly, he never short counts us, and is a gentleman at all times. He's a professional who knows how to run a successful business."

"Do you know approximately how much of the merchandise sold in the Fontana and Sons store comes from your company? And if so, please tell us."

"Yes, my products make up the lion's share of the store's inventory."

"Thank you, Mr. Silverman. Mr. Glassman will now take over."

"Thank you, Mr. DeMaio. Mr. Silverman, based on a review of your tax records, it appears that you operate a multi-million dollar a year business. Is that correct?"

"Yes, that's correct."

"How many paid receipts does your company generate for all of your accounts every year, roughly speaking?"

"Oh my God, it would have to be in the tens of thousands."

"Mr. Silverman, you have cooperated fully with this investigation. However, your office was unable to produce copies of paid receipts for the forty-five cases of merchandise in question. Isn't it possible with the size of your business and the magnitude of paperwork that goes along with it, you could be missing some of the copies of the receipts?"

"It is not only possible but probable."

"Please explain to the Court how this could happen in a multi-million-dollar business like yours."

"After we file our annual income tax returns, which are prepared by our accountants, per the IRS guidelines, we are required to retain our records for a number of years. That amounts to a mountain of paperwork, the vast majority of which is packed in boxes and stored in the basement. My business is located in a building in the West 30s, and the basement is a potential firetrap, especially since it houses multitudes of paper. If a water main breaks in the area, the basement often floods. And don't even get me started on the rat infestation down there. And of course, there is always human error; which happens in every business."

"Thank you, Mr. Silverman, for your time, and for making the trip over here from New York City. We know that you are a very busy man but, your answers have shed some light on the potential pitfalls of record keeping for a large magnitude of paperwork. No further questions."

Irv, still maintaining his best poker face, turned toward the prosecutor and, in a honeyed and polite manner, said, "Your witness."

"Mr. Silverman, the fact remains that forty-five cases of merchandise do not have paid receipts. It would seem to me that the paperwork hasn't been found on either side because it simply never existed to begin with, and that supports the charge against the defendants of being in possession of stolen merchandise. How else do you explain that these two businesses are missing the exact same records?" This line of questioning seemed to have given the prosecutor renewed confidence, and he was now nonchalantly twirling his eyeglasses in his hand.

"Normally, as our two businesses have been working together for so long, our transactions are very smooth. However, within the last year, we have both had staffing issues that resulted in a much higher than normal amount of paperwork errors. It's my understanding that the bookkeeper at Fontana and Sons, Louise, was out for a chunk of time while she was taking care of her sick mother, and a temp was brought in. On my end, I have had significant turnover in my billing department and have had more than a few new hires. You see, many of the young women I have hired have gotten pregnant in the last year. There must be something in the water!"

That did it. The entire courtroom erupted in laughter. Even Judge Harvey had a difficult time trying to hide his amusement as he pounded the gavel in an attempt to restore the courtroom to order. He gestured to the prosecutor and said, "You may continue."

The prosecutor muttered, "No further questions, Your Honor," quickly walked back to his table, and slumped down in his chair.

Judge Harvey dismissed Mr. Silverman, and asked the defense to call their next witness. Al stood and said, "The defense rests." Judge Harvey then said, "Closing arguments will begin tomorrow morning. Court is adjourned."

On Thursday morning, the trial drew to a close, and as is procedure, the prosecutor presented his closing argument first.

"Ladies and gentlemen of the jury, regardless of what Mr. Silverman and the defense have told you, the fact remains, neither the supplier nor the defendants have been able to produce any proof that the forty-five cases in question were ever paid for, making them stolen merchandise. Therefore, I ask that you render a verdict of 'guilty.'"

Judge Harvey then said, "Mr. DeMaio, the Court is ready to hear your closing arguments."

Al stood, and stated that his closing argument would be on behalf of both defendants. Irv stood and confirmed this point for the Court, Al walked over to the jury and began.

"Good morning. I'm sure you are all eager to return to your busy lives, so I'll be brief. As we have shown during the trial, the records of even the most successful and well-run businesses are at the mercy of fires, floods, and rats. Fortunately, the locusts are not on this list of potential pitfalls in long-term file storage."

I couldn't help but chuckle a little, and neither could the jury, or the rest of the courtroom, with the exception of the prosecutor. Al flashed a small smile as he continued, "In business, even when every effort is made to preserve a paper trail, human error is always a factor. Therefore, we're asking you to return a verdict of not guilty on the grounds of reasonable doubt. Members of the jury, we thank you for your attention and your time."

After four days, the proceedings had come to an end. The Judge gave the jury their instructions, and they were led out of the room. All parties were advised by the judge not to stray too far, just in case the jury brought in a speedy verdict. Al, Irv, Big D, and Bobby J went to the secluded waiting area for the defense, and I opted to go down to the cafeteria for a cup of coffee. I knew we weren't out of the woods yet, but I had been highly impressed with the way Al and Irv demonstrated their talents during the trial. And I certainly wasn't expecting an amusing Biblical reference in the closing arguments. In choosing these high-priced lawyers to represent Big D and Bobby J, once again, Uncle had known best.

Less than forty-five minutes later, Al DeMaio rushed into the cafeteria and said, "We have to return to the courtroom immediately, there's been a development. Something big must have happened, because the judge won't divulge a word until all three lawyers are present in his chambers. All I know is that he is not a happy man, and your father-in-law and husband have been brought back into the courtroom."

"Is this a good or bad sign?"

"Based on my many years of experience as a trial lawyer. I have my suspicions as to what may have happened. But I know your godfather well enough to know better than to speculate with you about this unexpected turn of events. After the judge enlightens us in chambers, he will come out and address the Court."

I was back in the courtroom for no more than fifteen minutes when the judge appeared with the prosecutor, defense lawyers, and the court stenographer. He began, "Robert Francis Fontana, Sr. and Robert Francis Fontana, Jr., please rise.

"It has been brought to my attention that one of the jurors gained information last night that has a direct bearing on these proceedings. Before this trial, the juror had never heard of the Fontana and Sons business as she doesn't live near there. Yesterday, she stopped by her mother's house, which does happen to be located near the store. She mentioned that she was serving jury duty on a case against a business called Fontana and Sons. Her mother was shocked to hear that the owner and son were on trial for anything. Her mother expressed her strong opinion that there was no way the defendants could be guilty of any crime.

"For those of us in the legal field, this represents an obvious conflict of interest for the juror. However, after questioning her extensively, it is clear that there was no mal intent on her part when she opted to stay on the jury. She truly believed she could remain unbiased and impartial. She tearfully expressed remorse when I explained the ramifications of her actions. For the record, I believe that the juror made an honest mistake and that no criminal charges should be brought against her.

"However, after weighing all of the facts, the risk is too great that the jury has not been tainted. Therefore, in all fairness, I have no choice but to declare a mistrial.

"As for the prosecution, my advice is that you never entertain the idea of re-trying this extremely weak case in anyone's courtroom ever again.

"Robert Francis Fontana, Sr. and Robert Francis, Jr., you are both free to go. Case dismissed." With that, the judge pounded the gavel one last time, and it was all over.

Big D and Bobby J breathed a great sigh of relief. As they were being escorted out of the courtroom to sign paperwork, they turned to me, smiled and gave me a big thumbs up.

Later, Al told us that after the courtroom had emptied out and there was no one left but the three lawyers, the judge said, "Al and Irv, I'm inviting both of you to join me in my chambers. Mr. Prosecutor, please join us as well."

After the judge removed his robes, he began, "Al and Irv, bringing in Mr. Silverman as a witness was brilliant. Not only was he entertaining, but in my opinion, he was most convincing. I was left with more than a reasonable doubt."

Then he glanced toward the prosecutor. "Now that my robes are off, I will call you by your first name. So, Steve, this mistrial has most certainly saved you from further embarrassment. Also, I know all about the suicide that took place at the jail some time ago. I know certain lawmen are still ticked off. I suggest you spread the word to them that they should let it go. Don't bring a dog of a case like this into my courtroom or anyone else's ever again. Please take that as sound legal advice.

"Gentlemen, it's been interesting, but the time has come for all of us to move on. Have a good day."

It didn't take very long to complete the necessary paperwork that would put this case to bed for good. Once again, I dropped Big D and Bobby J off at the store, and then went directly home to call Uncle. "Uncle, you probably won't believe this, but the judge had to declare a mistrial because of one juror's misguided actions, and the case was dismissed. Based on what Al and Irv told us, the judge read the prosecutor the Riot Act, and it's unlikely that there will be a re-trial."

"Kiki, it's been my experience that such twists of fate aren't accidental. I have it on very good authority that those pesky forty-five cases will, once again, become Fontana property before next weekend. The good news is that I can assure you that this terrible chapter in your life is over. However, sadly, I must tell you that another difficult chapter is about to begin. The Fontanas are sure to engage in their obligatory celebrations over the next few days, including tomorrow night.

"Kiki, you've always been there for these two clowns, and you handled Senior's and Junior's latest calamity, from raid to release, quite capably. You stood up, stood tall, and stayed by their sides the whole way. Through everything, you have remained a dutiful wife and daughter-in-law, as well as a wonderful mother. No matter what happens, remember that.

"In the meantime, your Aunt Esther and I have delighted in our extra time with Bobby III, but I know you are eager to pick him up. We will discuss everything when I arrive at your house tomorrow morning at ten o'clock."

Chapter 10

When the doorbell rang the next morning, Bobby III ran to the front door and said, "Hi Uncle Milt, come to my room and see my bowling game."

"Sure, my best boy. I'd love to see it."

A half hour later, Uncle said, "I had a great time playing with your bowling game, but now, I need for you to be a good boy and keep playing, because I have to speak with your mother. Can you do that for me?"

"Sure, Uncle Milt, I have lots of toys to play with!"

"That little boy of yours knows how to perfectly line up all the pins. He's one smart boy who loves that game."

"Uncle, that's the one thing Bobby J has taken the time to teach him. After all, bowling is definitely one thing in which he is an expert."

"I have come here today with such a heavy heart because I need for you to do something that will cause you great pain. I must take the next step in securing your future right now. Before I can go forward, I must go back and tell you of the unexpected timing and extraordinary circumstances surrounding your birth.

"Kiki, when your mother went into premature labor a little more than two months ahead of schedule your father called me with the news and told me that he would be staying at the hospital as long as necessary. Then he called Frankie and told him to run the bar until he returned to celebrate the birth of his first child. There was no chance that I wouldn't be at my best friend's side when my godchild was born, so, Aunt Esther and I rushed to the hospital.

"As a precaution, Dr. Edwards, Angela's obstetrician, had the foresight to call a pediatrician to be on hand. Fortunately, it turned out to be Dr. Manny Rosenthal, and it's a good thing he was there. Later, he told Hemmy that while most babies cry when they come into this world, you never did. You were so tiny that you fit in the palm of his hand. Dr. Edwards came out to tell us the good news while Dr. Rosenthal examined you. During the exam, you started turning blue. He immediately started to blow life back into your lungs, and then he massaged your tiny little chest to make sure your heart kept beating. He saved your life in those first few minutes that you were on this earth.

"After you were stabilized and placed safely in the incubator, Dr. Rosenthal introduced himself, and addressed Hemmy."

"Mr. Cipo, congratulations on the birth of your beautiful baby girl. Although she is healthy, she will probably never grow to be much more than fairy-size. I've delivered over fifteen hundred babies in my career, and not one of them ever had a sparkle in their eyes that could even come close to what I have seen in your daughter's eyes today. I have some advice for you. Don't ever try to give her a rattle because her hand will already be filled. I am convinced that God has placed a magic wand in it."

"Kiki, as you know, your parents, I and Aunt Esther became close friends with Manny Rosenthal and his wife, Muriel, after your birth. Manny is as devoted to his Jewish faith as you are to your Catholic faith. On the day you were born, during those daunting moments in which he was saving your life, he was also praying to God. Dr. Rosenthal had an unshakeable feeling that this tiny baby, who had not only survived a difficult birth, but came into this world smiling instead of crying, must have been put here by God for a very good reason. And so Manny made a covenant with God that he would look after your physical well-being for the rest of his life. So you now know that Dr. Rosenthal didn't just happen to be at your house when lockjaw set in and he saved your life for a second time when you were four years old. He believed that it was his covenant with God at work.

"I chose to tell you this remarkable story today for a good reason, because by the end of this day, you will have to tap into your faith more than you ever have before."

"Uncle, you know how strong my faith is. But what is this pain you're alluding to, what's going on?"

"I have a few instructions for you. Make arrangements for a babysitter this evening. Go to a place called Caesar's Lounge in Bayonne around nine o'clock tonight. I have written the address on this piece of paper. Just go in and walk around the bar. You will know where to stop.

"Take a deep breath before you open your mouth to speak. Do not lose your temper, and remember, it's not personal. It may look that way to you, but I assure you, it isn't. Then do what you have to do.

"In less than six months, you will have to make a very important decision concerning your future and your son's. After tonight, there will be no doubt as to what your decision must be.

"I would never send you into the arena empty-handed. Take your magic wand with you, it's a weapon of the fairies. Use it wisely. I will call you in the morning and we will discuss everything."

Uncle's request meant that tonight, before the witching hour, what I would be confronting head-on was going to destroy any shred of innocence I had left.

As a girly-girl, I had always loved to play dress up. My challenge tonight was going to be wearing, and maintaining, a brave face.

The babysitter arrived right on schedule. I handed her a piece of paper which had Uncle's phone number on it and, as I didn't know how long I would be out of reach, it instructed her to call him if an emergency arose.

Bayonne was about two miles away, so the drive was brief. But once there, finding a parking space in the area was typically another story. But tonight, I found a parking spot less than a block away within five minutes. However, I sat in my car for nearly half an hour. I needed a little more time to brace myself for what I would find on the other side of the lounge's door.

This was obviously a popular place, because I could barely get in the front door. People were standing three deep all the way around an enormous bar. The live band was very loud as they played 'My Girl' by The Temptations. Despite the fact that I was, as always, wearing my wedding ring, a couple of men offered to buy me a drink. Without looking at them for more than a second, I declined by saying I was meeting someone.

As the next song, 'Unchained Melody' by the Righteous Brothers, was a romantic slow song, more people got up to dance, providing a much clearer view of who remained seated at the bar. When I saw what Uncle had intended for me to see, I came to a dead stop, almost as if I had been paralyzed. Prepared as I thought I had been, I didn't want to believe my eyes. Bobby J was sitting about as close as he could get to a redhead, with his arm around her waist, while he whispered in her ear. I took a deep breath, walked right up behind them, and tapped him on the shoulder.

"Well, well, well, Bobby J, are you here celebrating the good fortune that found its way to you yesterday?"

Both of their faces registered nothing but complete shock, and their jaws dropped. I didn't give Bobby J the chance to reply, and continued, "By the way, who is this red-head? Care to introduce me?

"What's the matter, cat got your tongue? Never mind, I'll introduce myself." I turned toward the other woman and said, "I'm Kiki Fontana, Bobby J's wife.

"Don't you dare pretend that you don't know he is married; his wedding ring is on his finger in plain view. I suggest you get up right now and take a very slow walk around the bar. I'm taking your seat; Bobby J and I need to talk."

"Kiki, I hope you are not going to cause a scene here."

"Not as long as she vacates that seat immediately. Beat it Red."

She got the message and took a hike. I took her seat, and at that very moment, as if on cue, the band took a well-deserved break, substantially turning down the volume in the entire room.

"Kiki, she's just a friend. You know I come home every night."

"Whoop dee doo," I said sarcastically. "It's one of the ways in which you attempt to delude yourself, and others, into believing that you are a devoted husband and father."

"When you met me, you knew about all the different types of activities I spend my leisure time participating in. I live my life, and I've always done my own thing."

"Yes, I knew those things and accepted them. But this? Never. You should be celebrating with me tonight. Instead, I find you cozying up to another woman. You made the commitment to become a husband and father. How could you break my heart like that, and why would you even want to? I'm your wife."

Clearly unprepared to answer those questions, he chose to reply with only, "Kiki, are you going to tell your father and your godfather?"

"Uncle already knows. How do you think I knew where to find you? And since you always come home, consider yourself warned, I don't want to see or speak to you at all tonight.

"Oh, and one more thing. I'm packing. Don't look so frightened, it's not a gun. It's something much more powerful. I've got a magic wand, and I'm going to wave it over you very soon to make you disappear from my life and my son's life forever."

Then I got up, turned my back on him, walked straight toward the door, and never looked back. I would never allow anyone to see me break down. But now I was all alone, in every sense, and could let myself fall apart. I cried myself to sleep that night, knowing full well that my marriage was over. There were many things I could, and had, tolerated, but marital infidelity would never be one of them.

Of course, Bobby J came home later that night, but this time he found my note taped to the front door directing him to the guest bedroom. The next morning, I heard him get up, shower, and leave for the store much earlier than usual.

Uncle called at ten o'clock the next morning and asked if he could come right over. I decided to ask how he always manages to make time for me in his very busy schedule. He told me that he had flexibility to go in early or stay late so he could complete his work.

Bobby III was at my side when I opened the front door. "Uncle Milt, wanna make a puzzle with me?"

"Sure, my number one boy, what kind is it?"

"It's all the states in 'merica."

"Sweet boy, remember, it's called the United States of America, which is the country that we are living in."

"Okay, mom. United States of 'merica."

I smiled and said, "That's close enough for now."

Uncle took his hand and then watched as he put the entire puzzle together by himself in less than five minutes. Uncle helped him put a second one together, and then he joined me in the kitchen for a cup of coffee.

He surprised me when he said, "Kiki, your son will make a fine politician one day. I can promise you right now that if I'm still alive, and if that's what he wants, I will make sure it happens. You know how he started putting words together at ten months old, it was evident to me then that he was a future legislator in the making.

"Now tell your godfather what happened last night."

"Before I get into that Uncle, I want you to know what occurred to me early this morning. Yesterday's date, was in fact, Friday the thirteenth. How appropriate is that timing for a marriage to go down in flames?"

Uncle said, "Knowing full-well the significance of dates in your life, it was an omen. Last night's events had to happen the way they did, when they did."

"I had to see Bobby J and the red-head together with my own eyes. I know that's why you sent me into the lounge last night. You knew I wouldn't accept the truth any other way. How long has that been going on?"

"Kiki, it doesn't matter. What's important is that you now know the truth. So feel justified several months from now when you have the pleasure of ending your marriage to that fool."

"What I need to know is why my father encouraged me to marry that wrongo. I'm sure you know the whole story."

"Just know that I would have given the world if I could have spared you from shedding one single tear last night, and I'm sure that you did cry, so please accept my apology. All the wheels concerning your future are in motion, but right now, I need to know how you left off with Bobby J."

"He's well aware that I will never forgive or forget the way he hurt me. Considering the situation, it was all quite civil.

"Godfather, you know I never call you that unless I have something extremely important on my mind. I have never once seen any indication that you or my father ever crossed the line of impropriety where other women are concerned. I would never want to believe that to be the case for my own father or godfather. Please tell me that has never or would ever happen, I need to know the truth right now."

"Kiki, don't ever think your father and I are wiseguys. We are so much above that sort of behavior. We both know the way to live and love. That's the way it's supposed to be, and that's the way God expects it to be. Please don't ever give that another thought.

"I am acutely aware of the pain I caused you last night. The outcome certainly went against your Catholic upbringing, but I want you to know that I had Hemmy's blessing all the way. I want you to keep a civil rapport with Bobby J. If Bobby III were to feel tension or hostility in this house, it could become detrimental to his well-being. He is such a happy child. Let's all see to it that he stays that way.

"I won't be returning to my offices in Las Vegas for the rest of the year. I'll send Aunt Esther down to our estate in Palm Beach whenever she wants to go. I'm staying here, just in case Hemmy's new medicine isn't as effective as we are hoping."

"Uncle, is there something you aren't telling me about my father?"

"Not to worry my princess, just remember what I said about Bobby J."

In the following weeks, I avoided him as much as possible. But when the time came for me to look him in the eyes, and tell him I was leaving him for good and taking my son with me, I'd have more than an ample supply of words. Bobby J's day of reckoning was coming soon enough, and there wouldn't be a damn thing he could do about it.

Chapter 11

On the morning of October 23rd, Uncle called. He told me to pack up enough of Bobby III's clothes for several days, his limo would arrive within the hour to pick us up. When we arrived at his penthouse, I noticed that he was surprisingly pale. As a matter of fact, he looked downright sickly. Suddenly, Uncle picked up Bobby III, twirled him around, and said, "My best boy, Uncle Milt is about to become the man who will always look after you." Chills ran up and down my spine, and I got a dreadful feeling that something was terribly wrong. "Yolanda and Kim will be taking care of you today until Aunt Esther comes home. Your mommy and I have some very important things to do today"

Bobby III, blissfully unaware of the melancholy tone in Uncle's voice, said, "Okay, Uncle Milt, see ya later!" as he began to scamper off.

"Before you go off to your room, come over here and give your mother and me a big kiss, and remember to be a good boy.

"My driver will be taking us to The Medical Center because Hemmy was rushed there by ambulance this morning. Your mother and Aunt Esther are waiting there for us."

"What's wrong with my father? And please don't tell me it's a problem with his ulcers. I don't think that would qualify for a ride to the hospital in an ambulance."

"I'll explain everything in the car because I need to talk privately with you.

"About six months ago, your father started to experience a sharp pain in his back. You know how he loves Cipo's, so he stubbornly refused to take time off to go see his doctor and ignored the pain, even though your mother constantly badgered him. But after weeks of getting nowhere with Hemmy, Angela finally reached her wits end and confided in me.

"I'll get right to it. After undergoing a multitude of tests, my best friend was given the grim diagnosis that he had a rare form of lung cancer, galloping cancer to be exact. It moves very quickly, and he was given six months to live. That was about five months ago."

I began crying hysterically.

Uncle put his arms around my shoulder and said, "Sweetheart, cry as much as you need to. I was shocked when my lifelong friend told me his diagnosis, and my eyes certainly teared up. You know that Hemmy has always been like a brother to me, and much more. I took the news hard, too.

"There is more I have to tell you before we get there. Your father was given the bad news shortly before Sr. and Jr. took the bust in June. In fact, he knew about the bust before I did.

"He told me about his cancer just as soon as he found out. All the doctors could do was prescribe heavy doses of morphine to help shield him from the pain. They prepared him for the worst. The doctors made it very clear that in the end, he would likely slip into a coma and pass quickly.

"He needed to be in control of who found out, and when. The only other thing he revealed to your mother was that I would be available if he needed me for anything. We were both well aware of the grief that had been dumped in your lap at the hands of that reckless Fontana daily double.

"I have since taken Hemmy to all of his medical appointments. Since I am the owner of a real estate company, and all of Hemmy's papers are in meticulous order, taking care of your mother's future will prove to be the easy part. Our challenge has been in securing your destiny. Every ride in this limo afforded us precious time so we could spend it together formulating and finalizing a plan for you.

"We will be arriving at the hospital in a few minutes. You must stop crying and get it together right now. There will be plenty of time for tears later on. For now, your father is still coherent, and wants to speak to you in person. It's very important that you hear certain things directly from him."

My mother and Aunt Esther were sitting with my father when we entered his room. I rushed up to him and kissed his forehead. Then my father looked up at me with such sadness in his eyes. He was fully aware that his impending death would leave a giant void in his little girl's life.

"My daughter, I want you to listen very carefully to me. There's something I've got to get off my chest before the nurse comes in to give me another shot of morphine. I humbly apologize for allowing you to marry into the Fontana family. Fortunately, it can and will be dealt with. That is the first wrong that will be made right soon after I'm gone.

"I had already put a plan into motion for your future, when I learned that I was terminally ill. Milt was not on board with my plan at the onset. However, the friend who stood by my side at the start of your life, as soon as I reminded him of what Dr. Rosenthal said that day, he knew I had chosen wisely for you. He stands by my side again today, at the end of my life, you must have no fear, your godfather will implement all of our plans.

"Kiki, because of who you are, I think you will be equal to the task, and Milt agrees with me wholeheartedly. We concur that you will exceed all of our combined expectations.

"And one day, you will meet your prince. At long last, you will have the fairy-tale ending you so richly deserve. I'm positive it's in the cards for you.

"By the way, I heard that you recently tapped into your fairy's arsenal when you went into battle. Nicely done, my daughter!"

My father smiled as he said, "Kiki, on the day you leave Bobby J, there will be no turning back. You will never be able to see or speak to him ever again. That also applies to every member of his family. Promise me you can do this, because it's very important."

"Dad, I promise."

"Hemmy, I want to add something with both of you here. When I implement the plan to bring you into my universe, I know you will rise to the very top, and in doing so, you will become 'the legend.'"

"Milt, I'm counting on you to make it happen. When she achieves that undertaking, then, and only then, can you tell her the whole story about my life."

"Dad, Uncle, what are you talking about?" My father was talking to Uncle about my future, knowing full well he wasn't going to be a part of it.

Then the nurse entered the room and said, "I know this is a very difficult time, but I must give Mr. Cipo his shot of morphine." When she finished and left the room, my father continued.

"When I'm gone, Milt will immediately take on the role of being Bobby III's grandfather. Your son needs a stand-up man in his life, and there is no one more qualified than your godfather.

"You must remember, you are not a Fontana, you are a Gallo-Cipo and always will be. Certain principles have always been attached to the Gallo name, and you will be expected to stay the course and stand up at all times.

"I have one last thing to say to you, and it's very important. Above all else, never forget these words, 'I'll always be with you.'" As he reached up and brushed away the tears from my cheek.

Then he told Uncle and me that he was very tired and needed to get some rest. Uncle left the room to find my mother and Aunt Esther. My father's mission was now complete. He had disclosed everything to me that he thought I needed to hear from him.

Uncle was well aware that the entire staff at his penthouse was more than capable of taking care of my son, but at the same time, he knew that Bobby III wasn't accustomed to staying long periods of time alone with them. So, he asked his wife to take the limo and go home to look after him because my mother, Uncle, and I would remain at my father's side until he took his last breath.

Since I had already ceased most communication with Bobby J, I didn't keep him abreast of my comings and goings. Nevertheless, that did not apply to the whereabouts of my son. Then, to my surprise, Uncle asked me to call Evelyn and give her a heads up. I steadied myself and called the store's private line from my father's room. Evelyn answered, which was pretty much standard procedure.

"Hello Evelyn. Please tell Bobby J that my son will be staying at my uncle's penthouse for the next few days because my father was rushed to the hospital this morning. My mother, Uncle, and I will be staying here for the foreseeable future."

I was shocked by Big D's girlfriend's reaction to my call. She started crying, then quickly asked me if there was anything she could do to help. I thanked her and said, "My father is in very good hands here."

The hours wore on and at a little after midnight, all three of us noticed that my father's breathing had become extremely labored. Uncle rushed out of the room and returned with a doctor. After a quick medical examination, we were informed that my father had just slipped into a coma. The merciful side of this grave development was that his face was now completely relaxed and he could no longer feel any pain.

We had been keeping vigil at my father's side for twenty-six hours straight, when we were jolted by the sudden loud rattle coming my father's throat. Uncle jumped up, nodded to my mother and said, "Angela, the time has come for you to kiss your husband goodbye." Then as I kissed my father on the cheek, I noticed that the clock on the wall read three twenty-seven in the afternoon. Uncle squeezed my father's hand ever so tightly as he said, "Godspeed, my lifelong friend." Then he put his hands on my shoulders and said, "Let's step out into the hallway so that your mother can have a few private moments with her husband."

He understood that for all the anguish I had endured at the hands of the Fontana men, it was nothing compared to the pounding I had just taken. A few minutes later, he gestured for me to return to my father's room as he went in search of the doctor to come and pronounce time of death.

"Ladies, it's time. Let us each say good-bye to Hemmy. There's nothing more for us to do here. I made a phone call and employees from Palumbo's funeral home are en route to collect his body"

"Kiki, I would like you to go home with your mother when we leave here, but I know you want to go to your home. Try to get some much-needed rest. I will go home as quickly as possible because there is much work to be done. Angela, please be ready to leave promptly at noon-time tomorrow. You and I will go to Palumbo's funeral home and make all of Hemmy's arrangements."

Later, Aunt Esther told us that Uncle had made countless phone calls after he arrived at the penthouse. Then he attended a clandestine meeting with more than twenty highly trusted men. It would turn out to be the most crucial meeting ever held, ensuring that the family's future was solidified.

When I was dropped off at my house and entered, at that moment I understood how important it was for me to be here alone. I instinctively walked into my son's room and became conscious of the fact that my father would never enter this room again. Nor would I have the pure enjoyment of watching him hug and play with his beloved grandson.

I went into the living room next, because it contained the bar that my father tended at all of the family gatherings. Then my mind wandered over to Cipo's, which was now temporarily closed. Prior to the terrible disease that had invaded his body, nothing would have ever kept my father from working behind his treasured bar. The tears started to run down my cheeks once more.

At that moment, when I was at my lowest point, I had to tap into my faith, knowing it would have to become my life preserver now, so that I could have something to hold onto for the foreseeable future.

My mother called me at four o'clock and told me that my father's wake would be held on Saturday, Sunday, and Monday, afternoons and evenings. On Tuesday morning, a full Catholic Mass and funeral service would be held, which would be officiated by Father Grady. After its completion, we would all proceed to The Holy Name Cemetery, which was located in North Arlington, New Jersey. My father's parents, Angelo Cipo and Gemma Gallo-Cipo, and her parents, Gabriel and Antonia Gallo, were all buried there.

When we hung up, the phone rang again almost instantaneously. "Hello Kiki, I'd like to come over to see you right now if I may."

"Of course, I'd like that, please come." I still had a soft spot for Big D and Mario.

When Big D arrived, and after giving me a big hug, he conveyed sincere condolences on behalf of the entire Fontana family, and everyone who was employed in his store. There had never been a doubt in my mind that Big D truly liked and respected my father. It occurred to me that everyone seemed to respect my father immensely.

Then, he went on to say, "Bobby J truly cared for him because your father was a great family man."

"He expressed that sentiment to my mother when he called her last night. It's too bad he didn't take a page from his father-in-law's playbook on how to treat his own family."

"I got it straight from the horse's mouth, you are the only woman he will ever genuinely love, you can be sure of it."

"Big D, you certainly can believe that if you want to, but I'm not buying it for one second. And, if somehow it were true, let me give it to you straight from this horse's mouth. That would be his misfortune, because I don't give a damn about him anymore, and you can be sure of that."

"Please don't make it sound so final that your marriage to Bobby J is over. Look at Rose and me. Neither one of us are going anywhere, no matter what happens. We will always stay together."

"It's a good thing that you sell general merchandise and not love advice. Because if your marriage is your best sales pitch for the latter, then you would have to change professions. The only reason Rose stays married to you is because she is tucked away in Saddle Brook and you have yet to be caught red-handed in your dalliances as your fool of a son was.

"You know what, Big D, this is not the time to discuss the state of my marriage. It's time for me to mourn the beloved man who was, without fail, always there for me when I needed him.

"Big D, thank you for coming, I really appreciate your kind words about my father, I know you had tremendous respect for him."

I was certain that he knew that I would never forgive his son for not even coming close to being the man we would be burying in the next few days, and there was no way he could hide his sadness.

Shortly after Big D left, Uncle called and told me that his driver would be picking up my mother and then me within the hour. We would be going to his penthouse, where dinner was being prepared for us.

When we arrived, Bobby III came running up to me. "Hi, Mommy, hi, Nana!"

"Well hi, yourself handsome boy, please give your mother hugs and kisses. Come to think of it, Nana could use some big hugs and kisses also."

Bobby III eagerly complied, and then I saw the first smile on my mother's face in days.

I went over to Aunt Esther, gave her a big hug and asked, "Has Bobby III been a good boy since yesterday?"

"Yes, Kiki, he has been my angel, as always. Naturally, I will be at your father's wake and funeral, but in between, I will come back here to keep my eye on him, and he will be just fine."

After we all had eaten, I went into Bobby III's room and put some puzzles together with him. Then I gave him his bath, put him in his pajamas, and he began the "Now I lay me down to sleep" prayer. When he finished and said, "God bless Pop-Pop," I stopped him with tears in my eyes and said, "Pop-Pop has gone to Heaven. Would you please ask God to give him an extra hug from me and you?"

"Mommy, why did Pop-Pop go to Heaven? Isn't he coming back?"

"No darling, Pop-Pop won't be coming back, but Heaven is a good place."

A rare pout crossed his little face as he said, "Well, I don't want him to go away."

"I know sweet boy, but don't be sad, because Pop-Pop told me an important secret. Would you like for me to share it with you?"

"Sure, Mommy, I like secrets."

"Put your hand right here, over your heart on your chest. Hold your hand there. Pop-Pop said to me, 'I'll always be with you.' You see?"

I entered the living room and walked over to the wall of windows, staring at the beautiful Manhattan skyline. I found no joy in it tonight and I started to cry again. Uncle came from behind me and said, "Kiki, did you tell Bobby III?"

"Yes, and the realization has set in that as time goes by and he gets older, he will lose all memory of my father. My son will never have the chance to get to know his grandfather. That is almost more than I can bear."

"Sadly, it's true. In time, Bobby III will not be able to visualize Hemmy anymore. But we four, Angela, Esther, you, and I, will become the keepers of his memory and the guardians of his legacy. As Bobby III ages, our stories about his grandfather must become more detailed. By the time he becomes a grown man, he will know the entire story of your father's life. We will never allow Hemmy's essence to be forgotten. You don't have to be alone now, go home, pack a bag, and come back here with my driver."

"Thank you for the offer, but the memories of my father are in my house, and that's where I need to be. Besides, I want the pleasure of telling Bobby J that he won't be accompanying me to the wake. But he will be welcome to attend any time after the official two o'clock start time. This might not be the right thing to do, but that's the way I want it."

"Bravo Kiki, you are indeed a Gallo-Cipo. Tomorrow, we'll enter Palumbo's together. Aunt Esther and I will be in the limo and outside your door at twelve-fifteen sharp. We should arrive at the funeral parlor no later than one o'clock. That will give us at least one hour of privacy with Hemmy.

"I don't think your mother will be able to cope. It will fall upon your shoulders to greet all the people attending your father's wake. Hemmy knew so many people in his lifetime, many of whom became dear friends. Others became faithful customers, and the rest could be called staunch business associates.

"Your Great Uncle Dominick and his two sons, Gabriel and Salvatore, will be sitting to the left of you and your mother in the front row. I will be sitting on your right side along with Frankie Daily and your Uncle Vito. The second row will be reserved for all of our wives. We will help you greet everyone because many of the people will be known only to the men sitting with you in the front row."

When Bobby J came home, I informed him that I didn't want him at my side during the wake, and that he was being relegated to the third row where he could join his family. The look of shock on his face told me that he never expected to hear that, nor did he like it.

It hit me that this was the first time in my entire life I had done something so spiteful. I had deliberately hurt another human being.

I suppose there is some truth in the saying, "payback is a bitch."

Chapter 12

When Uncle picked me up the next afternoon, I sat next to my mother and noticed how pale and tired she looked.

The owner of Palumbo's Funeral Home, Richard, was waiting outside the front doors to greet us. He said, "My family and I are extending our deepest condolences to you Mrs. Cipo, Mrs. Fontana, and Mr. and Mrs. Kaye. Mrs. Cipo, even though you reserved the largest room, I want you to know that this entire building is available for your use."

My mother managed to nod her head in thanks. I thanked Mr. Palumbo as well. Uncle shook hands with him.

When we entered the room, before we approached my father's casket, we all noticed that the room was already filled with floral arrangements. Mr. Palumbo told us that additional flowers had arrived and had already been placed in the other two viewing rooms.

Uncle escorted mother up to view my father's body first. As soon as she looked upon the forever sleeping love of her life, she broke down completely and started yelling, "No! No! No!" Uncle had to practically drag her away from the casket and steer her toward her seat.

I walked up to my father next. Controlling my tears wasn't an option just yet, but when the doors opened at two o'clock, Hemmy's little girl would put her tears on lockdown, adopt a brave face, step up to the plate and get the job done.

Aunt Esther then viewed the man who meant so much to her husband. She cried her eyes out before taking her seat in the second row.

To my surprise, Evelyn walked in right behind Uncle Dominick, his two sons and their wives. Then Evelyn started walking toward the front and Uncle did something that totally astonished me. He intercepted her, and personally escorted Big D's girlfriend up to my father's casket. She quietly sobbed, said a prayer, and became solemn and dignified. Then she came up to my mother and me, offered her heartfelt condolences with genuine sadness in her voice, and then took a seat in the back of the room.

First of all, I was bewildered that she would show up here before the official start of the wake. So I asked myself, who is this lady?

Uncle Dominick and his sons, as part of the Gallo family, had been crushed by my father's death. Then Uncle Dominick took a place at the head of my father's casket while Gabriel and Salvatore planted themselves firmly at the foot, but not before the three of them had a very serious conversation with Uncle. At that moment, it occurred to me that the Gallo men were standing guard for my father.

Three young men were sitting in the front row next to Frankie Daily. They took the seats that had been vacated by Uncle Dominick and my father's cousins. Uncle Frankie introduced the two younger ones to me as his sons, who I didn't recognize as I hadn't seen them since they were young boys. The third man looked to be a little older than me, but I was positive I had never seen him before.

At exactly two o'clock, dozens of people started to file in. Then from the corner of my eye, I noticed the Fontana family standing at the back of the line. As they made their way toward the front, I saw that Rose, Jeanette, and Mario were walking right behind Big D and Bobby J. When Big D made eye contact with me, I could tell he was showing a complete disapproval of me for the first time. He was aware that his son was going to be humiliated in front of anyone who knew us. Protocol dictates that he should be sitting at my side in the front row. I'm sure this imposed seating arrangement drove home the point of the inevitable end of my marriage to his son.

Within less than forty-five minutes, Uncle told me that the line of people waiting to view my father's body stretched out the door for at least a block.

Later in the afternoon, I realized that the three men sitting with Uncle Frankie were there specifically to stand at my father's casket when Uncle Dominick and his sons took a break. I guessed it was simply their way of showing respect.

Soon, all of the Fontanas had paid their respects to my father and extended sincere sympathies to everyone in the front row. Then, Rose quickly apologized for not being able to attend the rest of the viewings, however, she did assure us that she would be attending the funeral and repast.

Then, Bobby J announced that he would attend every viewing through to his father-in-law's burial. I thanked all of them for their support.

Bobby J kept true to his word by not making a move to leave until we did.

After we had already stayed an extra hour, Uncle realized that we all needed a much overdue dinner break. He sent word to Richard Palumbo to disperse the crowds and lock the front doors. As soon as Uncle Dominick and his sons moved away from my father's casket, the three young men who were waiting in the front row, jumped up and replaced them immediately.

The entire family met on Newark Avenue at a fine Italian restaurant called Nardi's. The owner, Michael Nardi, was waiting to greet us. We were escorted to one of the party rooms in the back which he made sure was ready for us.

I was shocked to see my mother looking so relaxed as she enjoyed a glass of red wine with her meal, because she seldom ever drank. Then, to my surprise, I noticed that Bobby J had joined us. At least, he had the good sense to sit at the other end of the table. The service was impeccable and the food was excellent.

We entered Palumbo's through the back door and once again were able to visit privately with my father before Richard opened up the front doors. To my utter amazement the three young men were standing exactly where we had left them. I asked Uncle, "Why would a humble bartender warrant being treated this way and why would hundreds of people be filing through here non-stop?"

"Shortly before your father died, you know I promised to tell you the entire story one day. He trusted me to do that. Now, I'm asking you to do the same."

"All right, Uncle. I'll wait."

Richard opened the doors right on schedule. People kept coming. Suddenly, a very elegant man walked in, flanked on either side by burly men. He by-passed the entire viewing line and walked right up to the front of the casket. My father's uncle, then moved from his post and stopped the line of people, which once more, stretched out the door and down the block. He made way for this gentleman so that he was the next person to view my father. After he finished saying a prayer and as he approached us, Mother and I recognized him immediately as John V. Kenny. He was still called Mayor. At the time, when he served as Mayor, he was considered to be a very powerful man who was reputed to have had a very large political machine behind him.

"Angela, Kiki, I am so sorry for your loss. Hemmy was a great man. I knew him for a long time. Our friendship went back before either one of us was married. Our bond was built on mutual respect. Both of you can count on me to return for the funeral. By the way, has the floral arrangement I sent arrived?"

"Mayor Kenny, my mother and I haven't had a chance to view all of the arrangements yet. Our family will read each card and view every one of them after the doors close tonight.

"Thank you for your support. Your loyalty to my father is duly noted. And I'm quite sure your floral piece is exquisite. We expect that you will be riding up front in one of the limos on Tuesday morning. Our family is most honored that you have asked to give one of the eulogies at my father's repast. Mayor Kenny, thank you for coming."

The viewings were the same for the next few days. The line of people filing through had slowed down a bit, but was still steady by the last evening which ran an hour over schedule once again. Uncle had placed a sign-up sheet in the back of the room for anyone who wanted to attend the repast after the funeral.

The next morning, our family would have one hour to view my father for the last time, bid him a final farewell and then proceed to the church where Father Grady would begin the funeral mass promptly at ten o'clock. Upon completion, the funeral procession would slow down and halt for a few moments in front of Cipo's Restaurant before continuing onto the Holy Name Cemetery for the final prayers and internment.

After my father was laid to rest, Uncle took me aside and told me that the sign-up sheet for the repast clearly stated that a maximum of 300 people had to be enforced because that was the capacity at The Tavern in the Park and it was about to be met.

By one o'clock the burial was completed and as we proceeded to the restaurant, I began to think about all the people I had met over the last three days. These people represented all walks of life, councilmen, committeemen and women, several judges, lawyers, union representatives, police chiefs and lastly, the present mayor of Jersey City, Thomas Whelan. I thought, Wow! That was a pretty impressive list.

By the time we arrived at the restaurant and were escorted by the owner to the main ballroom, I couldn't help but notice that the sound coming from the room was deafening. The room was already full and the mood was anything but solemn.

I think my father would have liked that, and I'm positive that as a bartender his entire life, he would have wanted the last drink to be on him.

I was curious to see how some of the seating arrangements played out. Of course, Mother and I were sitting with Uncle Dominick and his wife, their sons and wives and Uncle and Aunt Esther. The other uncles, Frankie, Vito and Joe, who had come up from Florida along with their wives were at the next table. That table held a surprise. Evelyn, who is widowed, was sitting with them.

The Fontanas occupied another table. They were all present. I did catch Big D staring at Evelyn from time to time.

The entire room finally quieted down when Uncle Dominick as the first person to give a eulogy walked up to the podium. First, he thanked everyone in the room for coming to celebrate Hemmy's life. Then he started his eulogy by reminding all of the guests that his nephew had only been six and a half years younger than him which made their very close relationship more like brothers rather than uncle and nephew.

Gabriel went up next and talked about the way he grew up admiring his much older cousin. Clearly the guests knew that what he really meant was he unabashedly idolized his cousin Hemmy.

Next, Mayor Kenny started to walk toward the podium. He began with great enthusiasm to reminisce about the good old days when he enjoyed palling around with Hemmy after prohibition as two very determined bachelors. Then he affirmed how my father could always be counted on to lend a hand whenever asked during his tenure as mayor from 1949 through 1953. He concluded by acknowledging how Hemmy had remained his steadfast friend and how much he would be missed as the entire room full of people cheered.

The best was saved for last. When Milton Kaye walked to the front, one could have heard a pin drop in the vast room. He began by regaling the crowd with the story of his very first meeting with my father as boys which was the start of their lifelong friendship. He continued with a much more exciting tale of how Hemmy saved his life from two thugs. At the end, he said, "I'm going to wrap it up by reciting three passages that I think best describe the essence of this man.

"The first one was written anonymously and goes like this, 'As long as we live, He too will live, for he is a part of us, as long as we remember him.' The second was written by, believe it or not, Michelangelo and I will recite it in honor of Hemmy's Italian heritage, 'If we have been pleased with life, we should not be displeased with death since it comes from the hand of the same

Master.' And lastly, I will repeat a Hebrew proverb, 'Say not in grief He is no more, but live in the thankfulness that He was.'

"My world will forever be a lesser place because Hemmy is no longer a part of it." Then Uncle raised a glass, looked up toward Heaven and said, "Good bye my brother and my hero." With that all 300 people stood up and raised a glass to Hemmy Cipo. I was sure that Uncle had just raised the bar on the delivery of a eulogy because there was hardly one dry eye in the entire ballroom.

The timing couldn't have been better when within a few minutes of Uncle's eulogy, the prime rib dinners were served.

My father's life and death had come to an end. My mother never saw a bill for the repast. Uncle dropped my mother off at her house first because she told us that she was exhausted. Uncle told her that he would go over my father's papers with her by the end of the week. He made it very clear that Cipo's would not be reopening as it had already been sold per Hemmy's wishes. That information shocked both of us.

Then the driver took us straight to Uncle's penthouse. He knew how much I missed seeing my son's happy face. For me, it would be much more than the superstition that goes with the broken pieces of a mirror. My broken pieces were caused by two deaths: the death of my marriage to a selfish man and the death of my father, a selfless man.

Bobby III greeted me with hugs and kisses. "Where did you go? I didn't see you for a long time."

"My best boy, lots of people who knew your Pop-Pop wanted to say good bye to him. It's called paying your respects."

"Why can't kids say good bye too?"

"Well, they can but in a different way. Every night when you say your prayers and you get to the part God Bless Pop-Pop, that's your way of doing it. You won't ever forget to do that, will you?"

"No, Mommy, I'll always remember."

"Good boy. When we finish playing, we have to go home because you and I are going to visit Nana tomorrow."

Aunt Esther said to me, "I'm confident Milt and I will be able to talk your mother into coming down to Florida with me in a week or two. Angela and I will return before Thanksgiving as we all need to be together in order to get through the first holiday without Hemmy."

"Thank you, Aunt Esther. I hope my mother will accompany you to Palm Beach."

Then Uncle took me aside. "With everything that went on today, you missed the showdown between your Uncle Dominick and Big D. He started out by informing your father-in-law that he would be taking over the leadership role of looking after you and Bobby III immediately and he told Sr. to enjoy his grandson as much as possible because you would be leaving the Fontana family for good and that it was non-negotiable. He then made it very clear, "Kiki is not to be insulted and her feelings are not to be hurt in any way between now and then. And one last thing, make sure you keep a tight leash on that puppy of yours, Bobby J. Consider yourselves both warned," as he turned his back on Sr., and then we both walked away.

"Kiki, I have called you 'Princess' for much of your life, but from this moment on, I will only be calling you by that name because I want you to get used to it when you start working for me early next year. Princess is the only name you will be allowed to use. No one will ever be allowed to know your true identity.

"Princess, everything is moving along smoothly because your father made sure that it would. Don't worry about Bobby J's behavior, it doesn't matter how much his feelings were hurt at the wake and funeral. He won't dare say a single word.

"You already know how to keep it respectful and peaceful for Bobby III. I'll be checking in on you every day. Carl is waiting to drive both of you home."

I'd like to think Bobby J came home a little earlier than usual that night because he wanted to see his son who hadn't been home since the day before my father died, but it didn't matter because Bobby III was fast asleep when he showed up. He said, rather sheepishly, "Welcome home Kiki."

"Thank you, Bobby J. I know it will take a little time, but I'm hopeful Mother and I will be able to come to terms with our loss."

The next day, my mother looked rested, but I could tell that something was bothering her so I asked, "Mother, what's wrong? How can I help?"

"In a little while, Kiki. Let me have some time with my grandson first. Bobby III, I want you to come over a lot more now that Nana does not have to go to work anymore."

"Nana, Pop-Pop doesn't go to work either. He went to Heaven."

"I know sweetheart. That's why the restaurant is closed. Will you come back to visit with me?"

"Sure, Nana. Mommy will bring me here."

"I made gravy so you can have some macaroni."

"Okay, Nana. I love macaroni."

"Sit here like a big boy and eat your lunch while I go into the living room to speak with your mother."

"I feel like I'm drifting at sea almost as if I'll never be able to dock anywhere. I relied on your father to do most everything. I don't even have a checkbook because he did the business bills and the house bills at the same time. I spent most of my life cooking and now I don't know what I'm going to do without your father."

"Mother, I hope you haven't forgotten just how good I am with numbers. After Uncle sits down with you and goes over all the necessary papers, I'm sure you will have a much clearer view of your future. I will take you to the bank to close out the business account after I pay the last of any outstanding bills. Then you can open a personal checking account. I'll show you how to do it.

"Mother, please tell me you are not having second thoughts about wanting to reopen the restaurant."

"I've never been alone since I married your father. What am I going to do with all of my free time, especially in the evenings?"

"Well, Mother, you could read, watch TV, start going to bingo, or you can flop at Uncle's penthouse any time you want. But Mother, I've got a better idea. What would you say to having some company here two or three nights a week? Don't you think you've earned some quality time alone with your grandson? Please give it some thought, Mother."

"Maybe I should give it a try. Tomorrow, I will go shopping and buy my grandson a whole new wardrobe to leave here in my home. Please bring him here to stay over as often as you want. Thank you, Kiki. I needed that."

Then the phone rang and as my mother went to answer it, I high tailed it into the kitchen to check on Bobby III. "Wow, I see that you finished eating all of your lunch."

"Yeah, Mom. Nana makes the best macaroni ever!"

"I know she does. Nana is a great cook. She would like me to bring you to visit with her and she wants you to sleep here in your room so you both can spend time together. Would you like that?"

"Sure, Mom. I like my room here. And I love Nana."

"I'll tell Nana that both of you will be having lots of good times together real soon."

Mother came into the kitchen and said, "Milt wants to speak to you."

"Hello Uncle."

"Princess, I'm coming over there at three o'clock on Friday to go over your father's papers with Angela. We will do that privately, but I'd like for you to join us around four-thirty."

"Uncle, of course I'll be here, but I was going to bring Bobby III to spend time with my mother on Thursday. I won't bring him if you think he will be a distraction when you take care of your business with my mother the following day."

"Princess, your son is never a problem. When we get down to business he will be told to go to his room and play as always."

When I arrived at Mother's home on Friday, Bobby III ran up to me just as excited as he could be. "Mommy, come see my G.I., Joe's. They're soldiers!"

As I gave my mother a hug, I asked her if she had already concluded her business with Uncle. After I entered the kitchen and kissed Uncle on the cheek, my son came running in with a G.I. Joe figurine in one hand and a Jeep in the other.

"I bet Uncle Milt has already seen your G.I. Joe's."

"I've seen all of them and I think they're swell, but right now, Bobby III, I'd like for you to take them into your room and play for a while longer because I need to speak to Nana and your mother alone."

"Ok, Uncle Milt, see ya later."

Then Uncle got right to it and said, "Princess, as per your father's wishes and Italian tradition, everything he owned has been passed to your mother and that includes the restaurant. I already have a buyer and your mother has approved the offer. Hemmy provided extremely well for your mother."

"Excuse me, Milt. I'd like to say something to Kiki. I took Milt's recommendation that the price for Cipo's was more than fair. I hope you realize just how difficult it is for me to say those words. It is time for me to become a devoted Nana and I know I'm going to love my new role. You see, because of your little boy, I now know I'm going to get through all of my sadness."

"As for the Princess, you and Bobby III have been left in my capable hands, but I suspect you always knew that. I'd like to read a letter that was written by Hemmy."

"My ladies, without your knowledge I have lived s large part of my life carrying a heavy burden. Your love has always lightened that load because you both have given me more joy than any one man ever deserved in a lifetime. But I am concerned about the big change that will come after I am gone. I want to ease some of your heartaches by letting you know that I am at peace now and pain-free. Since one of us had to go first, isn't it better that it was me? So this is my wish for both of you, live long, healthy, and happy lives. Always seek Milt's advice and trust his judgement, as I always have, above everyone else in my world for all these many years. He will assist you in making all the choices that I have put in place for you to go smoothly. Both of you are the loves of my life and remember 'I'll always be with you.'"

After the three of us regained our composure, Uncle kept his word and went to play with Bobby III. Mother told me that she had made the decision to go to Florida with Aunt Esther. They would be leaving Tuesday and would be returning on the 26th right before Thanksgiving. I said, "I'm hosting the holiday at my house. Enjoy your time in the Palm Beach area. I'll have everything under control when you return. All of us must try to adopt happy faces for my son. We cannot allow sadness to overshadow this holiday season."

I informed Big D that I would be staying close to home for the holidays, however I did go to the store and invited Big D and Rose to come to my house to visit with their grandson on Thanksgiving eve and the day before Christmas Eve. My invitation was met with an icy glare from Big D. In the end, he agreed to come over on Wednesday to visit with Bobby III. I understood that Rose couldn't come as she would be busy cooking in her home. Big D never knew how to mask his disappointments very well and that was clearly seen through the sadness in his eyes.

Since Uncle Dominick had the talk with Sr., the dynamics had changed immeasurably. When he told me that he would be stopping in on Thanksgiving Day, he made it very clear that the Fontanas were not to be invited and I sure got that message because it was not a request.

Chapter 13

The next two weeks passed quickly. I did notice a slight change in Bobby J's behavior when he started to come home at a reasonable hour to spend some quality time with his son for the first time in his son's entire life. Bobby III didn't seem to care one way or the other for this new-found attention now being paid to him. However, my son did ask me several times when Nana was coming back because he wanted to stay over at her house again.

After my mother returned from Florida on Tuesday, she stopped at the grocery store before going home. I waited before I called to welcome her back. The first thing Mother told me was that she would be making a lasagna the next day to bring over to my house on Thanksgiving. Before my mother hung up, she promised to tell me all about her trip to Florida.

On Thanksgiving morning, I arose earlier than usual because I needed to stuff the turkey and get it into the oven. All of the side dishes had been prepared the day before and would only require reheating.

About fifteen minutes later, I heard the sounds of my son's little feet running toward me. I knew for as long as I lived that particular sound would always be remembered as one of the essentials in life. "Mommy, Mommy, is it Thanksgivin'?"

"You mean Thanksgiving. It sure is."

"I can have lots of people to play with today so I want to get all of my stuff ready."

There it was. The all too familiar sound coming from a lonely, only child.

"Go in and start filling up the tub for your bath. Make the water temperature just the way you like it. You know how to do it. Be careful. I'm going to get your clothes."

Later, as I was setting the dining room table and Bobby J was organizing the bar, the phone rang. Rose was on the phone and as usual, sounded overwhelmed. Big D wanted to wish us a Happy Thanksgiving but he couldn't hide the fact that he sounded down in the dumps.

When my mother arrived, I barely had time to greet her before she was commandeered into her grandson's room to play.

"Bobby J, here are my keys would you please go out to my car and carry in the food."

Aunt Esther and Uncle Milt were the next family members to arrive. They were toting bottles of both red and white wine and a strawberry cheesecake which Uncle bought in New York City.

Aunt Carrie and Uncle Frankie showed up within the hour and he was carrying one of the largest antipastos I had ever seen.

Before we all sat down to begin eating our feast, Uncle Vito called to wish all of us a Happy Thanksgiving. They were enjoying the holiday with Aunt Mary's family. Then Uncle Joe called from Florida.

When we were finished eating, the men went into the living room and proceeded to watch a football game. Uncle took a particular interest in the Detroit Lions-New Orleans Saints game. Later I learned that particular game was dubbed "The Mud Bowl."

We ladies went into high gear on kitchen duty. While we were cleaning up, Mother informed me that my son built something special for me.

I promised my son that as soon as my chores were completed, I would join him in his room to see the surprise he had built for me. Just as I was headed toward his room, the doorbell rang, so I said, "Come on Bobby III, let's go see who is ringing our bell."

"Mommy, now I can show more people my special building."

When I opened the door, Uncle Dominick was standing there all by himself.

"Do you want to see my Legos? I made a surprise for Mommy. But you can't tell her."

"I have to say hello to everyone. Then I'll be in to see what you built and I promise not to say a word because I know it's a big secret."

"I'm going Uncle Dom," he said as he ran off.

"Kiki let me give you a big hug. I bet you could use it."

"I have to be okay. Please come in. I'm so glad you stopped by. I've got coffee brewing. Can I get you something to eat?"

"Honey, I already ate, but I will have coffee. I just wanted to check in on you and Angela."

"The guys are watching the game."

As he walked into the living room, Uncle Milt stood up, shook his hand and said, "Happy Holiday Dominick and before you even ask, you're going to love this one, because the Saints have held the Lions scoreless."

"That's music to my ears Milt. I think you would know better than anyone, are Angela and Kiki really doing as well as they would have us believe?"

"Dom, you know how much Kiki has come through these past four or five years, everyone knows what she has done for the Fontana family. Is that a fair assessment, Jr.?" Who happened to be sitting nearby and had overheard.

"Yes, it is," he answered as Uncle Dom glared at him with such contempt the depths of which I had never seen before. There was no way Bobby J would ever go up against both uncles who made up a very powerfully stacked deck.

Uncle Milt continued, "I would have been more concerned about Angela making it through her husband's death if not for Bobby III. I have no doubt that he will become her salvation."

The coffee was ready and the ladies had displayed all of the desserts on the dining room table. Uncle Dom got to his feet first and said, "Bobby J, I'm so glad you stayed home to be with your family today. Who did you place your action on?"

"I passed today."

"With four games being played today I find that hard to believe? I promise that one day your son's mother will know nothing but happiness and success."

Uncle Milt, who by this time was standing alongside Dominick chimed in and said, "Amen to that! Dom, let's go see what the big surprise is that Bobby III built for his mother."

"Good idea, Milt."

Bobby J was left in his own thoughts to stare at the TV set all alone. As Uncle Dom passed the dessert table, he said, "Milt, is that a New York cheesecake?"

"It sure is."

"Kiki, after I finish enjoying some playtime with your son, I'd like a piece of that cheesecake."

"Sure Uncle Dom. And I'll wrap some up for you to take home if you like."

"Yes, I would. Are you ready for us to come in? Bobby III is the surprise all set up?"

"Okay, come in. I'm ready. Look what Nana helped me build for Mommy."

"Wow! That is a spectacular castle."

"Well, Uncle Milt calls Mommy a princess and everybody knows all princesses have to live in castles. Someday when I grow up. I'm going to buy my mommy a real castle, because she is a pretty princess."

Uncle Dom said, "I bet you will."

Then Uncle Milt said, "Bobby III, please don't take this castle apart, I have a feeling your mother will want to keep it forever. Well done, young man. Let's go get some dessert. I promise you; our lips are zipped!"

"I'm having ice cream, Uncle Milt, just like Pop-Pop. It was his favorite."

"Then you must be having Butter Pecan."

"Yeah, Uncle Milt. That's the kind I like."

When Uncle Milt and Dom entered the room, I was caught off guard to see these two tough guys brushing away tears from their eyes.

The men seemed anxious to get home before the start of the next game. In true Bobby J fashion, he said good night while staying glued to the TV set.

Mother stayed behind and got her grandson ready for bed as I was back on kitchen duty once more. When she was finished, they both came into the kitchen to get me. "Mommy, come see my building for you before I go to bed."

"First I want you to go inside and say good night to your father. Mother, would you like to take your grandson home with you for some company?"

"I'd like to be alone tonight. We haven't had the opportunity to talk about my trip to Florida, but I can tell you that I loved the sunshine and the area."

"Mother if there's one thing, I truly believe, it's that you will know where you need to be when the time is right and so will I."

Then my son came running into the kitchen saying, "Let's go, Mommy, it's time for you."

"I'm ready."

"Look, it's a castle for you cause you're a princess. Uncle Milt says so. Do you like it?"

"Bobby III, it's so beautiful."

"Some day when I get bigger, I'll find a real one for you."

"I have no doubt that you will." As I said it, I felt a presence in the room. So I turned around and saw Bobby J standing in the doorway listening to his son's conversation.

"I want to keep it for the rest of my life. It will always remain my treasure."

After I tucked my son in for the night and closed his door, I hugged my mother and was about to walk her out when Bobby J appeared at my side and hugged my mother good night before she drove off. When he came back in, he found me tidying up in the kitchen and said, "I'd like to talk to you when you're finished."

"No problem Bobby J."

About twenty minutes later I entered the living room.

"I'm not too happy with the way both of your uncles have been ganging up on me lately and more than that, I don't like the way your Uncle Dom is keeping my family from coming into our house to visit with my son. My father just happens to own this house. So what's going on?"

"Bobby J, it always worked that way until one particular night which changed the course of all our lives. You did that with the help of a red-head, but Holy Moly! I'm impressed that you don't have to be struck by lightning to see that your family is being kept at a distance from my son for a very good reason. My family knew that part of the Caesars crowd shop at your family's store. That made your indiscretions more of a humiliation to me and the Gallo-Cipo family. Instead, I've been instructed to stay here through the holidays for my mother and my son's sake. So, I suggest we keep it cordial until I leave this house, you and your family forever. If your family can't handle the way this situation is going to play out, then let me say this, they can always try suing my uncles. Good luck with that one. Good night, Bobby J." Then I walked into my bedroom and shut the door.

I hosted a third birthday party for Bobby III in December. It would turn out to be the smallest and most intimate party I had ever given. The three uncles, Milt, Frankie, Vito and their wives were present along with my mother. I did call the store and invited Big D to come over on Saturday before he drove home. He accepted my overture and told me he would be bringing all of his gifts from the entire family with him.

Several hours before Big D was due to visit with his grandson there was a knock on my side door. Bobby III didn't have to run too far because his room was directly across from it. When I opened the door, he said, "Hi Uncle Mario, want to see my soldiers?"

"I would like that big guy, but right now I have to speak to your mother, it's very important."

"Sure, Uncle Mario, I'll go set them all up."

"It's good to see you Mario. Let's go into the living room to talk so your nephew can't hear our conversation."

"He is a great kid so why are you so suddenly keeping my entire family away from him. How could you of all people do that?"

"Mario, it's not that sudden at all."

"This is the first time I heard my father lay the hammer down. He told the entire family that it was Bobby J's actions that caused all the trouble in the first place."

"Wow, I'm shocked to hear that, so please listen carefully. I'm sure you have heard about the night I was sent into Caesar's Lounge. Your brother broke my heart that night. And on top of that my family was deeply insulted by his behavior in public. My marriage was over at that very moment because Gallo-Cipo's have always believed in martial fidelity. As a result of those actions, I will be leaving your brother very soon. When I leave, I can't ever have any more contact with any of you. My son's safety is our priority so he must be kept away from the fallout that will always surround the Fontana family.

"I've always had a soft spot in my heart for you and that started long before we were held hostage together in the La Piazza Restaurant. I need to say something to you now as I may never have this opportunity again. I'll always love you and 'I wish you all that Heaven allows'"

"Please don't leave this family. I want you to remain in my life because I will always love you too. Why can't you stay in touch with me alone, I won't say a word to the others?"

"It doesn't work that way; it has to be a clean break. Please try to understand. I'm not at liberty to say any more than I already have."

"Kiki, you have been a better big sister to me than Jeanette has ever been. Make a mental note of this, if you or my nephew ever need me, get in touch with me somehow and I'll come running."

Later, when I walked my brother-in-law to the side door, I gave him the tightest hug because I knew he would be the one person in the Fontana family I would truly miss. I always thought of him as the younger brother I almost got to keep so many years ago before he was taken from us. All of the sudden it hit me just how cruel life could be and the tears welled up in my eyes.

Several hours later, Big D arrived with shopping bags full of presents for the birthday boy. "Hi Grandpa, are all those presents for my birthday? I'm getting big. I'm three years old. Come see my soldiers and my copta."

"Happy Birthday Grandson. Don't open these presents until tomorrow when you open all of the others, okay?"

"Sure Grandpa, aren't you going to help me blow out the candles on my cake?"

"No big boy. I have a lot of extra work to do tomorrow. Besides I want to see all of your soldiers and the helicopter that goes with them right now."

While they were playing in Bobby III's room, I went to get the coffee ready.

When they had finished playing, Big D joined me in the kitchen for a cup of coffee. I had a feeling he wanted to speak privately with me before I had to get Bobby III ready for bed. "I'm going to try one more time to convince you not to leave my son. No one wants you two to get divorced. I know what he did was wrong. But why can't you find a way to forgive him for having one affair?"

"Big D, I'm going to try to keep this conversation within the boundaries of respect. First of all, your attitude toward affairs will never cease to amaze me, what's one affair if it was just one affair? I'm quite sure this is exactly the kind of behavior Bobby J has seen his entire life. The result is probably partly the reason his miscues are done in such an insulting and cavalier way.

"When I was married in the Catholic Church, I took my vows very seriously. It wasn't just the affair that did it which turned out to be the last straw for me and the incentive I needed to throw in the towel on my marriage. I have an entire list of the fiascos I have suffered through at the hands of your first born. However, I will make it my business to go over that list with your son on the day that I leave him. I realize that this was not what you wanted to hear but I assure you that it is a done deal."

Big D had nothing left to say so he shook his head from side to side and sighed. As I started to walk him to the front door, Bobby III came out of his room and when he caught up to Big D, he gave him a big hug.

Later, I thought how prophetic my words would turn out to be because with the exception of the day before Christmas Eve, which was right around the corner, he would never see his grandfather again for the rest of his life.

Bobby III's birthday party went off without a hitch. I stepped aside while pretending to get the cake ready so that Mother and Aunt Esther could help my son open all of his presents.

I knew full well the importance of having someone to help fill the void in my mother's life. At the same time, I didn't want Aunt Esther to feel like she was being excluded from my son's life because she would always deserve a place in it. I knew that a balance would have to be struck so that both ladies could have access to the little boy who would always need them and someday the grown man who would always want them in his life.

Uncle Dom arrived around the time dessert was being served almost as if his sweet tooth had a built-in clock.

"Welcome Uncle Dom. My son's birthday cake is an Italian rum cake and a little birdie told me that it's one of your favorites."

"It sure is, but first, take this card and put the contents away for Bobby III's education. Before I catch up on the football games with the guys, I do have one question for you. How did it go with your father-in-law last night?"

"Well, I'll give you the short version, Uncle Dom. It seems that most of the Fontanas do not want me to divorce Bobby J."

"Of course, they don't want to let you go. Just remember to stay the course. All of our plans for you are in motion."

When he joined the men, it became all about the football. From what I overheard; Uncle Milt seemed elated the Jets were beating up on the Miami Dolphins. I glanced toward Bobby J's direction, but he showed little to no emotion one way or the other as if he hadn't made a wager.

Within the hour the party was over. Mother stayed to help me clean up. I asked her if she would like Bobby III to stay over at her house for a night or two. She agreed and said, "I'd like that very much."

Then Bobby III rushed me into his room to see some of his presents because it was close to his bedtime and a trip to Nana's house. As far as his soldiers were concerned, I could see that all four branches of the military were now represented. He very excitedly showed me a Navy frogman, an Air Force scramble pilot, a Marine paratrooper and an Army MP.

I thought, *Oh my God, I may actually have a Patriot growing up right before my eyes.*

With my son staying at Nana's house, I had uninterrupted time to decorate the house and shop for Christmas presents. I would buy all of the seafood for the "Feast of the Seven Fishes." The Christmas day meal would be taken care of almost entirely by my mother and Aunt Carrie.

I asked Big D and his family to visit with Bobby III on Monday. Clearly, they were once again, being ostracized, but nothing was said.

Uncle called me that morning and said, "Princess, remember when I finished reading your father's letter to his ladies, I handed you a few papers to sign. You didn't realize you were signing the petition for your divorce. I had no choice but to do it that day because of a promise I made to Hemmy, I'm making sure Bobby J doesn't receive his copies until you are out of your house.

"When you say good bye to the Fontanas tonight, do it knowing it will be for the last time. I'll see you tomorrow. You know how much I love seafood and can't wait to dig in."

"Don't worry. I'll get it done the right way." The doorbell rang and the welcome wagon was right there at my side.

"Hi Grandma, Grandpa, everybody. Come see my new soldiers I got for my birthday."

Mario knocked on the side door and Chris let him in. then Bobby J arrived and we gave them all of their presents and the gifts they brought to us were put under the tree not to be opened until Christmas.

My son had about three hours of play time with his grandparents and his father's younger siblings. Mario watched over the kids with a sadness that they couldn't have noticed because of their youth. I walked over to him, placed my arm around his waist and hugged him ever so tightly. He would be missed.

I gave each one of them a final hug at the door but when Rose said good night, I gave her an extra hug because she was such an uncomplicated, very kind, and a genuinely nice person. I would have loved having her as a mother-in-law for the rest of my life.

Big D waited until everyone had left and then he took me aside and said, "Kiki, I'll always think of you as a daughter, you have always done the right thing by my family. I want you to know that I take full responsibility for my son's actions."

"I know that Big D. I don't want to preach, but you have other sons that are not yet fully molded. Father-in-law, as we leave each other this evening, I'm going to make you this promise, I will raise your grandson as a man who will honor any and all vows he will ever take. Someday he will do us all proud." Then I kissed him on the cheek and said, "Stay well, Big D."

Chapter 14

We all made Christmas Eve and Christmas Day happy occasions for Bobby III, but one time I caught my mother crying all by herself in my bedroom.

Bobby J seemed a little restless. He was staying at home with his own family because that's what he was told he had to do.

My mother, Aunt Esther and Uncle were the only guests left when Uncle took me aside and made a very unusual request. He asked me to schedule a Super Bowl Party here on January 12th. "The entire party is going to be catered on me. It's been a rough few months and we could all use a good time. Do me a favor and call Evelyn and invite her to join us."

"Of course, I'll do as you ask, but you must realize how curious I am. Who is Evelyn to you and my father? Are you ready to tell me?"

"She's a friend and that's all you need to know for now. I want you to start, very discretely, packing up Bobby III's and your personal belongings and store them in the basement. I'm having moving boxes delivered to you tomorrow after Bobby J leaves for work. I will have you moved out of this house on Friday, January 17th. You will be taking care of business in the city with me on that day.

"You see Princess, when we return from the city, I will be taking you to your new home and since you will never be able to see Bobby J again, coming back here even once more will not be an option."

"I'm more than ready to move forward with my life."

"Bobby J will probably be expecting you to join him and the Saturday Night Gang on New Year's Eve just like all the others since you two started dating. I shouldn't have to tell you that's out of the question now. Aunt Esther and I would like you and Angela to ring in the holiday with us. I'll send Carl to pick you and Bobby III up at five o'clock. Plan on staying overnight because our time together will be spent going over our moving arrangements for you."

"Uncle, I'll be ready."

"Dom and the rest of the people in your father's trusted circle will be at my place. First, we will all raise a glass to Hemmy and then have a toast to the year 1969. This is going to be the year that you will take your place in the world which you are destined to rise to the very top. And as much as you can see the Fontanas are being frozen out, I can tell you that it goes much deeper than that.

"On the day that I come to pick you up for a meeting in the city, I'll be watching you very carefully. When you walk out of that door for the last time and climb into my limo, I don't want you to look back one last time.

"One more thing, we would like to keep Bobby III at our house for the next three days because Angela has been stealing a lot of our thunder lately in that department and we both miss him."

"I know that Uncle, but it has done my mother a world of good."

Then my mother who had joined us chimed in, "I've had an in depth talk with Milt and I've made a very important decision which I will announce after you move into your new home.

"Honey, your Uncle Milt has valid reasons why he must keep certain details from you but don't ever make the mistake of thinking that it applies to me. I know a lot more than you would ever believe. Remember I'm the lady who was married for all those years to his best friend."

"Angela, thank you for understanding what I must do."

The Super Bowl Party turned out to be a wonderful respite for all of us. The catered food Uncle brought in was delicious and all of the ladies doted on Bobby III including Evelyn. Shortly before the game was to begin, she asked to speak to me privately. I took her into my bedroom because it was always quiet in there as she said, "Kiki, I know you have many questions about why I'm always around. Please believe me when I tell you that I couldn't love you any more if you were my own daughter. That's all I can tell you for now. I think we should go back out there and rejoin the others for the start of our crazy rummy game while the guys watch the Super Bowl."

That unexpected disclosure certainly took me by surprise, but I didn't dwell on it because I saw that one of the ladies had already started to deal the cards. We had already agreed to take turns sitting out a hand to give Bobby III some attention and playtime.

When I entered the living room, all of the men were fixated on the TV because the game had already kicked off. Considering that they never took their eyes off the game, I concluded that big money had probably been wagered on this game by some, if not all of the men in the room. I made the decision not to disturb them and went into my son's room instead to see what he was up to.

"What's all this stuff I see lined up?"

"I'm getting all my soldiers ready to go to war."

"What war?"

"The one in Nam. Uncle Frankie told me my men have to fight the Commies. It's on the TV. I saw it. Didn't you see it?"

I tried to stifle my laughter at the very colorful way Uncle Frankie comes across with his mouth. He always cracked me up. "Our country is involved in a place called Vietnam and it is reported on the TV every night."

All of a sudden, some cheering erupted in the living room, so I told my son, "Keep building up your troop's sweetheart. I'll be back in a little while."

I went inside to find out what was the cause of all the excitement and said, "What's going on?"

Uncle answered, "Namath brought the ball up the field and Matt Snell took it in for a touchdown. The Jets are winning 7-0."

"Isn't he the cocky quarterback from Beaver Falls, PA? You know, the one that's always being written up in the newspapers? I think you must like him."

"Princess, you're not even close, my interest is solely in the point spread. I would never lay 17 points on a Super Bowl game so all of us uncles and cousins took the 17 points." With that, he looked at Bobby J and asked him, "Who did you put your money on?"

"I bet on the Colts and only laid 16 points."

"Where did you find 16? Nobody's got that number. That's cheap."

"I know that, but I managed to find it. It's only the second quarter and I believe the Colts with Earl Morrall at the helm will come back with a vengeance."

The men did take a coffee and desert break at half time and the only thing said about the game was that the Jets were still winning 7-0.

The game ended about an hour later and all of the men were so overjoyed with the outcome of the game with the exception of Bobby J of course, who then did something I had never seen him do before. He went over to the bar and poured himself a tall glass of Johnny Walker Red scotch straight up and proceeded to chug-a-lug it.

I heard Uncle say, that the Colts quarterback Earl Morrall had thrown three interceptions and even a last-ditch effort from Johnny Unitas couldn't save Baltimore so they went down to the Jets 16-7. Uncle Dom added that the very charismatic quarterback, Joe Namath sure made good on his "guarantee."

Uncle said, "One day this game will probably go down in sports history as one of the biggest upsets of all time."

It occurred to me that since the uncles and cousins had won the game, then it became obvious that Bobby J was the only loser here. Not one of them spoke a single word to him as he returned to the living room looking white as a ghost while drinking another glass of scotch. Without a shadow of a doubt this was positively the first time I had ever seen Bobby J with sweat running down from his forehead. I assumed that he must have lost a ton of money on Super Bowl III.

Then I remembered something Big D told me that last time he came to my house. He said perhaps it was time for him to practice tough love on his son by not bailing him out of any more of his gambling debts.

Uncle stayed behind to speak to me as Aunt Esther helped my mother tidy up the kitchen.

Uncle gestured toward my bedroom. Once in there, he said, "Princess, you know that your father and I devised this plan for you and I know you have said that you are ready to move forward to start a new life. Before we take that final step on Friday, I must clarify something to you. There is absolutely nothing that I have done, up to this point, that can't be undone whether it's the divorce papers I have gotten started or the new place I have obtained for you and Bobby III to live in. It doesn't matter. I can stop it right now. All you have to do is say the word.

"Sweetheart, don't do it because we cooked up this plan for you. This is about your life and the life of your son. Do you want to go through with this on Friday?"

"Yes, I do Uncle."

"Bravo Princess. I will arrive here at ten o'clock to take you to my offices in New York City. During our ride over, I will have ample opportunity to brief you on the way this final chapter of your marriage will play out. After we arrive there, Carl will go back, pick up Bobby J and bring him to my office to join us. During that time, after you scrutinize the photos I have chosen for you to see, only then will you be able to get a front row seat into exactly what the

Fontana men have been up to. Subsequently, you will finally know why we must get your son away from that family. Now let's go into the kitchen and join your mother and Esther."

When we walked in, both the kitchen and dining room were completely cleaned. Besides that, my mother had given Bobby III his bath and had dressed him for bed. Then I heard the sound of little feet running my way. "Mommy, Nana made me all ready for bed. Come tuck me in and hear my prayers."

"Bobby III, since your daddy is home tonight, I think you should go into the living room and ask him to tuck you in."

"Okay. I'll do it."

Aunt Esther shot me a very serious look and started to say something when she was interrupted by Bobby III who had come running back into the kitchen pretty much out of breath. "Daddy can't do it because he said he's sick and he doesn't want me to get sick. Let's go, Mommy."

My mother stepped in and said, "I got you ready for bed so I should do it, okay?"

"Sure, Nana, I'm ready."

Aunt Esther picked up from where she was interrupted. "Kiki, I have something very important to say to you. Let me take your son to our penthouse to stay for the last few nights. Why should you give that soon-to-be-ex-husband of yours any more time with your son? Look at what he just did to him. I'm so angry, I'd like to go into the living room and slap his face." Meanwhile Uncle, who usually is the one doing the talking, just sat there and listened intently.

"Aunt Esther one reason I do the things I do is because of my conscience. Bobby J doesn't even know about us leaving on Friday, but since I do, that is the reason I want to give him every opportunity to see his son. With that said, both of you are not going to like what I'm about to say next, but my mind is already made up. I've decided to take Bobby III to the store on Thursday to visit with his grandfather one last time. You both know that all I ever wanted was a simple life, and a house blessed with three or four children. I also wanted to be a good wife, mother, and a devoted family member to my in-laws. I need to know in my heart that I did it all the right way up to the very last moment so that I can lay my head down on the pillow at night and sleep like a baby."

Then Uncle spoke, "Princess, first of all, your husband is sitting inside still in shock and also half in the bag. You see I know how much money he lost on today's game, and I know who he owes the money to. By the way, he doesn't have that kind of money to pay off his bookies. Sweetheart, all degenerate gamblers are the same, it's all about the action. They must have the action. If you feel the need to keep your son here until Friday, then by all means do what you must, we will drop him off at my penthouse and then proceed to the city. And Princess, one last thing, Friday, will be your day to take the stage. I want you to say everything and anything you want and don't be too soft on him. Tomorrow I want you to start preparing your good bye speech because, quite frankly, I can't wait to hear it. Now, walk us to the front door, my little Tinker Bell."

I finished my packing by noon of the next day, then I started to write a good bye speech to Bobby J.

I kept my word on Thursday and brought Bobby III to visit with his grandfather for the very last time. He enjoyed his company as much as he had enjoyed Pop-Pop's at the restaurant. I grasped the fact that in the near future, because of the circumstances, one day my son would never have any recollection of either one of his grandfathers. That night I had to remind myself, "With faith all things are possible, as I fell asleep for the last time in that house."

Uncle took out a folder filled with photographs en route to the city. "Princess, I have hundreds of folders just like these but I chose to show you the only ones that are pertinent to your divorce from Bobby J. Someday I will turn all of them over to you and they will become your property to do with as you wish."

"Are these what I think they are?"

"Yes, they are. I promise you that before he leaves my office, you shall have exactly what you want."

Uncle made it very clear to me that this was going to be my show and mine alone. Before I knew it, my soon-to-be-ex came walking through the door. Uncle invited him to sit down and spelled out one simple rule, "She speaks, you listen."

"Bobby J, this is my farewell performance. When I'm finished getting everything off my chest, then I'll give you five minutes of my time to say your peace. First of all, let me say that you are the brown thumb of gambling. I wish you could have respected the Catholic vows we took and believed as I did that our life together should have been punctuated forever with 'I love yous' instead of 'How can I use you one more time?'

"Let me refresh your memory by revisiting just some of the crazy events I endured during our marriage. I'll start with one of the photos I just slid across the table to you. I'm sure you'll remember being in Caesar's Lounge with the red-head after you left the hospital while I was having emergency surgery.

"Next, I was held hostage in Newark because of your gambling debts. Of course, I can't possibly ever forget staying up for days at a time to serve the players at your professional card games. Then again, every new mother should celebrate her first Mother's Day in a house that had the gas and electric shut off for non-payment. Oh, and all daughters-in-law all over the country should walk in on their fathers-in-law right after they've been stabbed by a crazy broad while innocently delivering dinner and then, soon after that stand at the side of both father and son after the store was robbed on Valentine's Day. Then, there's the unforgettable incident of smuggling out guns in my son's stroller or standing up to every law enforcement agency that ever came knocking on my door. I bet my resume would be more colorful than any other female in the entire state of New Jersey. At least, I will be able to say I stood up each and every time.

"It's time for me to wrap up this rather sordid trip down memory lane by reminding you that I stood by both you and your father throughout the raid and trial. So now is as good a time as any to inform you just in case you didn't know, it was Uncle who made all of it go away. I will add that as of today, you and your family will no longer stand under the umbrella of Uncle's protection. Sadly, I must follow that statement with this thought, there is no doubt in my mind that it will be just a matter of time before the Fontana men self-destruct and I don't want my son to be around as part of the collateral damage.

"The thing is, Bobby J, you always lived for the moment. You never saw the bigger picture, because you are a complacent, conceited, self-centered ass who never knew how to take care of the truly important things in life.

"When you elected to cheat on me you also cheated on your son. Then, that awful deed fell upon his shoulders because he will be deprived of the stable happy family life as God intended for every child who comes into this world to have a shot at.

"One day you will wake up and realize that you alone threw away what so many others would gladly have died for because you never gave one thought to where you would be when you reach the age of fifty or sixty years old.

"At first, I thought your indifference to me and my son was the result of my inability to give you any more children but, then I realized you would never have been able to handle them because, quite simply, they cramp your lifestyle.

"You never got it, Bobby J. My heartbreak has never been the fact that I'm an only child. My heartbreak has always been the fact that my son will always remain an only child.

"When I caught you with the red-head, I wanted to crawl into the wilderness like a wounded animal because my values, dreams, and expectations were shattered, and I knew then that my marriage was over. I will raise a good boy to become a great man someday. I have no doubt that it will happen as long as he never has any more contact with you or your family ever again.

"I'm being moved out of your father's house this very minute, and I want you to know my son is already gone. Our personal belongings, Bobby III's furniture (just because I want you to look into his empty bedroom) and the beautiful bar my father presided over in happier times are the only things that I am taking out of that house.

"You will be served with divorce papers this afternoon. So, in the not-too-distant future, spousal privilege will no longer apply to us.

"If I ever hear that you have died, I'll come right out of the woodwork and be more than happy to pay for your burial. In fact, I will pay extra to have you buried six feet deeper than the norm so that you will be that much closer to the final destination for your eternity in Hell. I'm sure the first person to greet you and shake your hand will be Hitler. Hopefully, you will enjoy the ride.

"Now, I want you to take a good look at that plastic bag. It contains the suicide note written by one Leroy Thompson. I don't have to tell you whose fingerprints are all over that note.

"Uncle, the document please. All I want from you is your signature on that paper which will allow me to change my son's name. Then, Uncle is going to do something for you. As soon as you sign on the dotted line, he will pay your Super Bowl debt."

Although, he remained stoic, I detected a sadness in his eyes as he signed the document and just like that, my marriage to Bobby J was over as far as I was concerned from that moment on.

"I have only a few words left for you before you will be allowed the five minutes that were promised to you. I hope you just saw this fairy use her greatest weapon, her magic wand, because I just made you disappear from our lives forever. I know you never loved me. I was just the ticket that kept you out of the Vietnam War. So, I can say these words with a clear conscience, 'good riddance to bad rubbish.' Bobby J, the clock is ticking on your five minutes so you better get started."

"Kiki, I'm very sorry that I hurt you, but you knew who I was when we met. You probably thought marriage and fatherhood could change me, but think about it, and look at my family, the examples I was surrounded by and the lack of boundaries I grew up with.

"I wanted the idea of having a wife, knowing full well I would never be faithful, then I wanted to be a father, knowing full well I would never give my child the time he deserved. So, the fact that you couldn't give me any more children never entered my mind. Kiki, almost everything you have said about me is the truth.

"Don't ever blame yourself for the way I chose to live my life. From the very first moment I laid my eyes on you, oh how you shined and I knew how special you were on the inside and out. I wanted to have the best, knowing full well that I didn't deserve you. You've been around men your entire life who wear very big shoes and I knew that I could never have filled them. You were a wonderful wife and devoted mother to your son. I will always have to carry the sadness of knowing that I should have been a better husband to you. So instead, I wish you every happiness and the hope that you will find a good man worthy of you one day. Never forget these next words that I am about to say to you from deep down inside, if you or your son ever need me for anything, just find a way to get in touch with me. I'll be there and I promise you that I will right all of the wrong I did to you no matter what it costs me. Kiki you said I never loved you. But that's the one point I dispute big time, because, on the contrary, you're the only woman I will ever truly love."

It was too little, too late so I just shook my head in disbelief and turned my back on him for the very last time.

Then he turned to Milt and said, "One day I'll repay the $50,000 and the vig for my Super Bowl debt."

Uncle said with a smile on his face, "Forget it. You already paid it when you finally showed my little girl the respect she so richly deserved." Then he hit the intercom button and told Betty, his secretary to phone Carl in the limo and tell him to come up immediately and bring a token from the glove box with him. "Carl, give it to Mr. Fontana."

Without any warning Carl flipped it to Bobby J who proceeded to catch it even though it was an unexpected toss. There it was again, his uncanny reflexes and God-given, natural ability. I guess it was my destiny to witness it one last time.

If I had closed my eyes for a moment, when Uncle continued, I would have visualized his mouth with icicles instead of teeth because I never heard his mouth that sharp and cold when he said with such contempt, "Good bye Bobby J, the subway station is three blocks south of here, now you can go." And just like that, poof, Bobby J was gone forever.

Chapter 15

Uncle and I stayed in his office for another hour after Bobby J left because he had to make some phone calls. I knew the first call went out to Uncle Dominick. After we came through the tunnel, Uncle asked me if I was alright. I assured him that I would be just fine. Then I asked him where we were going and he said, "Kiki, I want you to spend the first day out of your house with Aunt Esther and me because some of your possessions haven't made it to your new place yet. I can now tell you that's it's located in my building. How's that for a surprise?"

"I'm so shocked."

"After dinner, I will take you to view the apartment that I have selected for you. I thought long and hard before I committed to this place. In the end, it became a judgement call for me and Hemmy. I'm convinced this is where you and your son belong for two very good reasons. First you know this place has 24/7 security. The second reason is that Aunt Esther and our staff can look after Bobby III when you start working for me. Spend as much time as you need over the weekend getting familiar with it. By the beginning of February, you will be working for me.

"Angela told me that she would like to go with you to buy the furniture for it. I have a friend who owns a furniture store in the city. Don't worry about the cost.

"Carl will drop me off at my office on Monday morning and then take you ladies to my friend's place and when you have concluded your shopping spree, go and have a nice lunch with your mother. When you are finished, call me from the restaurant and I'll be there to pick you up."

When we arrived at the penthouse, Uncle took care of his business and after we had dinner, as promised, he said, "Princess, we have something important to do right now. Let's go see your new home."

We took the elevator down to the sixth floor and stopped there. When we exited, Uncle turned right and stopped in front of apartment 622. He took out a key and opened the door. As we entered, he said, "Welcome home, Princess."

"Uncle, is this a coincidence? You know my birthday is June 22nd, or 622."

"Sweetheart, I'll tell you once more, where your life is concerned, there are no coincidences and nothing ever happens by chance."

The first two rooms I entered were the living and dining rooms. But it was the view from the living room that really caught my attention. It was just as beautiful as the view from Uncle's penthouse only on a smaller scale and seen from a lower level.

Then I entered a small, but well laid out kitchen. Next I looked into a full bathroom which was located directly across from my son's room. All of his furniture had been setup and his clothes were already hung up in the closet. Lastly I stepped into an enormous master bedroom suite which had an oversized bath area in it. I had only one other place to look at so I opened the door and was shocked when I looked into the largest walk-in closet I had ever seen besides the two that were located in the penthouse twelve floors above.

"Uncle, this place appears to have been newly renovated. Has it been?"

"Yes, Princess. I purchased this place for you prior to the trial. Then I had it completely gutted and the renovations have been ongoing ever since. When it is painted, furnished and decorated with your style, I know it will be a spectacular home for you and your son. Tell me the truth. Did I do right by you?"

"Oh Uncle, I positively love it! Thank you so much."

"Sweetheart, tilt your head toward the Heavens and thank your father because he paid for it. Hemmy trusted me and your Uncle Dom with the welfare and the lives of his two ladies, and both of us would rather die than let him down. Princess, take these keys, they open the door to your future and your destiny. Let's go back upstairs now because I have something else to discuss with you and it is a priority."

Just then, Aunt Esther walked in. "Kiki, do you like it? I sure hope so because I want you and your son to live here in the same building with us so I can help you when a babysitter is needed for your little boy. Please tell me that you want to stay in this building."

"I love my new apartment and I'm so grateful that Uncle found it for us. It just feels so right to me, like I truly belong here. Since my son didn't greet me at the front door, I have to assume that he's already gone to bed."

"I'd like to send in my interior decorator to work with you as a house warming present. I'm afraid I have to insist. All she'll have to do is tie it up with window treatments, bedding and accessories. When you are both finished, your apartment will be magnificent. Her name is Stella Duvall."

"Thank you, Aunt Esther."

"Uncle, I have a feeling that we may both have the same things on our minds. Is this about the name changes?"

"Your instincts are correct. The time has come. I will be submitting both of your name changes to the courts on Monday morning. What do you have in mind?"

"I've thought about it a lot. But in the end, it was a given for me. I want to take back my father's surname, Cipo. My new name will become Kiki Cipo, not Catarina. As for my son, as of this minute, he will become Robert Frances Cipo or RF as I will begin to call him."

"That's my girl. Tell your son that you are giving him a big boy name now that he turned three years old. Explain to him that his real name has always been Robert Francis so you will now begin to call him RF for short. It won't take him very long to adjust to his new name. There's one more thing that happened today that I must make you aware of. While both of us were concluding our relationships with Bobby J, Dom was paying Big D a visit in the store. He was told that, number one, Jr's marriage was over, number two, you and your son had already been moved out of his house, and number three, that he would never be able to see his grandson again.

"Dom made it very clear to him that if either one of them or anyone else for that matter went looking for you or your son or started making inquiries about your whereabouts then there would be hell to pay. Dom went on to tell him that the level of disrespect that his son had shown the Gallo family through his actions to you were only tolerated because he was the father of your child. He concluded by telling him that since you two were now split, all bets were off. Finally, he told Big D that the forfeiture of his grandson would be the price he would have to pay for raising his son to become one of the biggest wrongos he had ever met. I want you to be convinced that the Gallo family took care of it. Are you okay with that?"

"There are no more yesterdays in my world. There are only tomorrows. Now, I've got a promise for you. I will give you my best effort every day when I start working for you."

"I have no doubt that you will become the best at what I am going to teach you. It's been a long day. Why not take a long look at the skyline before you retire for the evening. I know you enjoy reading the Star Ledger every day. I left a copy on your bed. Princess, let me suggest that you start reading the sports section. I think you will find it very illuminating. Good night."

I glanced at the skyline on the way to the guest bedroom once more with awe. That weekend I measured and memorized all the wall space in each room. I moved paint color chips around from room to room, but in the end, as always, my favorite color green would dominate, followed by peach and earth tones.

By Monday morning, I was eager to get the show on the road. Mother arrived and was so excited to be the first person to park in the guest parking space reserved for apartment 622.

After Uncle dropped us off at the furniture store, we were led into an office that was occupied by a man who just about jumped out of his overstuffed chair when we walked in. He came over and introduced himself as Shelly Krantz. As it turned out, he was one of the owners so he took it upon himself to personally show us every square inch of the entire eight floors which were filled with furniture.

We got started at a little past ten o'clock and by twelve fifteen, I had selected all of the furniture I needed to fill-up my apartment. After we arrived at the restaurant, Mother started the conversation. "Kiki, I know Dominick and his sons paid Big D a visit at the store before they came to my house to assure me that no one would ever come looking for your son when he is visiting with me.

"The job you are about to start for Uncle will be very demanding and will require many hours of your time. Your father and Milt planned this a long time ago.

"Armed with that knowledge, I have made the decision to sell my house and move to South Florida before my grandson starts school. I won't be living too far from Esther. Together, we can take excellent care of Robert Francis. I'd like for you to send him to me before school begins. I'll also have your Uncle Joe and his family to help out as well. Honey, in about a year and a half from now, you will be so entrenched in your new world, I'm pretty sure you will want your son to have a fresh start far away from here. You are going to need help raising your boy because of the many hours your job will require. I will buy a three-bedroom house so you will always have a place to stay every time you come to visit RF. When your destiny is fulfilled, I'm quite sure you will want to put this chapter of your life behind you. Maybe you will want to join the rest of us in Florida. Please think about my offer."

"Mother, that's a tall order. The thought of sending my son away. I'll have to dig deep. I have said it many times before that RF will always need all of our love. What I don't understand is why you think I won't have enough time for both my job and my son. Can you explain?"

"Kiki, I cannot. That information can only come from Milt. Now, tell me what you think about my move to Florida next year."

"I'll be very happy for you. But you must know how much we will miss you." When we finished our lunch, Uncle picked us up and we returned to Jersey City.

I was kept very busy during the next week. As soon as my new bedroom set was delivered, my son and I moved down to the sixth floor. As much as I loved to stay over in Uncle's penthouse when I was a little girl, since I became a married woman, I preferred to be in my own place.

As soon as I closed the door on Apartment 622, RF ran to his room to begin setting up his toys. The first thing I did was take in the view. I truly felt safe and peaceful here. I was a grown-up now and realized that it was all on me as a single parent, and at that moment, I became more determined than ever that no matter what it took I would get the job done for Robert Francis.

Uncle called and asked me to be dressed and ready at six o'clock because he wanted to take his three best ladies out to dinner. He added that Kim would come down and babysit my son and get him ready for bed.

When we returned to the St. James, Mother insisted on coming up so she could say goodnight to her grandson. We pulled into the parking garage and noticed a car with a big green bow sitting on top of it which was parked right next to Mother's. Uncle steered us toward the new car. As we ladies oohed and ahhed, he pulled a keyring from his pocket and said, "Princess, I think you will find that these keys open the door to that Cadillac, and they belong to you."

I was in shock, but before I could say a word as we entered my apartment RF came running to the door to greet us.

"Hi everybody, I almost had to go to bed so I asked Kim if I could stay up to see you mommy. Can we stay here?"

"Yes, my Big Boy, we are going to stay here. This is our new home."

"That's great, Mommy, when's Daddy coming here. Can't he live here too?"

I had no choice but to lie.

"Sweet boy, Uncle Milt has many businesses. Your father went far away to work at one of them and he'll be gone for a long time."

"Mommy doesn't he have a job in Grandpa's store?"

"He did, Robert Francis, but Uncle Milt found him a better job."

"It's okay, Mommy, he always came home too late to see me before I went to bed anyway."

Wow, that was like taking a bullet, but at the same time, it was probably a blessing in disguise because it proved to me that one day Bobby J would be totally forgotten to my son.

"It's time for you to go to bed."

"Nana, want to come hear my prayers?"

"I sure do!"

Aunt Esther said, "Milt, I know you want to speak to Kiki alone, so I'm going upstairs."

Uncle said, "Let's go talk in the living room."

I spoke first, "Uncle, that's one big, beautiful car. Thank you so much, but why a Cadillac? That's way too expensive."

"Princess, I told you to leave your Chevy behind for a reason. It was bought and registered to Bobby J. I bought this car through one of my businesses because your name can never be attached to it. If by chance you are ever stopped by the police, tell them the car belongs to your uncle. Show them the paperwork and I'll take care of it.

"Sweetheart, your new job will require you to be on the road a great deal of time, therefore I wanted you to have a big, heavy car around you for your protection.

"Princess, remember I want you to ditch the name Kiki from this moment on. You cannot ever slip in front of any of the men. You will be known as The Princess or just Princess. No one can ever know your true identity.

"I'm going to go up now so you can get a good night's sleep. I'll be here at one o'clock tomorrow to take you to the place I rented in Hoboken which will become your office. Aunt Esther will take R.F. up to the penthouse. I want you to drive us to the place in your new car so I can show you how to get there because starting tomorrow, you will be driving there twice a day, seven days a week and at least 364 days a year.

"I'll be bringing you into my world, which will necessitate a tremendous amount of dedication on your part.

"Tomorrow, after we go to where it will all take place, I'll tell you enough of the why I chose this business for you. But, for now I'll bid you goodnight Sweetheart."

The next day we drove down one of the streets in Hoboken, which are named after presidents. This one was called Washington Street. Then Uncle pointed to a store front as he told me to take the next right and park in the lot where he had paid for and reserved a space for me on a monthly basis. We didn't have to walk very far when Uncle stopped in front of a store that read, X.Y.Z. Real Estate Company, and proceeded to unlock the door.

As we walked in, I noticed that the windows were covered with pictures of properties that were for sale. He pointed toward the back and said, "That's where the restrooms are located." I counted four desks in the middle of the room and most of the walls were lined with file cabinets.

"You once asked me what the two words that were printed on my business card, 'Business Consultant' stood for.

"Now, I can tell you that I am the biggest oddsmaker for all the professional sports in the country. That's what I do for a living above any of the other businesses that I own. So, I'll get right to it. The largest and most profitable part of 'the family business' is the illegal multimillion dollar a year money maker called 'Bookmaking' and is controlled by mob families all over the country. Before you can make 'book' as it is called, you must have the proper odds. I supply the odds or 'the line' as it is also called, to most of the bookmakers in the entire country. I not only control this world, I own it. I have people working for me all over the country, but as you know my headquarters are located in Las Vegas. Soon, you will see for yourself that the most necessary tool in my business is the telephone.

"I'm positive that you will go to the very top because I'm the man who's going to take you there. Starting tomorrow I will introduce you into the world of bookmaking from the ground up."

"Did you just tell me that it is your intention to teach me how to become a bookie? I've met a lot of bookies, thanks to you-know-who and none of them were women. Women aren't bookies, that's strictly a man's world. Why would you do that? You're an oddsmaker, that's not illegal, but bookmaking is."

"Simply put, it is your inescapable destiny."

"I'm just thinking that it seems a little unusual for the family to endorse this kind of a path for me."

"Sweetheart, there is another reason why you have been brought on board with us, and it's much more important, however, I cannot talk about it at this time.

"I can't promise you that you will never have to stare a lawman in the face, but I can promise you that I'll do whatever I have to do to take care of it. I have so much to teach you in a short amount of time, so we must get started. On the other hand, it would be fair to say that this is the kind of job in which you will have to learn as you go, because it will take practice.

"I'll start with lesson number one, and it's the most important so, here goes, and make it your new mantra from this moment on. Bookmaking is a business of numbers, nothing more, and nothing less. You either lay them or you take them, it doesn't matter which teams are playing each other, not our home teams or your favorite team, if you had one. It doesn't matter what the teams' uniforms look like or their helmets, caps or how attractive their logos might be. Even the players themselves do not matter to us. Always remember, you can never have a favorite, and there lies lesson number two.

"Princess, let me drive this home one last time. In the world that I control the true essence of the games aren't played out on the fields, the courts, or the rinks, they're played in the magic of the point spread. So remember, no favorites, ever!

"Next, understand that in this world, half the men that you will be dealing with are Wiseguys and the other half are not Boy Scouts. Make no mistake, this world is run very strictly by men only. However, I must warn you that some of these men will fall in love with you and some of the others will just want to be able to say 'I banged my bookie.' So, don't get a big head honey, it's really not about you, it's more like a lack of options on their parts because if they're heterosexuals and most of them are, that makes you the only game in town. I know that there are a few female writers around. These gals usually work the phones in the afternoon, from twelve o'clock until two o'clock when the men are out taking care of other business. All they can do is write the bets down exactly as they are given to them. There is another very serious aspect of this business called past posting, Which I'll explain to you at a later time.

"You are going to be trusted with everything. I will teach you every phrase of my world. Since you're a female I know you love to shop. That's going to come in handy now because you will learn how to shop for numbers for me. Since I supply the line to most of the big bookies throughout the country, I must hook you up with some of them. You will only ever be a voice on the phone because you will never meet any of them. I'll explain, as the oddsmaker, I can't make any bets myself because it would appear that my lines are tainted. I always put out a legitimate line and when I see a game or games that I think are good bets, I have to use what is called a 'beard' to place my bets. When you say someone is putting on a beard, it means they are fronting for someone. I am going to teach you how to become my beard. When I say me, what I am really saying is for the entire family.

"As you know, the Super Bowl game was played several weeks ago. More money is bet on that game than any other in the entire year. I told you then that we guys would never lay seventeen points on a Super Bowl, so we all took the points. Nevertheless, we still shopped for the best number on that game, so here goes the lesson. The line in this area stayed at Baltimore -17 because, since the Jets are one of our home teams some diehard Jets fans did bet on them. But in the Baltimore area the bookies were getting bombarded with Colts action, so they raised their line to -17 ½ and then to -18. That's called moving the line. It can be moved up or down, depending on which way the action is coming. I will give you the green light to move your lines when I think you're ready for it. So, if I'm looking to take the points, why would I take seventeen points around here if I could shop in the Baltimore area and find eighteen?

"To an average better who probably has only one bookie, he has to take whatever the going line is. But, when you're in this business it's imperative to have access to bookies all over the country as a way to compare the numbers. Do you get the picture?"

"Uncle, I got it loud and clear. When you want me to take the points, I should shop for the highest amount of points and when you want me to bet on the favorite, I should search for the lowest one."

"Oh my God, Hemmy must be beaming with pride right about now. You certainly have gotten lesson number three down to a science, because that's exactly how it works.

"This next lesson deals with the denominations of the money being wagered on the games.

"Listen carefully, the smallest bet you will take is called a 5 timer, which means the better is laying six to five or $30 to win $25. Those odds change when the bet becomes a 10 timer where the wager drops down to 5 ½ to 5 or a bet valued at $55 to win $50. The difference is called the vig, which on the surface doesn't seem like much but, if you are doing a robust business, at the end of the week it adds up to a lot of money. The vig is expected to pay for the rent, supplies, and salaries, etc. and it always meets its mark.

"The bets run like this 5, 10, 20, 30, 40, 50, and so on until you get to a 100 timer, then that's called 'A nickel' or a wager of $550 to win $500. Then you go to a 200 timer which is called 'A dime,' or $1100 to win $1000. After that it's just multiplication to accommodate the size of the bets.

"You can bet on the odd numbers as well, the 15 timers or the 25 timers. For that matter you can book any number over a 5 timer, just change the math to 15 times 5 ½. The 5 ½ never changes, but I can tell you from experience, I've seldom ever seen an odd numbered bet, the guys almost always stay on the even numbers. Any questions?"

"I do have a question. When I'm booking the bets, how high can I go? How many dimes can I take on a single bet that is if I can even take a dime?"

"To answer your question, you can book up to five dimes on any one game. I will bankroll your book. Most of the major cities in the country have multiple teams in all four of the professional sports that we book all year long. I have people on my pay roll in every city that has a professional team; I pay off sports writers, hotel employees, hospital staff, and even local newspaper gossip columnists. The up to minute weather reports come out of the major airports. I have someone in place in every airport in the cities where the games are being played that day.

"You see, I need to gather as much information as I possibly can to make the most accurate line for my clients. I pay extra to obtain that one tidbit of information out there that nobody else knows about so that I can put all of my resources in motion and ultimately make a lot of money for the family and me.

"When I obtain something so concrete it will not be necessary for you to shop for any numbers. I will just say go "bet the farm" on such and such team. Naturally, and it should go without saying that any action you happen to book on that game from your clients, go out and dump all of it. Make sure you tack on a sizeable bet for yourself."

"Excuse me Uncle, this sounds vaguely familiar from something I overheard between you and my father. I distinctly remember you two talking about "fixes" on the fights. So when you tell me to bet the farm, are you saying that the game is fixed? Is that even possible?"

"Sweetheart, when your father and I were teenagers, a man named Arnold Rothstein fixed the 1919 Chicago White Socks, Cincinnati Reds World Series. Whenever big money is involved you can be sure that there will always be people around who can be bought. I'm going to teach you something very important right now. You can never fix a game or a fight to win, but you sure can fix them to lose.

"I think I've taught you enough for today. I want to be here tomorrow morning at eleven o'clock to get you started in my world. I have business to attend to, so let's go home."

Chapter 16

As we were making our way back to Hoboken the next morning, Uncle explained to me that he would be giving out his line from my office today so that I could get a feel of what it sounded like.

"Princess, I will start giving my line out at eleven o'clock to about thirty select people, who each in turn will give it out to another twenty-five to thirty people. Within one hour, my line is out all over the country and my initial job is over.

Once inside, he said, "Take a good look at the clock on the wall. It is very expensive for a very good reason. The time is always accurate to the minute. Your working hours on the phone are from twelve o'clock to two o'clock on the dot and from six o'clock to eight o'clock in the evening. Remember what I said about past posting. Of course, you will need to be here about a half hour ahead of time to receive my line and set up your paperwork.

"Please go into the kitchenette and bring back a bowl filled with water."

I heard him say "Atlanta 7 ½, Boston 14 ½, Detroit 1 ½, L.A. 12, and Baltimore 2 ½." Then he gave out a long list of college basketball lines. After he made about thirty phone calls, he packed up his work.

"Princess, go over to the S file cabinet. There is a bundle of plain white paper in the back. Please pull out a sheet and bring it over here. Do you remember Tommy Glue Stick?"

"I try not to revisit that part of my past, however, that image of Glue Stick's pants going up in flames will never be completely erased from my memory."

"If you can remember, later that evening I explained to you that he used what is called flash paper to write his bets on. At that time, it was the paper of choice for some bookies. I made a reference that there was something else. Then I let it go, but now I'm about to demonstrate what I alluded to that night.

"Princess, I want you to take that piece of paper you took out of the S file and drop it into the bowl of water. Observe what happens to it."

Almost the second it hit the water, it started to dissolve right before my eyes. Uncle told me to pick it up, I tried, but it felt like a glob of mush when I lifted it out of the water. I was amazed.

"What is this paper?"

"That's what is known as 'sugar paper'. It is also purchased in magic shops just like flash paper. As you can see, once it hits the water, it cannot be retrieved. This paper is the only kind I ever want you to write your work on. You will always find a supply of it in the same file cabinet.

"I bought you a cosmetic case. It's empty except for eight rolls of quarters. Keep the quarters in your glove compartment at all times. Fill the top tray with an assortment of cosmetics. Put your work in the case underneath the tray because it will always have to be transported back home with you. You can get some of your paperwork done before you go to bed, if you want to. I will give you a telephone number to call in New York City. It updates all of the sports scores every twenty minutes. All of the games being played in the evening on the West Coast don't start until eleven o'clock our time. Those games won't end until approximately two o'clock in the morning. Use your imagination and find an ingenious hiding place for the work in your home.

"The only paperwork I want you to carry into the office is a list of the bettors' figures from the day before and their totals for the week. If one of your clients disputes the figure tell him you will bring it with you the next day. Then you will go over the figures and get it straightened out before he can make another bet.

"I've told you most of the basics of how your business is to be run. The family is giving you about twenty-five clients of your own. Most of these men bet between 10x's up to a dime. All of the money that you earn form your clients is yours to keep. Three of your clients have packages of their own. That means they have men that bet with them. Then they only have to make one phone call to you. For that, they receive twenty five percent of their total losses.

"You will be able to get R.F. up, dressed, make his breakfast, and have some quality time with him before you have to leave for Hoboken. On some days you might have a couple of hours to spend with your son before you have to be on the road again. You should leave for Hoboken no later than four forty-five, just in case you run into some traffic.

"Hemmy and I both realized that bringing you into this world would isolate you from the rest of it. We decided that along with giving you your own clients, you should be the one to go out and settle up with them after you close up shop for the evening. You will probably have to meet three or four of them every night. Your clients are going to want to meet you anyway. I already told you that since there are no other women of your caliber in the bookmaking world, they will become intrigued with you.

"If your clients have money coming from you, then you choose the spot to meet them. If the money is coming to you then they get to choose the place, within reason. That's the rule of thumb in this business. I will have a list ready for you tomorrow morning. It will spell out all of the places that you will be allowed to meet them in. I have chosen fine Italian restaurants and some of the best lounges in the area. They will be sanctioned for you. Every one of them is owned by Wiseguys. These places have been chosen for your protection. Just in case you should ever have a problem, we need to know that you are in the best of hands and that you will be protected at all times.

"Princess, all of the places on my list are located in Hoboken, Union City, North Bergen, Fort Lee, Secaucus, and Weehawkin. You see, you can never go south toward the area that you left behind.

"I think that I have covered most of the ABC's of the business except for the granddaddy of them all-that is you answer to nobody but me! Anything that I might have left out, you will learn on the job.

"Take this list of names I have prepared for you and study them. The first two are the bookies that you will place my bets with. I have arranged for you to have a 2-dime limit on any game. There are no limits to the number of games you can bet. I may give you one game to bet or twenty-five. You will be talking to The Sandman and The Skull. They are partners. I'll send someone to settle up with them, remember, you are 'The Princess' to them and no one else.

"Princess, we move a lot of money all around the country, when we need to. For the record my handicapping expertise is the sharpest on College Basketball. I make more money on that sport than any of the others. If I give you twenty-five games, you can expect that I will win the majority of them. You will be my first beard to ever give all of my bets to those two partners I just told you about."

"Uncle, if you can do what was just said, then you could potentially carry out The Sandman and The Skull."

"Precisely, my beloved fairy. I do believe that your brand of magic is going to bring me more luck than I've ever had before. I may give you a few bets to place for me this weekend. The week runs from Monday to Sunday. Your career will start on Monday, when you start booking your own clients. Take a look at this list of their names. What do you think of them?"

"Wow, Uncle, as I glanced down at this list, I can't help but think that even the powers that be in Hollywood would be hard pressed to cast this kooky list of characters. Do they really use these names on the telephone?"

"Absolutely! When you settle up with them in public, obviously they won't use those names. They'll give you a first name, which is usually their real names. For the record, we know who they really are and where we can find them if they ever try to stiff you out of your money.

"They may like to use crazy names on the phone, but let me assure you that most of these guys are very successful businessman. The majority of them are fixed pretty well financially. The three men that I told you that have their own packages are Speed Boat, Marco Polo, and Skinny Sully. You can expect to pick up sizable amounts of money from these three clients most of the time. What I can tell you is that you will win a helluva lot more than you will ever lose. I want you to listen carefully one more time to the sounds of the line.

"When we return home, you will have ample time to pick up your cosmetic case before you go down to your place.

"I want you to go to Hoboken tomorrow at the appointed time. You need to get used to the routine that you will be following for your indeterminable future. Princess, do you think you are ready?"

"Yes, Uncle, I may not know why, but I am convinced it is my destiny."

"If you ever start to become over-whelmed, think very carefully about my next words. My best friend, Hemmy, concluded a long time ago that a child doesn't have to be a male to set the world on fire. You will set my world on fire, I'm sure of it.

"Should anyone ever come knocking on your office door, tell them that all of the agents are on the road. Make it clear to them that they should call for an appointment. Never open the door for anyone except me. Then bring out the bowl of water and take out the Sugar Paper before you get started."

It was no surprise that I had all the clout with the oddsmaker, thus allowing me to be the first bookie to get his line every day.

Uncle called me the next day and gave me three bets to place for him in the evening. I called The Sandman and gave him Atlanta -10, New York -3 ½, and San Fran -7 ½ for 2 dimes a piece. When he answered the phone, I couldn't explain the feeling that came over me. It sounded like I had heard that voice before, somewhere in my past.

I stayed until eight o'clock on the dot, locked up the office, and walked to the parking lot. After I unlocked my car, I placed the Sugar Paper, which contained Uncle's bets in the cosmetic case. By the time I arrived home, my son was already asleep. I settled in and had a bite to eat, which Kim had left for me. I was able to get the results of Uncle's first two bets, which he won. Uncle lost the San Fran bet. That loss still had him up $1800.

The next day Uncle won three out of four games at 2 dimes a piece. He checked in with me at eleven thirty that evening. After I told him he was up $3800 for the day, I said, "You certainly do know your basketball."

"Princess, I've had some losing weeks with the pro baskets, but I told you that college basketball is really my forte. There is a long list of college games that are played every week. I didn't want to put you in that arena just yet. You will have the entire week to practice booking both pro and college basketball bets. Once in a while, you may even book a hockey game from your clients. By next weekend, I'll be sending you in to set your new world on fire. Your first order of the day will be the list of college games I'll give to you when I give you the opening line. That list goes only to The Sandman and The Skull for 2 dimes a piece. Remember to follow my lead on those games. Dump any action you take on them to the other bookies that I hooked you up with, and don't forget to tack on something for yourself."

I arose at six thirty the next morning, flushed with anticipation at the prospect of starting my new career.

I waited for the phone to start ringing. Uncle called at eleven thirty. After I finished taking down the line, he reminded me to stay focused, then he wished me good luck before he hung up.

The first call came in at twelve o'clock on the dot. "I'm Take This, I want the line." Not even a hello or anything else. He called back about ten minutes later and said, "Take This," as he proceeded to give me three 10-time bets. He certainly earned his nickname. Every time I gave the line out the phone rang again instantly. Most of the guys liked to bet early and were 10- or 20-times bettors. The Silver Fox bet 50 and 100 timers. Of course, the three men who had their own packages called for the early line, but they never called any bets in until the evening. I gave out the line and then wrote down the bets over and over again. And so it went until two o'clock, when I wrapped it up.

R.F. came running to the door when he heard me put the key in the lock. "Hi, Mommy, guess what? Nana's here. She brought over the macaroni. Do you like to go to work?"

"Slow down, little man. I can't answer any questions until you come over here with lots of hugs and kisses for me." Mother came out of the kitchen and said, "Kiki, how did your first day on the job go?"

"Mother, Uncle was right on the money, once more. I have this incredibly strong feeling that I'm going to become really good at it. That was the good news. The bad news is that I added up the number of hours that this job will require of me per week. My job will only afford me a few hours in the morning and maybe two in the afternoon to be around R.F. That is the only reservation I have about this whole set up."

"Kiki, go tell my grandson that you need a few minutes to talk to me while I finish preparing your dinner, then join me in the kitchen, I need to speak to you.

"Sweetheart, Milt had your father's blessing to bring you into his world. No one knows the hours that are required to run this kind of business better than him.

"Esther and I both have a stake in Robert Francis's well-being. Whether you want it or not, you are going to need our help in raising your son. One of us will always be here for him, until we both move to Florida before he starts school. Please, accept our help. We all want what's best for your son. I've said my piece, so go and enjoy some playtime with him."

I left promptly at four forty-five. Uncle called at five-thirty sharp with the line. He didn't give me any bets to get him down on, but promised to call at ten thirty to check in with me.

At six o'clock the phone started ringing again. Then I had the opportunity to hear from the rest of my clients. I suspected that they all called in on the first night, probably because they couldn't wait to hear the voice of the first ever full-time female bookie.

Uncle had already told me that some of these guys are only weekend bettors. Of course, I could always count on Speed Boat, Skinny Sully, and Marco Polo to call every day and night. The phone never stopped ringing for two solid hours. Once more, I got the biggest kick out of Take This. I did get one request that totally surprised me. It came from Marco Polo. He dared to suggest that I keep my phone open for a few extra minutes if he didn't have the time to get his bets in; he felt that because of the volume of his business, it was warranted. Needless to say, he got a resounding smack down from me. I told him that when the clock went off, I folded up my tent. I added that I would never make any exception for anyone.

Uncle called at ten thirty and said, "How did it go, Princess?"

"I loved it, Uncle."

"Set your alarm for seven o'clock. You will have more than ample time to get all of your paperwork done. I have only one question before I sign off. Did these men speak to you with the utmost respect, as they should?"

"Actually, Uncle, I have only one reservation concerning a bettor in the entire group so far. There's something about Marco Polo that disturbs me. I have a feeling that he wants to do business with a female bookie, but when the time comes to settle up, I don't think he's going to like forking the money over to someone of the female persuasion."

Then I told Uncle about his unusual request and how I had handled it. I continued by asking him if he would give me the latitude to end my business relationship with any one of my clients for what I perceived to be "just cause." He assured me that I could indeed.

"Princess, don't ever worry about Marco, I'll keep an eye on him. Now, it's time for you to get some rest. Good night Sweetheart."

To anyone else, my job might have seemed dull, but I found it to be exciting.

My job was about to get taken to an entirely different level on Saturday. After Uncle called me with the line, he gave me a list of twenty-three games that he wanted me to bet 2 dimes a piece on them.

"Got them, Uncle, do you want me to shop for numbers?"

"No, you don't have to. Make sure these go to The Skull and The Sandman. They already have the right numbers. Get their line first, wait about ten minutes, and then get my bets down ASAP. I think you're going to be my lucky charm today, Princess."

My curiosity got the better of me. I just couldn't wait to see how many games Uncle had won or lost the next morning because he had put up $50,600 to win $46,000. I went and got the scores a second time on account of the fact that I couldn't believe my eyes. Uncle won 22 of the 23 games he bet for a total win of $41,800. I was sure glad that I took Uncle's advice and dumped all of my action on those same games.

When Uncle called me later that day, and before he gave me the line, he said, "We did it, Princess"

"No Uncle, you did it."

"Princess, I knew you would bring me luck."

Uncle ended up winning $47,400 that first week, which included a few pro basketball bets from The Skull and The Sandman. I had a good week also. I told the smaller bettors, like Take This, who owed me around $100 each that they could carry their totals over until next week, to save me a trip to settle up with them. Only five of my clients had money coming to them. I asked them to meet me in Hobokon. One of them asked me to hang onto his money. Uncle was correct, on average, I would have to meet three or four clients per night. No one wanted to come out on Sunday evenings so I had that one night off.

I started out meeting some of them at the bars and in the sanctioned Italian restaurants. One of my clients, Mr. Whisper owned his own restaurant, so he asked me if we could settle up in his place. Once I saw it, I didn't mind going there at all. It was definitely upscale and very continental.

The rest of my clients elected to meet me in lounges. At least I got to listen to some very good music while we schmoozed.

Each one of my guys offered to buy me a drink with the exception of Marco. He insisted on meeting me in the parking lot of Club 46. On top of that, he kept me waiting for twenty-five minutes, which annoyed me to no end.

"Hi, Princess, you're not at all what I expected to see. No one as cute as you should be a bookie, let alone, hanging around with nobody but men like me."

"I am a bookie who gets paid extra to pick up and drop off the money. I'd appreciate it if you would be prompt as I have another client to meet tonight. Please hand over the $1800 you owe and I'll be on my way."

"Relax Princess, I was just trying to pay you a compliment. Besides, a woman shouldn't be carrying around this much cash."

"Marco, I have a schedule to maintain. It cannot be changed for you. I have the right to terminate my business relationship with anyone who gives me any kind of grief. Let's not get off on the wrong foot. The money please!"

Then he reluctantly handed me the money, exited my car, and said, "I'll talk to you tomorrow." Now that I had met him, I had more reservations concerning him. When all was said and done, I decided to keep him as a client for the time being. I made the executive decision to keep my conversation with Marco to myself.

Uncle didn't make any bets until the following Friday. I made the usual 2 dimes bets on three teams for him. He won two of the three which put him up $1800. Then on Saturday he took the plunge once again. I made 22 college basketball bets for him at 2 dimes apiece. To my utter amazement, he won 21 of the 22 bets. He finished out the week up $41,600 from The Skull and Sandman.

When Uncle called on Monday with the line he said, "Princess, you have no idea what you've done in just the first two weeks on the job. You did the unthinkable and got away with it." Then on Saturday, Uncle told me matter-of-factly, that The Skull and The Sandman had been put out of business permanently. "Start using the other bookies I hooked you up with when I want you to bet for me."

By this time, I had met all of my clients with the exception of The Silver Fox, because he was one of the men who asked me to carry over his figure often. His business was located in Harlem. Even with his carry over from the week before he now owed me $3800 so I had to go to him. I took Park Ave. all the way up to his place. He assured me that I would be able to park safely in front of his store. As I opened the door, I noticed the name Zito's was painted on the glass window.

The store was dimly lit. When my eyes adjusted, to my utter amazement, I saw four pay phones lined up on one wall. They were followed my three slot machines on the same wall. I was jolted back to my present surroundings by a very loud banging sound. I called out, "Silver Fox, is that you back there?"

"You sound like The Princess, follow my voice. I'm in the store room. I have to finish taking care of some business."

As I entered the store room, I said, "You're The Silver Fox?"

He answered, "Yes I am."

When I walked up close enough to him, I caught a glimpse of a rodent that was being beaten into submission. I had never seen a real rat up close. Well certainly not one that walked on four legs.

"I could almost put a saddle on that thing. I can't believe rats can grow to be that large."

"Princess, I've seen them even bigger. Please go over to the cardboard box marked outgoing and count out $3800."

As I walked over to the box, he turned the broom upside down and proceeded to stab the rat to death. After washing his hands, he walked over to me and formally introduced himself.

"I'm Richie, it's my pleasure to meet you, Princess, I apologize for the terrible first impression you stumbled upon. We have to deal with this all the time up here. You see, these stores in this neighborhood must be kept open 24/7. If we ever locked these places up, there wouldn't be one single item left in any of the stores by the next morning. The thieves would break through the ceilings, drop down, and carry everything out. I can already tell that I'm going to like doing business with a female. As long as I have to hand over my money to a bookie, you're sure better looking than any of the others."

"Richie, Uncle warned me not to get a big head, after all I'm the only game in town."

We were both laughing as he started to walk me out to my car. "Princess, please stay for a few minutes, I have something to discuss with you. Before we started doing business together you were vouched for by some of the highest ranking guys around.

"I received a phone call earlier this morning from a very important man. He was very upset that you were coming up here and he doesn't want you to come back here ever again. I was asked to do him a big favor and come to you in Hoboken no matter, win or lose. I agreed to the accommodation and now that I have met you, I'm glad I did. If I were ever to let anything happen to you, trust me, my ass would be in a sling. I was given a marker by him that I can cash in any time in the future."

"Richie, at least allow me to raise the amount to $5,000 before we have to settle up. It will cut down on the trips you have to make."

As he walked me to my car, he said, "Princess, you're a breath of fresh air. Welcome aboard. I have only one question for you, who the hell are you?"

"I'm nobody. I work for certain men and I do what I'm told. Thank you, Richie, I'll talk to you tomorrow when you once again become 'The Silver Fox.'"

I had now met all my clients and a few of them stood out from the rest, and became my favorites. I was already certain of one thing, if this was to be my destiny it was all right by me because I realized just how much I already loved my job.

Chapter 17

I moved into the NCAA Basketball Tournament season. The tournament went down to sixteen teams, then eight, and ended with the final four. The last game was played in Louisville, Kentucky, where UCLA beat Purdue 92-72 and won the tournament.

Uncle did very well financially on the NCAA playoffs by betting on UCLA. He raved about a young man named Lou Alcindor who coincidentally was named Most Outstanding Player. While Uncle never had favorites, he certainly had an eye for talent. He believed that Lou had the potential to become one of the greatest players in pro basketball history one day. I was barely on the job for a month and a half, but I could already see that when it came to numbers, Uncle made magic.

My business almost doubled in volume during the tournament. What surprised me the most was the way the action came in. I was shocked to see it was almost an even split. That's a dream come true for a bookie because it put me right in the driver's seat. I made a lot of money on the vig alone during that time. After all was said and done, I did all right on the College Basketball Tournament.

Soon after that I went right into the 1969 NBA World Championship Series. Then I caught a huge break. The Lakers were the favorites due to the three big guns on their team, Baylor, Chamberlain, and West. Boston was such an aging team that no one ever expected them to make it to the finals. It turned out to be one of the greatest upsets in NBA history.

I was surprised that Uncle didn't make a single bet on the series until the seventh game. A bookie by the name of Vinnie the Blade had replaced The Skull and The Sandman. When Uncle hooked me up with him, my job got a little easier because he took up to 5 dimes on a single game. Now, with Vinnie on board, I could cut out a few calls. It doesn't seem like much, but on those occasions when I was asked to bet a minimum of $50,000 or more on a single wager, time is of the essence.

Uncle had me take the points on Boston for 5 dimes. I didn't have to move out any of my Boston bets because most of my clients bet on LA. I just booked it all, sat back and watched as Boston defeated LA 108-106. Anytime a huge upset like that occurs, you can be sure the bookies are going to take down all the money.

I moved right into the baseball season next. This would be the first time I got a taste of what a money line looked like. They can range from a low of -120 +110 to a high of -220 +210, which becomes astronomical if you're on the losing end of a bet on a big favorite.

A lot of gamblers think that the favorites should always win so they lay big money on them. When they lose and are laying more than two to one, they would then need at least two wins just to get back to even. By the end of the season, three of my biggest bettors got crushed. However, they always paid on time.

The 1969 Orioles team was considered to be one of the finest ever. Baltimore had star sluggers like Frank Robinson and Boog Powell, and pitchers like Mike Cuellar, Dave McNally and Jim Palmer. That made them the heavy favorites. Most people believed that only the most foolish gamblers would put their money on the Mets.

It certainly appeared that way when Baltimore beat the Mets 4-1 in the first game. Uncle wasn't much of a baseball bettor. He only made a few dozen wagers all season and won about 75% of them.

When the Mets upset Baltimore by beating them 2-1 in Baltimore, the majority of my bettors went down in flames. Then in game number five they beat Baltimore 5-3 to win the 1969 World Series. The Mets accomplished one of the greatest upsets in World Series history, thus earning them the moniker, "The Miracle Mets" Once again, the bookies made all the money.

Football season, both college and pros were both in full swing by the time the World Series ended. Uncle only bet about ten games every Saturday and always won at least seven or eight of them. I would never again see Uncle bet 22 or 23 games like he did on the first two weekends that I ever took action. After following Uncle's lead on the games he did bet on and after adding in all of the vig, I had a very good college football season.

Pro football is the one sport where shopping for numbers becomes so very important. Uncle hooked me up with the five biggest bookies in the country because they would take up to 50 dimes on any bet from me. I could bet on more than one game because his money was vouched for by the most powerful men on the east coast even though he had to remain anonymous. I added Hot Wheels from Detroit, The Shoe Box out of Baltimore, Sunny Man from Miami, Voodoo Daddy based in New Orleans, and J.D. from Denver to my shopping list of bookies.

I didn't have to go shopping for Uncle until the playoffs. The Dallas Cowboys were favored and were playing at home. But Uncle wanted to take the points to the tune of fifty thousand dollars, so I went shopping. Voodoo Daddy and Sunny Man had the highest line and each took the maximum bet from me. By the end of the game, the point spread didn't matter because Cleveland destroyed Dallas 38-14. Uncle made a lot of cash on that game, and all of us bookies got to take the ride on that runaway train while taking down all the money.

With the conclusion of all the playoff games, the last two teams left standing were Minnesota and Kansas City which earned them the right to go to Super Bowl IV.

Before the Super Bowl was played, I had to book the four most popular college football games on New Year's Day 1970. Uncle bet on two of the Bowl games and split them. When I factored in the rest of the minor Bowl games, in the end they turned out to be an almost even split for me.

The Super Bowl was played on January 11, 1970 in New Orleans. Most of the fans and bettors continued to believe that the NFL was still superior to the AFL in spite of the big upset by the New York Jets the previous year.

Uncle set the line at Minnesota -12 ½ and the over/under at 39. He asked me to go shopping for the highest numbers I could find since he was taking the points on Kansas City. I suspected that I would find the best numbers on the East Coast so I called The Shoe Box first and was able to get 50 dimes down on Kansas City taking +13. Then I called Sunny Man and made the same bet for Uncle. Almost all of my clients laid the 12 ½ points on Minnesota and I booked all of it. In spite of the odds against Kansas City, they pulled off a 23 to 7 victory over the Minnesota Vikings and the AFL upset the NFL for the second year in a row. Needless to say, Super Bowl IV made a lot of money for many of the bookies all over the country.

Uncle had worked in Las Vegas for most of the football season. He did return for a few days to celebrate RF's fourth birthday.

Uncle assured me that he would return to Jersey before my official first anniversary on the job. My mother and Aunt Esther were leaving for Florida. They asked for my permission to take Robert Francis with them. I agreed because my business took up most of my time. I thought it would be in his best interest to send him to Florida so that he could play in the sunshine. Uncle made it very clear to me that I could fly down to visit RF and work out of his mansion anytime I wanted to.

When Uncle returned, he insisted on taking me to Nardi's restaurant to celebrate my first anniversary on the job. So many changes had taken place to my life in the last fifteen months.

A bottle of Pink Crystal Champagne was already chilling in a bucket at our table. Uncle started the conversation as he raised a glass, "To my Princess, congratulations on the completion of your first year working for me and the family. I know Hemmy would want us to observe this first milestone here. Remember, that it was in part the wisdom of your father and the totality of his confidence on your ability to rise to the top that took you down this road with me in the first place.

"Sweetheart, now the time is at hand for you to receive your first report card. I'll state the facts as I've observed them during the past year.

"Princess, you've had a hand in something that I've never seen in my entire career. You were barely in the business when I sent you out to go shopping and get me down on UCLA when they defeated Purdue. I'll always believe that you were my lucky charm.

"Soon after that, you booked the heavy underdog Boston Celtics as they defeated the LA Lakers for the NBA Championship. Next, the Miracle Mets destroyed the far superior Baltimore Orioles in the World Series. Then you went full circle by booking the AFL upset over the NFL in Super Bowl IV. If I had to predict all those upsets in one single year, and put a line on them it would have been so astronomical that we wouldn't have been able to use it. I do believe that you have a magic wand in your left hand, a pen in your right, and an infinite amount of fairy dust in between. So, as of tomorrow you will have my permission to move your lines whenever you have the inclination to do so. I think you're ready for it and more than that I think you will make "magic" with the hook whether you bring it up or take it down. You have earned an A+. What do you think, are you ready?"

"Uncle, I do believe I am ready for the next step. It occurred to me that maybe the reason I adapted so well in this business is because it's a world filled with nothing but men. I've been around men my entire life and I genuinely like them, so I guess this was always meant to be my destiny."

"Sweetheart, it was always your destiny, but for a much different reason. It is part of the story that I promised to tell you one day. Now, I will raise a glass to you and another successful year."

I was right back where I started, booking pro and college basketball games once again. Then I moved into that exciting time of year when the final twenty-five NCAA College Basketball Tournament started. As it turned out, I got a break with one big surprise which made us a lot of money.

Notre Dame snapped a record 12-year drought without a single NCAA tournament victory. Austin Carr scored an NCAA record 61 points and led Notre Dame as they rousted Ohio 112-82. Uncle bet the underdog, and I just booked my action because most of my clients bet heavily on Ohio. That one big upset put the bookies way over the top that March.

As I moved from one season right into the next, I realized that there would always be a game in one of the seasons that would forever stand out in my memory.

One such game happened on July 18, 1970 in the next baseball season that I booked. Willie Mays, at age 39 bounced career hit number 3,000 to left field.

Then two big changes took place in the football sports world in 1970. First, the NFL and the AFL merged. Second, Monday night football debuted on September 21st with Cleveland beating the Jets 31-21 in Cleveland. It seemed like I just turned around and I was about to log in another big game. Super Bowl V was being played in Miami, Florida on January 17, 1971. Baltimore was playing Dallas.

Uncle set the line at Baltimore -2 ½ with the over/under at 36. He would never let the biggest game of the year go by without having some kind of a wager on it. He didn't want me to go too crazy on this game so I only got him down for 25 dimes on Baltimore -2 ½, I decided to just book it.

I did end up losing money on Super Bowl V, but I didn't get hurt that badly because I made a lot of vig as many of my clients bet on the over 36. Super Bowl V went into the books as The Colts 16 and The Cowboys 13. Somehow

Uncle pulled that one out of the hat even though it was a small wager for him, but he still won $25,000.

Mother, Aunt Esther, and Robert Francis went back to Florida. My mother had already put her home up for sale. I couldn't put it off any longer, the time had come for me to do some serious soul-searching concerning my son's future. I turned to God Himself or as I call it, "The hand of God" to point me in the right direction. Then I asked Him to grant me the Wisdom of Solomon so that I could make the best decision regarding my son.

Mother returned home in the middle of March. While she was in Florida Uncle's X, Y, Z Real Estate Company found her a buyer.

My son ran up to me and said, "Mommy, I missed you so much."

"Only half as much as I missed you, R.F. Sit down best boy and tell me about your time in Florida."

"Wow! I saw sunshine almost every day. I'm learning how to swim. Nana takes me to a real pretty Church. I never forget to say my prayers every night because I promised you I wouldn't. Uncle Joe takes me out for a ride in his boat and he's teaching me how to fish."

"Did Nana take you to see her new house?"

"I saw it. It's nice and she's got a pool too."

"You know Nana is moving in six weeks. Now, I have something very important to tell you, I need you to be a real big boy and listen carefully to what I have to say.

"Nana wants me to let you move to Florida and stay in her house for most of the year because you will start going to school in September. When you make friends at school, you will be able to play outside down there. I might allow her to take you because Nana promised me that she will bring you back up here to visit me on the Holidays. I will come down to visit you from time to time when I can leave my work here. I can work with Uncle down there every once in a while.

"I have a very important question to ask you now. Do you like being in Florida with Nana, Aunt Esther, Uncle Joe, and Aunt Connie? I need for you to tell me the truth."

"Mommy, I did like it down there. I had a lot of fun and I love the sunshine, but I can't leave you alone because it would make me too sad. Besides, I have to build you a bigger castle."

"I want you to make lots of friends, play outside, and start playing any sport that you might like. You know, there's no better place in the world to make a bigger castle than in the sand. The big question is, and I want the truth, do you like it down there enough for me to let Nana take you with her?"

"Mommy, I really like it down there."

"I thought so, I'll tell Nana you can go with her. First, I have one big rule. I want you to call me every morning so I can hear your voice. Remember I'll always be your mother no matter where you go and I'll always love you."

"I'll always love you best, Mommy."

When all was said and done, I realized that sometimes knowing when to let go is part of being a good parent and the right thing to do. In the end, I asked myself, do you love him enough to let him go, knowing that living in Florida would be so much better for him. I believed that God pointed me in the right direction.

I went down to Florida at the beginning of June to visit my son and find a suitable school for him. I was flying back late on Friday night. By Friday I would have to make my decision and get my son enrolled.

With my son happily attending Don Bosco, making many friends, and enjoying his new home, he was doing just fine.

I plunged right into the football season next. For the first time on Christmas Day 1971, two divisional playoff games were played. Even though I had to go to the office on Christmas it turned out to be well worth it.

I opened up the phone at eleven o'clock and worked until three. Uncle asked me to take the points on Dallas for 50 dimes which I gave to J.D. Most of my action came in on Minnesota since they were the home team as were the Chiefs, so I just booked them.

My mother and son came up and she was hosting Christmas at my place. Robert Francis was waiting for me at 3:30 pm when I arrived at home. I got to spend some alone time with him before Uncle Milt and Aunt Esther came down to join us for Christmas dinner. Dallas had just finished beating the Vikings 20 to 12. Uncle had just nailed another one. By the time we finished eating Miami had tied Kansas City. The Chiefs had taken the early lead. It took a double over time, which was also a first, for Miami to beat Kansas City 27-24. When both of the underdogs win divisional playoff games, it's a pretty good bet once more, that the bookies could be found popping the champagne.

R.F.'s birthday fell on a Saturday. Since he was only two weeks away from coming home for the Christmas holidays, I decided to celebrate it on the same day because I came home early on the holidays. Both uncles, Dom, and Frankie stopped in for a few minutes that morning before I went to work, bearing their presents for my son.

The new toys that my son received grabbed his attention instantly. Uncle Frankie gave him something new called an Etch a Sketch. He loved it because he could draw on it, then shake it, which erased the drawings. Uncle Dom cracked me up by bringing R.F. something called an NFL Electric Football game. The Jets and The Raiders met on a twenty-seven x sixteen-inch NFL Field, whose action posted Jets and Raiders did battle on the colorful field. Quarterbacks passed and carried the ball. It had automatic timers with magnetic down markers, vibrating coils, and a click on grandstand. Only time would tell if he was old enough for that one. Uncle would not be outdone, he gave him something called a Rock Em Sock Em Robots, which puts you in control of every blow including knockouts. Players handle controls as boxers in the ring, jabbing, feinting, shifting, and then delivering the knockout punch.

My little guy was now six years old.

The three Floridians left before New Year's and Uncle went back to Las Vegas.

On January 9, 1972, when Uncle called me with the line, he asked me to go shopping for the best numbers I could find and bet 50 dimes on the Milwaukee Bucks That didn't surprise me since we were back into Uncle's favorite betting season. I did what I had to do, got Uncle's bet down, dumped off all of my Milwaukee money, and tacked on a substantial bet for myself.

I had just gotten the score the next morning when Uncle called me.

"Do you remember when you booked your first college basketball playoffs, I told you then that one day a certain young man would become a fantastic professional player in the NBA?"

"Sure, I remember that conversation very well and I remember that player's name. You're talking about Lou Alcindor. Didn't he change his name since that time?"

"That's correct Princess, he recently changed it to Kareem Abdul Jabbar. Last night he led the Milwaukee Bucks in a 120-104 victory over Wilt Chamberlaine and the LA Lakers breaking the Lakers' 33-game winning streak, which was the longest of any team in American professional sports."

"Uncle, what made you decide to bet on the Bucks?"

"Well, Sweetheart, it was the odds mostly, and the fact that Kareem had become an even better player than I had predicted, but let's see what happens with this Sunday's Super Bowl."

Chapter 18

Super Bowl VI was played on January 16, 1972 in New Orleans, Louisiana. Uncle set the line at Dallas -6 over Miami and the over/under at 34. Never one to pass up a Super Bowl bet, Uncle wanted me to get him down for 100 dimes on Dallas -6 only.

Personally, I never liked a flat number, without the ½ point or the "hook" as it was called, particularly on a Super Bowl.

I would always put the hook on it, bring it up or down a ½ point because I would always want a decision, no matter if I won or lost it, so I opened my line up at Dallas -6 ½. I waited and got Uncle down at -6 with Sunny Man and J.D. for 50 dimes each.

Because I opened my line up high, I was able to secure some Miami action which earned me a lot of vig. Before I wrapped it up, I gave Vinnie my Dallas overage, plus a bet for myself. The Cowboys thoroughly dominated The Dolphins and the final score went into the books as The Cowboys 24 and The Dolphins 3. Uncle won $100,000 and I did alright.

Time marched me on and I found myself booking what would become one of the most famous football games of all time. The AFC Divisional playoff game was telecast from Three Rivers Stadium in Pittsburgh, Pennsylvania on December 23, 1972. Uncle set the line at Pittsburgh -3 ½ over The Oakland Raiders. He loved Oakland and had me bet the max on them with all five of the big bookies. I got him down at +3 ½ everywhere except for The Shoe Box where I got him down at the even better line of Oakland +4.

I was listening to the game on the radio while driving along Kennedy Blvd. with 1:13 seconds left in the game when Ken "Snake" Stabler scrambled and scampered untouched into the end zone. The Raiders were winning outright. I could feel a celebration about to begin, or could I?

Pittsburgh took over, Terry Bradshaw threw two short passes, one to Franco Harris and the other to Frenchy Furqua, which brought the ball up to the forty-yard line. Only problem, there were only thirty-seven seconds left in the game. Two failed passes ensued. Then it was forth and ten at their own forty-yard line with twenty-two seconds left. Bradshaw threw the ball which somehow got deflected off of someone, no one knew for sure who it was. Franco Harris caught it just above his shoe and ran it in for a touchdown giving Pittsburgh a 13-7 win over Oakland, and the greatest loss of my career as a bookie. That play became known as "The Immaculate Reception," and the most famous play in all of football history. Uncle went down for $275,000. I took a hit of over $50,000 which was a lot of money considering most of my guys didn't bet too high except for the three who had packages of their own.

When Uncle called me later, he reminded me of something he told me when he was first teaching me the business, "Princess, we can't possibly win every single game, but I promise you that we will win the lion's share of them." All that mattered to him was his numbers and what they were intended to do. Tomorrow would be another day and he would start all over again.

Three weeks later, on January 14, 1973 Super Bowl VII was played in Los Angeles, California. The Miami Dolphins played the Washington Red Skins. Uncle set his line at Miami -1 with the over/under at 33.

Uncle wanted me to max out all five of the big guns with Miami -1 or 1 ½. That was easy enough to do. In all, Uncle had the same amount of money bet on the Super Bowl that he had on that disaster, The Immaculate Reception.

By the time I closed up shop, I was still top heavy on Miami. I passed it off to Vinnie at the same price. By the time Super Bowl VII was recorded into the books, Miami was recorded as the champs with a 14-7 victory over The Washington Red Skins. Just as Uncle had predicted, it hadn't taken him very long to get back all of the money he had lost on Oakland with the exception of the vig. I did get all of my money back plus a tidy sum on top of it.

It seemed like I had just turned around when I found myself in the height of the basketball season again. What would turn out to be one of the most memorable events of my career took place on October 20, 1973, when Uncle called to give me the line, he said to me, "Princess, go out and bet the farm on the Chicago Bulls tonight and numbers won't matter. Max me out with your five big bookies. Remember, way back when I told you that every once in a while, there would come a time when I would tell you to bet the farm with no questions asked. This is that time."

Uncle called me at nine o'clock from Las Vegas the next morning.

"Princess, how do you like them apples?"

"Good morning Uncle, I have to love them. It's almost as if the Knicks didn't even bother to show up for last night's game as they went down in flames to The Chicago Bulls 85-69."

"Sweetheart, you are close, but no cigar. I'll tell you all about it one day."

When Uncle called me with the line on Saturday December 30, 1973, he sounded frantic.

"Princess, the law is sniffing around today. Get out of there immediately and go directly to the stacks. I've got that number. I'll call you there in ten minutes."

"I'll be there."

I grabbed my purse and coat, then flew out the door and got to where I had to be, pronto.

I'll never forget what the weather was like that day. It was so bitter cold with the wind blowing in from the Hudson River. I made it to my car in record time, considering that my foot wear of choice was Stiletto boots. They may have come off as being super stylish to look at, but I assure you, they afforded very little warmth. I removed the eight-inch stack of newspapers that had been sitting in my trunk since February, 1969, along with a small jar of water, and all eight rolls of quarters from my glove compartment.

I walked up to the corner and turned onto the side street. There, right before my eyes stood the dirtiest, most disgusting phone booth imaginable. This clean freak was staring in disbelief. I had to take a deep breath which just about seared my lungs as I inhaled the bitter cold air, and then I pushed the door open with my boot. I placed the stack of newspapers on the floor to stand on. It was the way we bookies tried to keep our feet from freezing. Thus the term, "going to the stacks." I opened the jar of water and placed it on the floor, then I took out the roles of quarters, my pen and my sheets of sugar paper. I was ready to go to work, in spite of the bitter cold and the dirty surroundings. Uncle called within two minutes.

"Sweetheart, I prepared you for this day a long time ago. The phone booth you're about to start working in will probably become frigid within twenty minutes or so. Your fingers and toes will become totally numb. Enough of that, let's look on the bright side. There are only two divisional playoff games today. I want you to book The Cowboys-Vikings game first, which is going off at one o'clock. Then I'll give you the line for the Dolphins-Raiders game. When you are finished, I want you to go straight home. It's going to take some time for you to thaw out. I'll call you later, but for now I want you to know that I'm taking the red eye back tonight."

When Uncle called me at 3:30 pm, I told him that I left that freezing phone booth at exactly two o'clock. Then he brought me up to speed on everything that happened earlier.

"Of course, I dispatched two men to set up their business in your office immediately. When two detectives arrived within the hour, supposedly working off of an anonymous tip about suspicious behavior coming from your building, all they found were two licensed real estate agents who were hard at work.

"They asked if there were any female employees working there. The agents explained to them that of course they had several secretaries working there part time. Obviously, the detectives didn't find any illegal activity going on so they were satisfied and left.

"Sweetheart, if I had enough time, I would have told you to work out of my penthouse, in the warmth, instead of that raunchy phone booth. I don't care if your clients have my phone number. I'm doing everything I can to protect you, but remember I told you there are no guarantees in this business.

"On the lighter side, I'm told that the potential problem with the law has been neutralized for the time being, so you can go back to your office this evening. However, if you want to stay close to home tonight, feel free to use my place. I can have one of the real estate agents give out my number to your clients from your office again."

"Uncle, please call me at my office, that's where I'll be. I don't want my clients to get a new number for the second time in one day. They only had two games to bet on today so they will be chomping at the bit by this evening."

"By the way Princess, I want you to know that I'll be staying back east for the foreseeable future."

By the time I went back to my office, Minnesota had upset Dallas 27-10 in the one o'clock game. I did very well on that one. On the other hand, I didn't fare as well with the four o'clock game. Miami, the favorite, beat Oakland by the same score 27-10. I thanked my lucky stars when the day finally came to an end because I managed to make a few dollars and escape the law.

In what seemed like the blink of an eye, on January 13, 1974, I was about to book Super Bowl VIII, which was being played in Houston, Texas between the Miami Dolphins and The Minnesota Vikings. Uncle set the line at Miami -6 ½ and the over/under at 33. As always, he could be counted on to make some kind of a wager on the big game.

It didn't surprise me that he wanted a total of 250 dimes on Miami. Of course, I gave all of my Dolphins action to Vinnie and sat on all of my Vikings bets. We won another Super Bowl with the Dolphins beating the Vikings 24-7. Then it occurred to me that I had just booked my fifth Super Bowl.

Every year, my mother, Aunt Esther, and Robert Francis flew up the day before Mother's Day. My little man was almost eight and a half years old. This year had taken on a very special tone when I conspired with both ladies to incorporate a surprise 70th birthday party for Uncle on Mother's Day. He would never suspect a thing since his birthday had already passed on April 3rd. We arranged to take him to dinner on Saturday evening after I finished work.

When I entered the business in February of 1969, I made it very clear that on Mother's Day I would work an extra hour in the afternoon because I would not be returning to work that evening. All of my clients understood as they had family obligations of their own.

I had reserved the private room in Nardi's for the party. I even got R.F. on board with my Mother and Aunt Esther. The plan that we put in place had the three of them taking the limo to visit my father's grave which was located near his Mother's before going to Nardi's. Uncle was going to wait for me to return from work, at which time I would drive both of us to the restaurant and join them there.

When we arrived, my son played his part to a T. He rushed up to Uncle and said, "Uncle Milt, come quick and see what I found," as he led him toward the back room. Then R.F. opened the door and as they both walked in, about one hundred people who were all standing up yelled, "SURPRISE!"

I could tell by the look on Uncle's face that he was bowled over. After everyone quieted down, Aunt Esther led all the guests in the raising of a glass of Champagne by way of a toast to the man of the hour. She paid a loving tribute to Milton Kaye by reminding everyone that she had a long and happy marriage to her husband. My mother followed and told the crowd that she had known Milt only one day less than she knew Hemmy because he couldn't wait to introduce her to his best friend the very next day. Her eyes welled up with tears when she spoke of Milt's lifelong devotion to her husband and the way he had remained a good and steadfast friend to her since Hemmy's death.

Uncle Dominick, who, without a doubt, carried himself as the most important man in the room, gave a glowing tribute to Uncle as he took a trip down memory lane.

I was asked to make the last speech in as much as Uncle thought of me as being his own child.

"When I was a little girl, I daydreamed about the sort of man I would marry one day. I pretended he would be someone out of a fairytale. Well, it didn't work out for me, as you all know. One day, I realized that a very special man had been standing right in front of my eyes my entire life. First, alongside of my father as I grew up, and ever since my father passed away, he has stood tall in front of me, he has been at my side, and he has stayed behind me to watch my back. He is made up of good character and integrity, which has earned him the love, admiration, and respect of family and friends alike. I am honored to call this man my Uncle and Godfather. And on a personal note, this is the man who takes 'ordinary numbers' and turns them into 'the extraordinary'. I love you, Uncle, and I wish you many healthy, happy birthdays to come, and most of all. 'I wish you all that Heaven allows.'"

Then everyone joined in together and sang "Happy Birthday" to him.

Uncle went up front and thanked everyone for sharing the latter part of their Mother's Day with him. Then he ever so gently chastised his three favorite ladies by accusing us of "big time duplicity." He swore he didn't have a clue about this surprise party.

In between eating the various courses, everyone started to move around and mingle. I went over to Uncle Dom's table first. He stood up, hugged me and said, "Here she is, our little Princess. Your father would be so proud. You're doing one helluva job for the family."

Cousin Gabriel kissed my cheek and added, "You are loved and valued, as was your father."

Salvatore chimed in, "And you're so much like him."

My next stop took me to Uncle Frankie and Aunt Carrie's table. He stood up and as always opened up his arms as he said, "Give us a hug, little girl. We don't get to see you nearly enough since you went to work for Milt. We miss you."

"You know, Uncle Frankie, I miss seeing all of you also. What are you up to these days?"

"I'm sure you heard that when Hemmy died and Cipo's closed, I got a job at Caesar's Lounge. We don't talk about that place anymore. Besides, I'm semi-retired now. I only work on the weekends."

Then I went around the table and there she was, "Evelyn." She stood up and gave me a hug. Any mention of my former life with a certain ex family was strictly off limits. Clearly, she was very happy to see me. A man of about my age was sitting beside her. He literally jumped out of his seat as Evelyn introduced him to me as her son, Kenny and his wife Carolyn. He looked vaguely familiar to me, almost like the third young man who stood watch at my father's casket. I told him how pleased I was to meet him. Then I asked him if he had ever met my father, and he did something that looked a little strange to me. He turned his head away from me and glanced at his mother. Then he stared at me for a few seconds before he said, "I did get to meet your father." He clammed up after that and didn't say another word. I found that behavior a little odd so I excused myself and went over to greet Mayor Kenny. He was now in his eighties. Even as he was faced with declining health which had forced him into a wheelchair, and with the loss of his beloved wife Margaret, four years prior, he still loved the attention paid to him by a young lady who fussed over him. I wanted him to know just how much our family appreciated his presence.

Mayor Kenny had survived having to resign as Mayor of Jersey City in 1953 because of allegations stemming from widespread corruption on the waterfront. When all was said and done, some twenty-one years later, somehow he managed to remain just as powerful as he had been when he was the mayor. I could never understand that, but I sure could attest to his loyalty to old friends.

The party seemed to end a little too soon. Uncle thanked everyone for helping to make his day so special. It was obvious that he was genuinely touched by the love and respect that had been poured out to him by all of his guests on his special day.

When we returned to the St. James, Uncle stopped by my place first to thank my mother and me one more time. Then he thanked my son for his participation with the decorations and for his ingenuity at being able to lure him into the room. Robert Francis was beaming with pride. Uncle kissed me on top of my head and said, "Princess, you know what they say, 'the party's over.' Tomorrow, it's business as usual."

My mother and son were leaving the next day to head back down South. I told Robert Francis how very proud I was of the fine young man he had become. Then I reminded him that school would be out soon and that I would be flying down to visit him.

As always, time marched on and before I knew it, Super Bowl IX was looming on the horizon. It was being played on January 12, 1975 in New Orleans, Louisiana. Uncle set the line at Pittsburgh -3 over Minnesota and the over/under at 33. When Uncle called to give me the line, he started laughing because he knew that I would put the hook on it, either up or down, immediately. Then he told me to go out and bet 200 dimes on Pittsburgh for him, but he made it very clear that he would only lay -3, nothing more. I had no problem getting him down with Hot Wheels, J.D., Sunny Man, and Voodoo Daddy at -3. Since I opened my line up at Pittsburgh -3 ½. I did manage to bring in some Minnesota action my way. Right before I was going to close up shop, I dumped all of my Steeler money to Vinnie and I sat on all of the Minnesota bets. All I did was follow Uncle's lead. When it was all over, the Steelers beat the Vikings 16-6 and handed them their third Super Bowl defeat as another one went into the record books.

By this time, I thought that all of the lessons I had been taught by Uncle when he brought me into the business had been put to bed years ago. I was wrong. Another lesson was about to come my way that I never knew existed. On March 24, 1975, a much-publicized fight was being held in the Richfield Coliseum in Richfield, Ohio. Mohammed Ali was taking on Chuck Wepner, AKA, "The Bayonne Bleeder." Ali was guaranteed $1,500,000 and Wepner signed on for $100,000. Everyone looked upon this fight as little more than being a joke. It was predetermined that Wepner didn't stand a chance. Uncle was aware that the fight was taking on a life of its own, especially in the North East part of the country. It was a certainty that men were going to want to bet on it, therefore, he had to come up with a suitable line.

When Uncle called me, he said, "Princess, take this line down and make sure that you give it out exactly like this, Ali 40 to 1, in and out. I'll explain, it means that for every 1-dollar bet placed, you will pay them 40 dollars if they win. There is only one catch, they can only bet on the underdog. No money will be booked on Ali. Do you understand?"

"You're putting out a line that can only be bet one way?"

"Yes, I am, you will probably never see a line like this one again, but for this particular fight, it is appropriate."

"Do you really think the guys will put their money up on Chuck?"

"I think they will. Maybe they won't make large bets, but some of them will make a wager and look for a miracle to pay them big odds. Don't worry, just book it and have some fun."

"Will do, Uncle."

I almost had a scare when Wepner knocked Ali to the canvas in the ninth round before losing by a T.K.O. 19 seconds before the final bell in the fifteenth round. He just about went the distance by taking a brutal beating along the way. Later, it was determined, after the footage was scrutinized that Wepner never knocked Ali down, he either stepped on his foot or tripped him somehow. Whatever happened didn't matter because Uncle was correct. I booked a lot of action on that fight and I made all the money!

Chuck Wepner was so sure that he would win the fight, he bought his wife a beautiful blue negligee and told her to wear it because she would be sleeping with "The Heavy Weight Champion of The World" that night. It took the doctor quite a while to stich Chuck up and put him back together again before he was finally able to return to his hotel suite.

It didn't take very long for the story to circulate. His wife was sitting on the edge of the bed in the blue negligee when Wepner entered the room. Without skipping a beat, she quipped, "Is Ali coming here or am I going up to his room?"

I always loved that story and knew that I would enjoy retelling it in the years to come.

By September of 1975, I had decided that the time had come for me to fulfill my childhood pledge that someday I would buy myself the same kind of car that parked across the street from my house when I was a little girl. So I went shopping for a 1976 Lincoln Continental Mark IV. One of my clients was a manager at a dealership and promised me a good deal. They had a designer series that year. The Bill Blass was dark blue with a crème roof. The Cartier was dove gray with a gray roof. The Pucci was dark red with a silver roof, and the Givenchy was aqua with a white roof. As soon as I saw the aqua car, I thought to myself, *now that's a car for a girly-girl, "Tinker Bell."* It was love at first sight.

Of course, I knew that when it was time to sign the papers, Uncle would have to be there to put the car in the name of one of his companies to protect my identity. I gave Uncle one of my checks to pay for it in full. He didn't want to take it, but he acquiesced when I reminded him that I had made the vow to buy it for myself when I was just a little girl and now that I had earned my own money, he really didn't have a choice, so he took the check.

Less than a week later, on September 22, 1975, one Sara Jane Moore made an assassination attempt on President Ford's life in San Francisco just seventeen days after Lynette "Squeaky" Fromme tried to do the same thing in Sacramento. Sara fired the first shot about forty feet away from the president across the street, in front of the St. Francis hotel. After realizing she had missed, she raised her arm again and this time a former Marine knocked her arm away, maybe saving President Ford's life.

I had just locked the door to my office at 2:05 pm on the day after the assassination attempt and had walked about two hundred feet when two men approached me and said, "Do you work at X, Y, Z Real Estate Company?"

"Excuse me gentlemen, but I was taught that I should never speak to strangers. Who are you and what do you want?"

"We are FBI Agents and we need to speak to you. It's very important."

"Gentlemen, let's step around the corner, shall we? I'll have to see some identification."

After they both produced the proper ID, I suggested that we go to my office and speak privately. We walked in and I invited the agents to take a seat.

"Gentlemen, how can I help you?"

"As you've probably heard, an attempt was made on the president's life yesterday. This was on the heels of the earlier one several weeks ago. The FBI is in charge of the investigation, which, in turn, brought us to your door. One of the guests who was staying at the St. Francis hotel called the phone number which is registered to this address on Sunday both afternoon and evening. Then he called again on Monday evening and then again last night as well. Why was he calling this place so often? Is he buying or selling a piece of property? You are aware that we can access the records."

"Of course, you can. I do the paperwork here, that's my job. Who is this man? Can you give me his name?"

"Yes, it's William Sullivan. He's an executive with a consulting firm."

"I know Billy, he was in San Francisco on business. Didn't you check out his story?"

"Of course, and then we did a background check on him. We confirmed that he was there on business, however, it also came to our attention that he is a married man, which raised a red flag. Why is he calling you repeatedly? Maybe you two are cooking up something anti-American, or is it something more personal?"

"Agents, are you judging me, your credentials clearly identify both of you as working for the FBI, not the moral majority. Maybe we are just good friends and he likes to call me to say, 'Sweet Dreams,' or could it be that he just likes to hear my sweet voice? Do I have to draw you guys a picture? I don't like where this is going.

"Twelve years ago, your outfit told the American people that Lee Harvey Oswald acted alone when he killed President Kennedy. I never bought that lemon for one single second. What are you going to tell them this time? That a married man and a single lady from New Jersey conspired to knock off our current President. Is that going to be the latest addition to another one of your fairytales?

"If you had taken the time to do your due diligence, you would have contacted the voter registration office and found out that I have always been a registered Republican. I have no desire to kill my President, especially a fellow Republican. I think it's time for you gentlemen to leave. Please don't come back here again to waste any more of my time or yours. If you find yourself in a position where you think you must return here, I'm warning you that I will not utter a single word to you until I have a very expensive and high-powered attorney attached to my hip. Have a good day, gentlemen."

After they left, I called Uncle and gave him a heads up, I told him how I had handled the FBI this time around. After he stopped laughing, he said, "So now you're running around with a married man. How do you manage to fit him into your very busy schedule?"

"Uncle, I'm so glad that you can find humor in the grip of these unbelievable circumstances. After all, I couldn't exactly tell The Fed's that I'm his bookie, could I? I didn't even know his last name. I pulled that information out of them. What is it with me, Uncle? As the biggest oddsmaker in the country, what are the odds of one of my clients being in San Francisco on legitimate business the same day that someone takes a shot at President Ford?

And so where is he staying? Like San Francisco is a small city. Of all the hotels, he just happens to be staying at the same place where that kooky broad decides to shoot the president from across the street, which brought the FBI knocking on my door. Now, I ask again, what are the odds?"

"Well, if I had to make a legitimate odd on that scenario, I assure you it would be astronomical. Sweetheart, once that shot was fired, the FBI had to start looking for a conspiracy, hence, they grabbed every phone number coming in and going out of the St. Francis. Princess, you know that none of your clients ever leaves home without taking your phone number with them. You're bigger than American Express. Your client just happened to be at the wrong place at the wrong time, and you unwittingly got swept up into it.

"Princess, you handled yourself impeccably, as you were trained to do. I told you from the onset that while this business might seem a bit mundane at times, it would positively never be boring. Case closed, let's move on."

As it turned out, another one of the most memorable games of my career was played on December 28, 1975, and it had nothing to do with the money and the results on the wagers that were bet on that game.

A "Hail Mary" pass is a very long pass in American football, made in a desperate attempt with only a small chance of success. It's executed by having all of the receivers run straight toward the end zone while the quarterback throws a pass, which is, "up for grabs." The saying took on a life of its own when the quarterback of the Dallas Cowboys, Roger Stauback, (A Roman Catholic) AKA, Roger the Dodger, Captain America, and a Heisman Trophy winner, said about the game winning touchdown pass to Drew Pearson, "I closed my eyes and said a Hail Mary," Up until that time, most desperation plays were called "Alley Oop's."

With 24 seconds left in the NFC Divisional Playoff game at Minnesota Metropolitan Stadium, the favorite was knocked off of Super Bowl Road because of the "Hail Mary Pass and completion." The Minnesota fans thought they had a comeback victory so the last few seconds' loss left the fans in a state of sadness and shock, of such magnitude, that one perturbed or, perhaps mentally ill, fan hit one of the officials in the head with a whisky bottle, which, knocked him out, and later required eleven stiches to close the wound. To add a sad epilogue to one of the greatest playoff games in professional football, the Minnesota Viking's quarterback, Fran Tarkenton's father, the Reverend,

Dallas Tarkenton, suffered a fatal heart attack while watching the game at his home in Georgia. Fran didn't learn of his death until after the game ended.

The final score was Dallas 17 Minnesota 14. Uncle passed on that game and I just booked it. Most of my action came in on The Vikings. Because it was an upset, I did okay, but that Hail Mary Pass put the Cowboys on the road to Super Bowl X. So much happened that year, good and bad. As a result, I was so glad that 1975 was about to be put into my past.

Chapter 19

Super Bowl X was played on January 18, 1976 between The Pittsburgh Steelers and Dallas Cowboys in Miami, Florida. Uncle opened up the line at Pittsburgh -7 and the over/under at 36. After he gave me the line, he told me to go shopping and lay the points on Pittsburgh for 200 dimes. I opened my line up at Pittsburgh -7 ½.

I was able to find -7 for Uncle, but even with the hook my guys still bet on Pittsburgh so I moved it all out to Vinnie the Blade with some additional money for myself.

By the time Super Bowl X was made official, the Steelers won it for a second consecutive year behind Terry Bradshaw's 64-yard touchdown pass to Lynn Swann. Pittsburgh won the Super Bowl game 21-17, leaving Uncle and me sucking wind, we went down for a lot of money on Super Bowl X, because in my world, the world where the magic of the numbers is all that counts. Pittsburgh may have won the game but they didn't cover the point spread.

Just about two months later, another milestone was made on March 20th, 1976. Boston's John Havlechek became the first NBA player to score more than 1000 points in one season for fourteen consecutive years. That was pretty impressive.

Before I knew it, I was back into baseball season. One game stood out above all the others. On April 25, 1976, on Sunday afternoon, the Los Angeles Dodgers and the Chicago Cubs were playing in Dodger Stadium when suddenly two people ran onto the field. Cub's centerfielder, Rick Monday, had seen it all in the out fields over the years. Streaker's, drunks, and all-around whackos, but this time he sensed something was really amiss. One was carrying an American flag, which was common during the bicentennial year, he proceeded to unfurl it and then struck a match. Vin Scully cried out from the broadcast booth, "It looks like he is going to burn the flag."

Monday, who'd served in the Marine Corps Reserves for six years, didn't hesitate. He ran straight to the pair, grabbed the flag with his right hand, and kept running toward the dugout. The sodden flag was never lit up. The fans gave Monday a standing ovation and the scoreboard read, "Rick Monday. You made a great play."

I knew that one day, when I would be many years removed from the business, that would remain my favorite baseball story, and I didn't have one single bet on that game.

Time was moving along so quickly before I realized that I was about to book my eighth Super Bowl. This one was being played in Pasadena, California, between the Oakland Raiders and the Minnesota Vikings on January 9, 1977.

Uncle put the line out at Oakland -4 and the over/under at 38. As soon as he gave me the line, it was clear as a bell that in his opinion, Oakland was going to be the bet all the way, so Uncle wanted me to get him down.

The Vikings had already made three prior trips to the Super Bowl and hadn't won any of them. I always believed that my clients being the kind of gamblers that they were is what prompted them to think that the Vikings, who had a powerful team, could never go 0 for 4.

And that's the difference between gamblers and oddsmakers. You see, the oddsmaker knows that on any given game the odds are made for that particular game only, not yesterdays, tomorrows, last weeks, or even three previous appearances in Super Bowls. The bettors just can't grasp that concept. I, for one, was delighted that most of my clients took the points. When Super Bowl XI was recorded, it was Raiders 32-Vikings 14. The Raiders won their first NFL Championship and the Vikings dropped their fourth Super Bowl in as many tries. Super Bowl XI turned out to be one of the most profitable Super Bowls of my career.

Almost an entire year zipped by when on the evening of December 2, 1977, Uncle called to give me some scoop on a story that defied my logic.

"Princess, I hope you can remember when I told you that whenever there is big money involved, most anyone can be bought or allow themselves to get caught up in a crooked money-making scheme. I've heard of many over the years and I've been involved in a few myself. You've already seen it, but today I heard about a scam that was a first, even for me.

"Get a load of what this guy almost got away with. His name is Mark Gerard. He was a successful, American, Equine veterinarian who was born in Brooklyn and studied at Cornell. He had imported two horses from Uruguay, a champion named Cinzano, and a much cheaper not so good horse called Lebon. Well, this guy switched the horses and ran Cinzano in Lebon's name. By the time the race went off, he was a 57-1 outsider at Belmont Park. Needless to say, with that kind of odds, Gerard made a ton of money when his champion won the race. However, his luck ran out when a journalist, of all people, recognized the winning horse as Cinzano, which triggered an investigation. He was indicted today. I hope he's retained a very good lawyer because it's going to be tough to get out of that one. I've seen many horse races that were "fixed" during my long career, especially in harness racing, but I have never seen a fix involving the switching of horses. Every time I think I've seen it all in this business, I'm wrong, Princess. There will always be another scheme coming up the pike sooner or later."

"Well, Uncle, I'll tell you something, I will never forget that story for the rest of my life. This crazy business is not for anyone who can't go with the flow because you just never know what tomorrow might bring."

Several nights after Uncle told me that kooky switched horse story as we were enjoying a wonderful dinner at Nardi's, he brought up an unusual subject.

"The family is counting on you to remember everything about this business in spite of the fact that you can't ever write a single word of it down on paper. I promise you that when this part of your life is over, the family is going to give you a very valuable present, which will change your entire life one day. I'll leave you with that thought and say good night for now, because tomorrow we will start all over again."

Just three weeks later the NFL Divisional Playoff games began on Saturday, December 24th, 1977, between the Oakland Raiders and the Baltimore Colts. Both of these teams were power houses and just about evenly matched.

The game was being played in Baltimore, so when Uncle called me with the line, I was curious to see where he was going to put his money. He set the line at Baltimore -3 and told me to go shopping and take as many points as I could find. He was putting his money on Ken "Snake" Stabler.

Uncle wanted 150 dimes on Oakland, so that was enough to cause me to open up my line at Baltimore -2 ½. I was pretty sure that my number would be seen as "a bargain," thus bringing me plenty of Baltimore action, which I would sit on. I had no problem finding the right numbers for Uncle. By this time, I had so much experience to know that if I waited long enough, The Shoe Box should have the best number for Uncle. Sure enough, because he was located in Baltimore, he was inundated with Colts money, so he bumped his line up to Baltimore -3 ½. So I grabbed an extra half point for him. It might not seem like much, but a half point can make all of the difference in this world. I had to settle for +3 for 50 dimes each with Hot Wheels and Sunny Man.

This game would go into the sports books as one of the most exciting and memorable in professional football for a play that would be called "The Ghost to the Post." It refers to a 42-yard pass from Ken Stabler to Dave Casper, nicknamed, "The Ghost" after Casper the Friendly Ghost, which set the game tying field goal in the final seconds of double overtime. Casper also caught the last pass of the game, a 10-yard touchdown, which gave Oakland the 37-31 win. Uncle lost some smaller basketball bets during the week, but I wasn't surprised that he won this game because when it came to the playoffs, the Super Bowls, and the NCAA Finals, he won the lion's share of them. That's when he really did shine. That game would always remain unforgettable to me, not just because we won it, but because of that spectacular play, which set us up for the win.

Even with the fantastic, "Ghost to the Post" play, etched into the sports history books forever, Oakland got knocked out of the running for the Super Bowl, which was played on January 15, 1978, between the Dallas Cowboys and the Denver Broncos. This Super Bowl would have the distinction of being the first indoor Super Bowl played in the New Orleans Superdome since it opened in 1975.

Uncle opened up the line at Dallas -6 with the over/under at 39 for Super Bowl XII. He made no bones about it and said that his gut told him to lay the points for 200 dimes on Dallas, he was willing to go as high as -7. He had referred to it as his gut, but I knew it went much deeper than that. I always remembered the first rule he ever taught me, "It's just a game of numbers, lay them or take them." He always acted nonchalant and played down his expertise, but I knew better. He was always on top of all the big money games and in doing so he made magic out of numbers.

With his bet in mind, I opened up my line with a bump to Dallas -6 ½, trying to lure some Denver action my way. Dallas action was dominating even with the bump so knowing that I was going against my own Super Bowl rule that I would never put out a flat number on any one of them, I moved my line up to Dallas -7. It didn't matter to me on this particular game because Uncle felt so strongly about the Cowboys. Ergo, I was going to move all of my Dallas action out and sit on all of the Bronco money.

By the time Super Bowl XII went into the books, it was almost as if someone had cast an evil spell on the Broncos because they turned the ball over eight times, which the Cowboys took advantage of and then walked away with the big win of 27-10. Uncle and I made out very well on Super Bowl XII.

Most of my clients had money coming to them since they had bet on Dallas. I didn't care because Vinny the Blade took all of my Dallas action so I was covered. As per protocol, it meant that they would be coming to me to collect. Most of the Denver action that I sat on came from one source, Marco Polo's package. Apparently his bettors took the bait. I had to pick up $4200 from him, therefore I had to meet in our usual spot in the parking lot of Club 46. In the nine years that I had been doing business with him, he managed to rattle my cage by still always showing up fifteen minutes late. I had gotten used to it because as much as he irritated me, his money was strong. Sometimes, I still got the vibe that deep down in his heart, he was a misogynist.

My patience for him had been tested and pushed to the max in the last two or three months. It became clear that he was beginning to drink way too much and was half in the bag each time he entered my car. I realized that the time had come for the two of us to have a serious conversation because my bad vibe was getting more pronounced toward him each week.

I was about to put him on notice and give him his walking papers.

"Marco, you're loaded again. I'm not usually in the business of preaching, but I must say this, how can you drive so intoxicated? I don't want you to enter my vehicle ever again in such a drunken condition, and take your hand off my knee this very second. Don't you ever put a hand on me again, EVER!"

"Don't treat me like that, Princess. I know you like me too. I only want to be friendly. After all, I bring you plenty of money month after month."

"You stop right there, buster! Bringing me money that you owe me doesn't give you any special privileges. As of this moment, I'm putting you on notice, if you ever show up in such a drunken condition again, that will be the last night I will ever book your action. Now, hand over my $4200 and get the hell out of my car. I mean it. Clean up your act or get lost."

I moved right along into the height of basketball season, which always carried with it a big increase in the action. I didn't have to meet with Marco Polo for two weeks because he only owed me a few hundred dollars the following week so I told him to carry it over.

The next time we met Marco really seemed to have cleaned up his act. He showed up sober so I guessed he didn't want to go shopping for another bookie. Then I moved right into baseball season and had just celebrated my thirty second birthday. Everything was moving along smoothly as I was looking forward to going to Florida for one week to visit my son over the Fourth of July weekend. I was in such good spirits on a balmy summer evening when I went to meet Marco Polo in the parking lot of Club 46.

After being kept waiting for the usual fifteen minutes, he entered my car. I never got a chance to notice the crazed look in his eyes or the smell of booze on his breath before he pounced all over me. I started screaming at him to take his hands off of me as he tried to pull my right leg over the center console toward him. I scratched the left side of his face which only succeeded in causing him to become more determined, clearly, he was hell bent on raping me. As frightened as I was for the first time in my life, I knew instinctively that I would never go down without a fight. Then he grabbed my right arm above my elbow while trying to pull me across to his side. I was able to reach down with my left arm and grabbed my left shoe. Never underestimate the power of a Stiletto. Oh, how I was aiming for his eye, but not being a lefty, I wasn't having much success in making the connection. All of a sudden, the passenger car door was yanked open, and in mere seconds, a man dressed in black from head to toe, right down to a ski mask, hit Marco so hard on his jaw that he knocked him out cold. Then, with super speed, he covered his mouth with electrical tape and threw him into the open trunk of a car that had somehow appeared out of nowhere right next to mine.

He yelled at me, "Princess, I'm Mr. Y, Mr. X is inside the lounge, using their phone to bring Milt up to speed. I know you've just been traumatized so what I need to know right now is if you can physically drive home safely. Milt will be waiting for you in the parking garage. Remember, you are not to be pulled over by the police. You have your work on the backseat. Can you do this?"

"After I take a few deep breaths and get my bearings, I'll be fine."

As I was driving back to Jersey City, I kept replaying what had just happened over and over in my mind. Although it had seemed like an eternity, I realized the entire dreadful event took less than five minutes from start to finish. I could only imagine what Uncle had up his sleeve. I envisioned him as being livid, and that was probably an understatement. I was pretty sure that all of this would end very badly for Marco Polo.

Uncle was waiting for me in his limo. When I parked my car, he came over and hugged me ever so tightly, then he made the assessment that I was okay physically before he hissed.

"That Bastard is going to pay for what he tried to do tonight. Let's head out, I have to brief you on your participation in a major event that must take place this evening. You and you alone are going to be responsible for tonight's outcome."

On our ride to Uncle's destination, I got an earful because he was so angry. As much as he wanted to take care of this situation himself, he had no choice but to let me handle it as long as I was capable of doing what had to be done.

As I exited the limo and looked around, my face must have showed my bewilderment and it didn't escape Uncle's eyes.

"Princess, this warehouse sits in the middle of a twenty-acre tract of land, thus affording the family much needed privacy. Before we enter this building, I need something from you. Since you endured so much trauma earlier, are you sure that you can do what we discussed in the ride over here. It's important that you remember every square inch of this place. You will need it somewhere in your future. Do you want in?"

"Uncle, I'm going to take this bastard somewhere he's never been before. He will rue the night he dared to put his hands all over Hemmy's little girl."

"Let's go, Kiki. It's time for you to enter 'The Butcher Shop.'"

When I entered, the sheer vastness of this building which was made of cinder blocks struck me at first glance. More than that, there was a smell of paint that permeated the entire building. It was so strong that it actually stung my contact lenses.

I was blinking my eyes so Uncle explained, "It is industrial strength paint which is why the smell is so strong. Now look down."

"I'll be damned, I'm standing on plastic, in fact, this entire warehouse floor is covered with it. Wow! It must have taken a tremendous amount of man power to cover this entire building."

"You're correct. Now, I want you to take a deep breath because it's show time."

We walked toward the back of the room and at about half way there we stopped in front of a chair where I saw a man's hands tied behind his back with his head which was slumped down onto his chest. He was out like a light. Two men all dressed in black were standing on either side of him.

"I'm going to wait in the office because it's time for you to take the stage. You are in excellent hands with Mr.'s X and Y. They will do your bidding. I told you that a Mr. Z will be watching as he stands by my side, if you need him just call out his name. Now, Mr. X, give the Princess her wrap. I don't want her to be covered in blood."

I asked Mr. X to pull his head up by the hair. Then Mr. Y waved smelling salts under his nose. As soon as he did, Marco started to stir. When he waved it a second time, he bolted upright.

Once I got a full view of his face, I gasped and covered my mouth to stifle a scream. The image was so grotesque I had to shut my eyes for a few seconds. His nose, or what was left of it, was scattered in all four directions on his face. As he raised his head up all the way the look of total shock told me that I was the last person on this entire planet that he ever expected to see standing right in front of him. Mr. X said to me, "Princess, we just tenderized him a little for you."

"Well, well, well, Marco you seem surprised, were you expecting a visit from Mother Theresa? From that very first week back in February, 1969, you have been nothing but a thorn in my side. But, enough of the chitchat, let's get down to business. Where would you ever get the idea that you could attempt to rape me anywhere in this world and think that you would not have to pay the piper. Don't you know what kind of people I work for? You must have been told that I am a valued employee, and so much above that because they trust me with their money. Now, you are about to find out what the consequences for your actions are going to be tonight.

"I am going to demand two things from you, starting right now. First, I want a humble and sincere apology from you. Second, I want you to beg me to show you some Italian generosity so that I can spare your life. If I don't get what I want by my count of five, I am going to give the orders to Mr. X and Mr. Y that will cause you more pain than most human beings are capable of enduring."

Then through a voice that sounded like a partial croak and a defiance that blew my mind, he said, "You don't have the balls to give that order."

I realized, at that moment, my instincts toward him were right on the money all along. Marco was a stone misogynist. He wasn't about to beg for his life from a female. Now, he had rattled my cage for the last time and pushed me too far. So I chose my words very carefully for the fullest effect.

"Well Marco, you certainly are correct about that. I wasn't born with that particular equipment, but let me assure you that I do possess something else. I certainly do have "The hairy patch" that is going to give the orders. I'm warning you that if I don't get what I want by the count of five, believe me, I will shout it out. One, two, three, four, this is your last chance, five."

"Mr. X, send his balls to the promised land!"

He spun around and kicked Marco in his privates so hard that the chair fell backward. Judging by the scream, which seemed to come from somewhere deep down as he toppled to the floor, it was obvious that he was in excruciating pain. It took both X and Y to set the chair and Marco back upright.

"Mr. Y, break his kneecap!"

Mr. X moved to the side and in an instant Mr. Y heel kicked Marco in his kneecap and shattered it. He let out a guttural sound before he passed out. Mr. X assured me that he wouldn't die from the blow to his groin because he had taken the edge off of his kick. Mr. Y asserted that in time his kneecap would heal, but he would probably be left with a limp for the rest of his life.

Uncle came out of the office and said, "It remains to be seen if he ever leaves this building alive. Get him back up, let's finish it, Princess, are you ready?" I nodded my head in affirmation. Then uncle went back into the office.

Mr. X waved the smelling salts under his nose several times before he started to come around. When he did come around, the only sounds coming from him were moans. I positioned myself right in front of him. As he raised his head up, I could see the hatred in his eyes, so I spoke up to him.

"You tried to rape me in my car, if I hadn't been under surveillance by these two men, you probably would have succeeded, don't think that I have one ounce of pity for you, when in fact, all I have for you is contempt. You are a piece of crap, so let's get this over with. I'm going to ask you one more time to tell me what I want to hear by the count of five. If I don't get it, I'm going to give the order to Mr. Z. He will come out of the office and pick up the chainsaw, which is sitting on the table over there by the door. Go ahead Marco, take a good look at the table.

"You see, he is called 'The Butcher.'" When he comes out here, I am going to step aside and he will proceed to carve you up, piece by piece. First, maybe a finger, then a hand, foot, etc. while you're still alive. Every time you pass out, Mr. X is going to wake you up with the smelling salts until you bleed out. After you're dead he will continue to carve up the rest of your body. I assure you, at that point, the only way you're leaving this building is in a black trash bag.

"Marco, you so arrogantly told me that I didn't have the balls to give the order when you were only playing for pain, and I proved to you that I do have the goods to get the job done. Now, I'm going to turn the tables on you. Do you think that I have what it takes to give the order that will raise the stakes and ultimately cost you your life? Take a few seconds to think about it before I start counting to five.

"Okay, Marco, that's it, times up. I've got to go to work tomorrow. Since I don't hear anything coming from your mouth, I'll start counting. One, two, three, four,"

"Enough, Princess." He said in a raspy voice. "I'm sorry for what I tried to do to you, it was the booze."

"Well Marco, that was a pretty weak apology. Blame it on the booze, shall we? In the interest of time I will accept your attempt at atonement. Let's just say that was door number one. I hope you haven't forgotten that I must see what's behind door number two. You still have something very important to ask me."

"Princess, are you serious about having me beg for my life?"

"Marco, pardon this pun, you bet your life I am, you misogynist pig. Start begging!"

"Princess, are you really going to keep your word and spare my life?"

"I gave you my word. Now, start groveling and stop wasting my time."

"Princess, I'm begging you to show me some Italian generosity and please spare my life. I don't know what I was thinking earlier this evening."

Before he could say another word, Uncle appeared at my side and took charge.

"Mr. Z will join you two men just as soon as I have a few words with him. Princess, please go into the office and shut the door.

"Marco, you piece of shit. The Princess is my little girl and you dared to put your filthy hands all over her. You have no idea how much I want to kill you with my bare hands, but not for the fact that she gave you her word.

"Here's the way it's going down. These guys are going to throw your broken body into the sleaziest park in this city. Shortly after that, one of them will alert the police to a probable mugging and give them your whereabouts within the hour. Your car has been removed from the Club 46 parking lot and moved to the park area. You will tell the police that you were mugged. Guys, take his keys, ID, and give the Princess the envelope with the money in it that he owes her.

"I don't give a damn what story you concoct for your wife, but you will have exactly 48 hours after you are released from the hospital to get to Las Vegas. Your family will be watched from this moment on. You don't have a choice, its Vegas or The Butcher. We have hundreds of eyes out there. If you ever set one foot back here in New Jersey, I will take that as a red flag and a threat to my little girl's safety and I will have you picked up and brought back here to this building.

"We don't usually involve family members in our beefs, but in your case, we are going to make an exception. If you come back here, the last vision you are ever going to see is The Butcher carving up your son right in front of you. When he is finished with your son, then he is going to carve you up. You've been warned, but just as an added sleeping pill for you, one day when you least expect it, you will turn around and I'll be standing there.

"Throw this trash into the park, it's time for us to go home."

It would be another three years before the events of that evening would ever be mentioned again.

Chapter 20

Time marched on with one season flowing into the next. I was about to book Super Bowl XIII on January 21, 1979, which was being played in Miami, Florida, between the Pittsburgh Steelers and the Dallas Cowboys.

Uncle opened up the line at Pittsburgh -3 ½ and the over/under at 37. Once more, I was anxious to see which way he was going today. Uncle surprised me this year by not betting on the game itself. However, his assessment of these two teams led him to believe that they were going to bust it open with a high scoring game. He was looking to make a quarter of a million dollars on the over so he sent me out shopping.

I bumped my line up to 37 ½ right from the start and made a sizeable wager on the over 37. When the final whistle blew on Super Bowl XIII, Pittsburgh beat the Cowboys 35-31.

Uncle wasn't kidding when he said that he anticipated a high scoring game.

It became a routine that I would go down to Florida to visit with my son over the Fourth of July weekend. Soon after I returned, I found myself fully entrenched in another football season. Up until and including the playoff games, I had made a very good living.

Now, the time was at hand for me to prepare myself to book another Super Bowl, number XIV, which was being played on January 20, 1980, in Pasadena, California, between the Pittsburgh Steelers, for the second year in a row, and the Los Angeles Rams.

As with all the previous Super Bowls that I had booked over the years, I always looked forward to the excitement that went along with the biggest game of the year. But there was another reason. The holidays had come and gone and we were thrust into the height of winter, where our fingertips and toes get numb which pushes us ever closer to the radiators and the fireplaces. Then right in the middle of winter, along comes Super Bowl Sunday, and that game breaks the cold spell with all the hype and anticipation that goes with it.

Uncle set the line at Pittsburgh -10 ½ and the over/under at 36. Once more he only wanted to bet the over. He wanted 100 dimes on it. I could go as high as -37. The Shoe Box and Sunny Man took the over 36 action.

I opened my line up at Pittsburgh -10 ½ and kept it there because I wanted the hook on it, but I bumped up my over to 37. I maxed out a bet with Vinny on the over 36 and he got some of my Pittsburgh money.

This turned out to be a close one, but when this Super Bowl was recorded, the Steelers covered the over/under spread by beating the Rams 31-19. The Steel Curtain dynasty continued as Terry Bradshaw set two passing records and Pittsburgh became the first team to win four Super Bowls, which earned him the MVP award for the second straight year.

I went down to Florida in the early part of June, rather than the Fourth of July weekend because my son was graduating eighth grade. It was so hard for me to believe that he was fourteen and a half years old. Uncle Joe picked me up at the airport and R.F. was there to greet me. Not only was he a stone gentleman, who possessed impeccable manners, but he was also very handsome, athletic, and well groomed. He was so happy to see me and when he gave me a hug he said, "Mother, I'm so glad that you are here to see me graduate. Besides, I'm going to be receiving a special award."

"I wouldn't miss it for the world."

When we arrived at Mother's house, I found her in the kitchen with Aunt Connie and Aunt Esther cooking enough food to feed an army.

"Welcome, Sweetheart, I know it looks like too much food, but your son has invited three of his best buddies over for dinner tonight to meet you. All he ever talks about is his beautiful Mother. I know you just saw him on Easter Sunday and Mother's Day. Still he misses you. Isn't he turning into a very special young man?"

"He certainly is, Mother, and I have you, Aunt Connie, and Aunt Esther to thank for that. I am most grateful for all that you three have done."

"Honey, it's not what we say to him that makes the difference, the magic is in the conversation that you two have every morning. I can see that he is beaming when he gets off the phone each day after speaking with you."

"Well, I'm certainly looking forward to meeting his friends this evening after I finish my work. I'll be coming over with Uncle. He'll be arriving down here at six o'clock pm, then he'll pick me up after I complete my work and we will head right over here."

The graduation started at two o'clock p.m. so I only missed the procession. R.F. did receive a special award for oration. Apparently, he loved to speak in front of a crowd and was very good at it. Of course, that set Uncle up once more to tell me that my son was a Politician in the making. I was happy to learn that all four of the boys would be going on to Neumann Prep High School together.

I went to work the next day from Uncle's estate and when I finished, I went straight to the airport. Uncle had already taken off. He wanted to be back in his office in the city to give out Saturday's line.

When I came back and settled in, it occurred to me that I had already been in the business for 11 ½ years.

After all these years I still kept Mr. Whisper as my last stop on Wednesdays. I loved his restaurant and the old European elegance that he was born with. He remained one of my favorite clients. The following week he asked me a question that he said had been on his mind for a very long time.

"Princess, would you like to come upstairs and see my etchings?"

Not believing what I had just heard, coming from this distinguished gentleman. I laughed as I said, "Are you serious? Mr. Whisper, that old saying has been going around since The Playboy Mansion opened up in Chicago. It's a pick-up line that all the single men are using on all the ladies. I would have thought that you are so much more sophisticated than that."

"No, Princess," he said in that wonderful European accent, "You misunderstood, I really do possess beautiful etchings upstairs in my apartment. I do own quite a collection and would be honored if you would come up and enjoy each and every one of them, I am hoping that you will pick out one as your favorite. Please come with me."

I loved beautiful artwork and really couldn't justify not going up for a few minutes. Besides, he had always conducted himself so properly all these years, so I threw caution to the wind and agreed to go upstairs.

When we entered, he flipped a switch and a lamp came on which illuminated enough of the room for me to see that this apartment was quite large. After he turned other lights on, I glanced around the room, it was so beautiful that it took my breath away, the same way as the restaurant had the first time I walked through the front door.

If I had to pick out one negative feature in the entire room, I would force myself to say that it was a bit too ornate.

Then I turned my attention to the artwork. Wow! He wasn't kidding, he certainly did have etchings. Every square inch of wall space was covered in oil paintings. I admit, I'm not an art virtuoso, but I always had an eye for the finer things. After all, I spent enough of my childhood growing up in Uncle's penthouse and mansions.

I didn't have to look far before I found myself standing in front of a magnificent portrait of the most famous clown in the world, Emmet Kelly Jr. Mr. Whisper came up behind me and ever so proudly told me that Emmett actually sat for the artist. It was not painted from a photograph.

As I slowly moved along, I came to a dead stop in front of a very bright painting of the finish line at the Hialeah Park Race Track. It was gorgeous. He said, "Princess, you do have an excellent eye for exquisite artwork. I can tell you've been exposed to some of the finer things in life."

"Mr. Whisper, I've been to this race track several times. This is a beautiful painting. The jockey's colors are so vivid as they cross the finish line and when I looked at the dust being kicked up from the horses' hooves, the painting almost came to life. In fact, it looks like Hialeah circa the early sixties. What do you think?"

"That's probably a pretty good guess. I do know the Hialeah Park went into the National Register of Historic Places last year. So tell me, which one is your favorite?"

"It's a tough choice, but I'd have to go with the clown, Emmett Kelly Jr."

"Well, I'm glad Princess, because I'd like to gift you with the painting."

"What? Oh no, Mr. Whisper, I could never accept that, it's way too expensive."

"Princess, I've been attracted to you ever since the very first time you walked through my door,"

"Stop right there. I think I'm beginning to see where this is going. Mr. Whisper, what exactly would I have to do to walk out of here with that painting? And please be honest with me."

"I'd like to make love to you just one time."

"Oh, I see, you're like so many of the other guys, only you come off in a much more gentlemanly way. In the end, it's all the same. All you really want is to "bang the bookie." I was warned about guys like you and told that this would happen when I started in this business."

"No, No, Princess, I didn't mean to offend you. I truly want to make beautiful love to you."

"Well, that's not ever going to happen. If any of my bosses ever thought that I had an intimate relationship with a client, they could easily think that I might be past posting them in favor of that man and steal their money. That would get me killed. If they ever found out that you tried to bribe me to get me into bed, then that would get you killed. Do you understand what I'm saying?"

"Oh my God, Princess, I am so sorry and I humbly apologize for being out of line. It will never happen again. Please forgive me. What can I do to fix this?"

"Mr. Whisper, you have always been my favorite two-time teaser bettor so let's pretend that this never happened. I won't give you up because you never put a finger on me. If I elect to continue to do business with you, there will be a price to be paid. I will never step into this building again. Win or lose you will have to come to me. I will choose the place. Take it or leave it. One more thing, tonight's events are never to be mentioned again."

"Thank you, Princess, I want to stay with you."

"Then it never happened."

"I noticed that Deimos, the bartender was still cleaning up. I thought he would have been long gone."

As I drove home, I tried to evaluate everything that just happened. I had been in this business long enough to know better than to attempt to come off as "a babe in the woods." Since I had been around men my entire life, and when you added in the fact that Uncle warned me about some of the men's probable behavior when he put me in his world, I had no choice, in good conscience, but to take it in stride.

That is why I made the decision to keep this unpleasant, fleeting situation to myself and keep Mr. Whisper on as a client.

The next day was business as usual. It seemed like I had just returned from Florida when I found myself once again hip deep booking another very exciting football season. I realized that I was about to book my twelfth Super Bowl, which was being played on January 25, 1981, between the Philadelphia Eagles and the Oakland Raiders, in New Orleans, Louisiana.

Uncle put the line out at the Eagles -3 and the over/under at 37 ½. He asked me to wager 150 dimes for him on the Eagles. As always, I wouldn't put out a flat line on a Super Bowl, so I put the hook on it right from the start. I followed Uncle's lead and dumped all of my Eagles overage.

By the time Super Bowl XV was over, another upset took center stage. The Eagles first appearance in a Super Bowl was squashed by Jim Plunkett's two first-quarter passes, including a Super Bowl record, 80-yard pass to Kenny King which led the Oakland Raiders to a 27-10 victory over the Philadelphia Eagles. Plunkett was named MVP.

Uncle went down for $165,000, but for him that was a drop in the bucket. I didn't get totally carried out because I made a lot of vig, which helped me out. Uncle kept his cool and waited to make it up with his bets during the NCAA Basketball Tournament, which is exactly what he did.

It seemed like I had just unpacked my luggage from the annual visit with my son in July when I found myself right in the middle of the dog days of summer. The 1981 baseball season concluded with the World Series being played between the New York Yankees and the Los Angeles Dodgers.

I got destroyed the first two games as The Yankees won them at home. Then I made most of my money back on the third and fourth games which were played in LA and won by The Dodgers.

Game six had been scheduled for Tuesday October 27, at Yankee Stadium, but it was delayed by rain. That allowed the manager to start Tommy John opposite Burt Hooton of The Dodgers. It also allowed Ron Cey to be in the line-up.

In game six with LA up 3 games to two, Hooton faced Harry Milborne and quickly walked him to face the next batter who happened to be the pitcher, Tommy John. (There were no designated hitters in this series.) That's when Bob Lemon did something so unusual that people were shaking their heads. He sent in a pinch-hitter for his starting pitcher in the fourth inning of a 1-1 game. Tommy John could be seen in the dugout with a look of disbelief on his face. It was all downhill for The Yankees from that moment on as they went down 9-2 in the Bronx and lost the 1981 World Series. That call by Bob Lemon will probably go down in World Series history as the most controversial of all time.

Uncle made $200,000 on that game and it turned out to be the most successful one game take of all the World Series games that I ever booked over the years because the Yankees were the big money line favorites at home.

Combine that with the fact that my guys insisted on playing double up and catch up. They all got carried out and I made all the money.

On Saturday November 14, 1981 at precisely 1:15 pm, my work got interrupted by a loud banging on the front door.

"Open up, it's the law. We have a search warrant. Open up immediately."

I sprang into action with such speed that could only have been inherited from my father. I threw the Sugar Papers into the bowl of water and hid it under one of the desks. Then I dropped down to one knee and disconnected the phone line which was located right above the floor behind my desk.

As I started toward the front, I remembered and was taken back to the very first day I walked into this building. It seemed a bit odd to me that every square inch of the front window was covered completely with pictures of property listings. Now, I understood, the detectives couldn't see in here. The front door lead into an alcove where a left had to be made to enter the building.

"Gentlemen, please desist from making any more racket. Who are you and how can I help you?"

"We are Hudson County Detectives and we have two warrants, one to search these premises and the other will allow us to arrest you. Now, let us in."

"Not so fast, gentlemen, first thing's first. Please take out your badges and hold them up to the glass. After I finish inspecting them, then you can hold up the warrants."

"Gentlemen, what are you looking for and what am I being charged with?"

"Kiki Cipo, you are being charged with bookmaking and we will be searching this building for betting slips. Even if we don't find any of the work in here after we toss this place, it won't matter. We've got you loud and clear on another bookie's phone line which has been tapped for a while."

"Detectives, thank you for being so straight with me. It will become my lawyer's job to sort out the evidence. Would you allow me to be just as straight with you gentlemen? You're not going to find any slips in this building because there aren't any here. I'm telling you that the only papers in this building are legitimate real estate records. In the interest of time and effort, would you take me at my word? I guess we will be going to the Hudson County Jail on Newark Avenue. I will come quietly and without incident."

"Miss Cipo, we have no doubt that you are cooperating to the max, but we still have to conduct a search," one of the detectives said, "and we will have to search your pocketbook and coat as well."

I was totally shocked, when, suddenly one of the detectives said, "Miss. Cipo, we've seen enough."

"Gentlemen, I will be sure to tell my attorney and anyone else who will have an interest in my case how both of you treated me with the utmost courtesy, I appreciate it."

When we arrived at the jail, I was taken to the booking area where I was immediately processed. Then, I was moved into a private room where I was stripped searched by a female guard.

As soon as the processing was finished, I asked to make the one phone call that every arrestee is entitled to make by law. The guard took me into a different office and handed me the phone. Naturally, I called Uncle and I got an earful.

"Princess, I know you are calling from the Hudson County Jail. By the time I received the word that the detectives were coming for you, they were probably banging on the front door. Then your phone went dead. Listen carefully, I'm on it. I've already dispatched my limo to pick up a very good friend of mine in the city to represent you. His name is Marvin Krautblatt and I assure you that he is one of the best defense lawyers on record in the city.

"Mr. X and Mr. Y went to Hoboken to bring your car back here. They are on the way as we speak. I'll be driving your car to the jail immediately. Do you think you can hang in until I get there?"

"Uncle, of course I can. I'll be put in a holding cell after I hang up. I'm not going anywhere until Marvin gets here."

"Sweetheart, I better not find you in a holding cell when I get there. You had better be tucked away safely in somebody's office. That's all I'm going to say on this phone."

Uncle arrived first and he did find me in the same office where they had let me stay after I made my phone call.

"Too many people have been taking gravy from me for a long time. If I don't start seeing some food on my plate, fucking heads are going to start rolling. By the way, as of this afternoon, you are officially retired. You've completed a little over twelve and a half years in this business without taking a bust. That's saying something. After we make this go away, we will discuss your future."

"Mr. X will man your phone tonight and inform your clients that today's work has been erased. Monday to Friday's work stands as is win or lose. Mr.

X and Mr. Y will settle up with them. Kiki, you have no idea what you've succeeded in doing for the family since I brought you into my world."

After a few minutes had gone by a tall thin man came in and walked over to Uncle and shook his hand.

"Hello, Milt. Thanks for sending your limo for me."

Then he came over to me and extended his hand as he said, "Miss. Kiki Cipo. I'm Marvin Krautblatt. I'll be representing you."

"How do you do? Please call me Kiki. May I call you Marvin?"

"Absolutely. I've been in this building for some time. Your bail hearing is scheduled at 4 o'clock. The Judge agreed to stay an extra half hour."

"Judge Riccardi, I'm Marvin Krautblatt and I'm representing Miss. Cipo. I'm asking that she be released on her own reconnaissance because she has a spotless record. Miss. Cipo has never even had a traffic violation. On top of that, she owns a home here in Jersey City. I assure you Miss. Cipo is not a flight risk."

"Mr. Prosecutor, do you have any objections?"

"None whatsoever, your Honor."

"Then I order Miss. Cipo to be released on her own reconnaissance."

Before we all left Marvin told me that he would be petitioning the court for a January trial date. He made it very clear to me that he was quite sure that I would qualify for Pre-Trial Intervention and that the Prosecutor should go along with it.

Then he promised Uncle that he would be in touch as soon as the court date was put on the roster.

Uncle said, "I'd like to take my little girl to Nardi's for dinner. I have some things to discuss with you while we relax a little."

After we arrived at Nardi's, Uncle ordered a fine bottle of champagne.

"Do we have something to be celebrating Uncle?"

"As a matter of fact, we do. We are celebrating your well-deserved retirement. I have a suggestion, let's go down to Florida and spend the Holidays with our family."

"Uncle, if I go down the family will know that I'm not working. They would only worry every day down there. After all these years they know how busy I should be, especially on the Holidays. What could I possibly tell them?"

"Sweetheart, I've got that all figured out. I'm going to tell them that a detective from the Organized Crime Unit contacted me and convinced me that the law had gotten onto you. Then I will add that Uncle Dom and I reached the decision that after twelve and a half years of faithful service, you've earned some time for yourself. We can sell that story.

"I want you to relax and get your bearings. When we return after the first of the year and dispose of your case, together you, Uncle Dom and I will discuss some of your options. What do you say, shall we go to Florida?"

I left on Monday afternoon and Uncle arrived late the next evening. Uncle Joe and R.F. were waiting for me at the airport. As I laid my eyes on my son, I realized that he was growing up too fast. When I didn't leave to go to the mansion for work, my mother and my son asked me why. I told them that Uncle got the word, I should lay low for a while. My son was overjoyed and spit it out, "Mother, please don't go back to work. Why don't you move down here? Nana's got plenty of room."

"Robert Francis, if I were to move down here, I will buy us a home of our own. I am staying through the Holidays. Now, let's go. Nana is waiting for us."

"Kiki, is everything alright?"

"It is, Mother. You know Uncle errs on the side of caution."

My mother was so happy that her eyes welled up with tears as she said, "Kiki, stay as long as you want."

Aunt Esther added, "Let's plan on doing some shopping." I believe that she too had tears in her eyes.

Uncle came over on Wednesday morning. After he grabbed a cup of coffee, he asked me to join him on the Lanai. He asked me how I was doing.

"Uncle, I'm bored to tears. In an instant, I've gone from not ever having enough time to do everything I needed to get done, to having way too much time with nothing to do. I think I'll borrow my mother's car and start exploring the area. I don't know how long it will take for me to adjust. I hope you can understand what I'm talking about."

"I sure do, Kiki. Let me bring you up to speed on what I've done for you. Since you are retired, I took it upon myself and sold your business to Vinny the Blade for $100,000. Even though he took his pinch on the same day as you, he fully intends to stay in the world of bookmaking. I took a $40,000 cash down payment. He will pay off the rest at $5,000 a month for twelve months. After I got the cash, Mr. X took Vinny into your office to give out his phone number to all of your clients. You will get your money monthly. I wrote out a check for Vinny's money from one of my businesses for you. I think that you should take it and open up an account down here. When your case has been disposed of, I'm hoping that you will consider moving down here permanently."

Chapter 21

"I spoke to Marvin; he will be meeting with the prosecutor in early December. We will have a much better view of our position after that meeting. By the way, Carl is on the way down in my limo. You know I can't stay down here for a couple of months without having a car. I almost forgot; Kiki please stay here for the next couple of hours. I'm going straight to a car dealership to get you a car rental. It will be delivered here."

"Uncle, I can get my own car."

"Like hell you will, just do as I say and come over here and give me a hug before I go."

Within two hours, a beautiful silver Lincoln Continental was delivered to my mother's driveway. Mother came out and was admiring the car. After the driver left in another dealership car, I asked her if she would like to take a spin with me.

My mother directed me to Saint Anthony's Church first. He had always been my favorite Saint and she happened to belong to that Parish. I went inside to light a candle for my father. Then we went to a shopping plaza which also had a bank in it so I opened up an account there. I enjoyed our tour together.

Thanksgiving was only a week away. My mother was hosting it at her home.

On the morning of R.F.'s sixteenth birthday, he was off to play some tennis matches with his friends. Before he left, I got a big hug. He was genuinely happy that I was staying through the holidays.

I was elated to see that he had a large circle of close friends. It reminded me of a conversation I had with him when he first moved down here to live with Nana. Shortly after I enrolled him into school, I sat him down and said, "Listen up, son, soon you will start school and meet a classroom full of children. I want to teach you how to make friends because you've lived most of your life surrounded by the same few people.

"Before you can ever make good friends, first you must know how to be a good friend. Do it like this. Be nice, kind, and polite. Don't be afraid to say 'Hi, I'm Robert Francis, do you want to play with me? We could be friends.' This is very important. You see, that's pretty much how your Pop-Pop and Uncle Milt met when they were just boys. And as you know, they remained best friends until the day Pop-Pop went to Heaven."

We did have a birthday cake for him after Sunday's dinner at my mother's house. My mother, as the former chef, hosted Christmas as well.

Marvin called Uncle on the day after Christmas to tell him we were set to go before the judge on Monday January 11th. Uncle was relieved as he wanted this case to go away for good.

New Year's Day fell on Friday.

"Kiki, on the following Monday after you were released without bail, Marvin met with the prosecutor and suggested P.T.I. (Pre-Trial Intervention) for you because he truly believed that you would qualify for it with your spotless record. He agreed and they shook hands on it. The paperwork was submitted and you did qualify very quickly. That deal was confirmed today and the prosecutor is preparing his recommendation for Judge Moore. Sweetheart, I'd like for you to start giving some thought about what you want to do with the rest of your life because this case is about to come to an end."

We were scheduled to appear in Judge Moore's court room at 10:00 a.m. After the Judge kept us waiting for fifteen minutes, the bailiff read the docket number and the proceedings were officially underway.

The prosecutor, true to his word, had submitted his recommendation and he did reiterate it to the judge that I had qualified for P.T.I. and he was going along with it.

"Ms. Kiki Gallo-Cipo please stand. As part of the background check that is a requirement of any P.T.I. candidate, I became aware of who you are affiliated with. It became crystal clear that your great Uncle Dominick is the highest-ranking Mafioso in the Gallo family and the list of your relatives goes on. I'm not sure who that man is sitting alongside of Mr. Krautblatt, however I'm sure he somehow fits into the Gallo family, but I do know that my courtroom is being contaminated by 'Organized Crime,' and I don't like it one bit. In fact, let's say, I detest it and I don't want it infiltrating my County, especially when it comes before me in the form of a female. With that said, Miss. Cipo, I am turning down the prosecutor's recommendation for P.T.I. and hereby sentence you to six months in the Hudson County Jail," as he slammed the gavel down.

Uncle jumped out of his seat and yelled out, "What the hell did he just say?" A rage had come up from down below and turned his eyes black. Marvin cautioned him and said, "Milt, put a lid on it. You are being of less than any help. Let me handle this."

Meanwhile, Judge Moore stood up and banged his gavel down a second time while shouting, "I will have order in my court. Do all of you understand me?" And as he pointed his gavel at Uncle, he said, "If you open your mouth once more, I will hold you in contempt of court. I suggest that you take Mr. Krautblatt's advice, sit down and put a lid on it!"

With that, Uncle stood up and said, "In all due respect your Honor, 'Organized Crime' has been in your County since before you were born and that's a fact." Then he sat down. Everyone started snickering, including both prosecutors as Judge Moore who had been made to look foolish and red-faced said, "Mr. Krautblatt, I don't usually get tough with a fellow professional, but if that man crosses the line again, I will hold both of you in contempt of court and levy a substantial fine on you and him. Please proceed."

"Your Honor, for the record, as soon as I walk out of this courtroom, I will be filing a motion to come back here in thirty days from today for a reconsideration of sentence hearing and I sincerely hope you will look it over very carefully."

I think Marvin spoke so harshly to the Judge to make amends with Uncle. I'm sure he realized that he had spoken to Uncle disrespectfully and out of turn. A dose of reality must have set in as soon as the words left his mouth and probably struck fear in his heart. No one, and I do mean no one on the entire planet would ever dare tell Milton Kaye to "sit down and put a lid on it," not once, but twice in one day.

At the end of the Judge's ruling, everyone was shocked and their emotions had begun to spin out of control.

Then it hit me, I had to get up and speak for myself. I raised my hand as I had done in school. My gesture got Judge Moore's attention. "Miss. Cipo, is there something you want to say?"

"Yes, there is your Honor, with much respect."

"Miss. Cipo, you have addressed my court correctly, I'm going to allow it."

"First, I'd like to thank the prosecutor and his assistant for trying to get me into the P.T.I. Program. They believed I would qualify, and I did. Secondly, your Honor, the man sitting next to Mr. Krautblatt is my uncle. I'm asking you to grant me a little time to speak with him before I am taken next door to begin my sentence. He is understandably disappointed and very upset with the verdict. I'd like the opportunity to calm him down a bit. Judge Moore, thank you for allowing me the opportunity to speak."

"Ms. Cipo I noticed that you never asked for anything for yourself and that impressed me. Not even a hint of trying to get me to change my mind about the sentence I handed down to you. You have distinguished yourself as a lady in my courtroom, therefore I am going to grant you your request. I will allow you to have fifteen minutes before you are remanded to the jail."

Uncle, Marvin and I stayed in the courtroom after it cleared out. It was time for Uncle to look me in the eyes so now his anger was replaced with such sorrow. He started the conversation, "Kiki, I have let Hemmy down. This was never supposed to happen when we put our plan in motion so long ago. Misters X and Y have already taken to the phones and informed Dom, Gabriel and Salvatore. I can't tell you enough how sorry I am. Hemmy must be turning over in his grave. I am the man who is responsible. With the two million dollars I put up on the table to spread around, it should have been more than enough to make sure that you would never see the inside of a jail. I never counted on this pontificating judge.

"I promise you, I'm going to destroy that rat-bastard. I will have you out of that place next door thirty days from today. I'm so sorry that I won't be able to do it one day sooner. I'm going to make Judge Moore wish he had never heard of the names Gallo-Cipo.

"I owe my life to your father. If he were still alive, this never would have happened."

"My father is exactly where he needs to be because he's got the best seat in the house. He will watch over me as his little girl stands up tall and gets through this rough patch. Please don't blame yourself for what happened to me. Maybe writing sports bets isn't the biggest crime in the world, but it is against the law and I knew that going in. I'm not the new kid on the block. I alone broke the law and even though I should have gotten P.T.I., big deal, so a bad break came my way. I don't blame you, Uncle Dom, or his sons, and most of all, I will never blame God. I know that I will come through this.

"Now, Uncle, I need you to focus on what you do best. The job at hand is to make sure I get released in thirty days and that my safety is guaranteed during my incarceration. I'll take care of the rest. Marvin, when you return to court next month, I'm sure that you will be signing the papers for my release. Uncle, please think of some way to make it right with my son when he calls tomorrow morning and the day after, etc." I walked over to Uncle, gave him a big hug and said, "I love you. It's time, gentlemen, they're waiting for me."

I was taken to the jail through a corridor in the basement. When I was brought in an officer fingerprinted me all over again to be sure they had the right inmate. Apparently, some prisoners were switched by family members and caused scandals for some of the jails in recent years. Then I was taken upstairs to the women's wing. I was escorted in by a female guard who carried a walkie-talkie. She brought me into what was called the day room. It was a large room which had a TV hanging on the wall. I noticed that all of the furniture was made of metal and bolted down to the floor with the exception of a sink and refrigerator. Later, one of the girls told me that the refrigerator only held pints of milk and small plastic bottles of orange juice in it. We were not allowed to help ourselves. It had a lock on it so we had to get permission from one of the guards. I did notice right away that the guards were addressed by their first names only, which surprised me. It was explained to me that was done for their own personal safety because they would be a lot harder to find without having a last name should a disgruntled former inmate ever go looking for them. A very long metal table with benches was bolted down in the middle of the room. Five young girls were seated at it. Maryanne, the guard, said, "Girls, I want you to meet our new addition, Kiki." Someone asked, "What are you in here for?"

"I was a bookie for the mob."

The inmate named Julie said, "No shit."

"Yeah shit. I'm going to take a seat. Why don't you ladies tell me who you are and why you're here."

Clearly, at thirty-five years old, I was much older than these kids. They looked to average out to be about twenty years old. I took command right away because I already knew the thing that mattered most in jail was the crime that put you there. The inmates never got to meet what they considered to be the crème de la crème, this is anyone who is "mobbed up." Nothing even comes close, so it takes down all the respect.

Julie spoke first, "Kiki, may I call you Kiki?"

"Of course, ladies, please do."

Julie continued, "No one ever calls us 'ladies,' we're just inmates."

"Well, ladies, guess what? That ends now. Just because we're in jail doesn't mean we have to give up our self-respect and dignity. As long as I'm here we're all going to be known as ladies. Now, please continue."

"I'm Sherry, I got nailed for shoplifting."

"You know I'm Julie and I'm here for kiting checks."

"I'm Amy, I got pinched for prostitution."

"I'm Eileen, they got me on drug possession."

Lastly, "I'm Gloria, I was driving my boyfriend's car. I didn't know he was going to stick up the gas station. Hell, I didn't know that he owned a gun. He told the cops that I wasn't involved because I didn't know what he was up to. That just might get my charge reduced."

"Well ladies, it's pretty obvious we're not here for high crimes, more like misdemeanors. We can get through this."

Julie spoke up and said, "Yeah Kiki, this is A Block, we're the good guys. The badasses are way down the other end in B Block. It's for sure none of those bitches committed any white-collar crimes over there. One of those low-lifes bounced her four-month-old daughter's head off every wall in her house and fractured her skull in 29 places. She was jealous of her baby because she believed that her husband loved the baby more. Can you believe that any mother could do that?"

"Kiki, wait, it gets better," said Eileen. "They've got a bitch over there called Casey. She is supposed to be the biggest badass. We hear she's not much taller than you, but none of us have ever seen any of the inmates over there. Neither side is supposed to cross over to the other without an invitation. It's an unwritten law in the Slam. We don't want to meet her anyway because we hear that she's crazy and dangerous. Rumor has it that she was busting her mother's chops for more money and when her mother refused, she hid behind the velvet drapes in the living room and waited for her mother to return home. Then she jumped out and stabbed her thirty-seven times with a butcher knife. Everyone is said to be deathly afraid of her. We hear that she takes whatever she wants. It's a fact that she picked out a bitch by the name of Carley to be hers alone. Get ready to hear some moaning and groaning tonight. When it gets real quiet after the night count, the noise travels loud and clear over to this side."

"Thanks ladies for the tip, but I assure you that Casey will not be a problem."

Within the hour, lunch was delivered. The women were not allowed to go upstairs to the cafeteria. Each one of us got a tray that was sent down. Mine had a beautiful long-stemmed red rose on it and a note form Uncle that read, "I'll see you at 8:00 pm." Needless to say, the ladies were impressed, but that didn't compare with their utter excitement when they realized we had gotten a large pot of perked coffee. They had never seen it in jail. Only instant coffee was served. All of the ladies turned toward me. I smiled at them and ever so sweetly said, "I don't drink instant coffee." To which Gloria said, "Kiki, who the hell are you?"

"I'm nobody except a good friend for the next thirty days if you wish."

Lois, who was a night guard, came into "the dorm" as it was called, at two minutes to eight and took me down to the visitor's room where Uncle was waiting for me. He came over to me and kissed me on top of my head as he hugged me ever so tightly. He looked as sad as he did on the day my father died. Clearly, he was crushed so I had a feeling that he was about to tell me something I wasn't expecting to hear.

"The first thing I want you to know is that the wheels went into motion while you were still in the courtroom. As soon as Dominick heard the bad news, Mr.'s X, Y, and Z, and others sprang into action. No stone will be left unturned. Your Uncle Dom added another $1,000,000 to our war chest.

"Everyone in the entire family is heartbroken because you are here. This was not supposed to ever happen. You have no idea how deeply this goes, but that's not important right now. I promise you that I alone will take care of Judge Moore. He belongs to me. I will get you out of here because I will be working on it 24/7. Since you are no longer in the business, neither am I. The word has already been put out there that my business is up for sale. I doubt that it will take very long to sell. And in the meantime, my very capable staff will take care of it for me. If they need my advice, they know where to reach me.

"The list I am about to give you is all you need during your incarceration. You will know how and when to use it because it contains everything you need to know about the bitches in B Block. All of the guards are already on board. They have been told to allow you to take the lead, but should a situation arise, don't hesitate to use them. I have made arrangements to visit you twice a day to check on you. I will have a rose, perked coffee, steak dinners, and many other extras sent to you, but the one thing I cannot do is unlock that front door for the next 29 days and my heart is heavy. I am tortured that this got by me and that you must be confined here temporarily."

"Uncle, please don't talk like that. How, and I say this with all due respect, did you make the moves to gather all of this information in little more than half a day?"

"Well, I took the advice of the smartest lady I ever met. I focused. With the war chest filled to the brim with money I can move many mountains. When you walk out of here for good, we are going to have a very special celebration. For now, please try to get a good night's sleep."

"I will memorize this list before I go to sleep tonight and I'll be just fine until I see you again tomorrow afternoon."

When I went back upstairs, all of the ladies were in the dorm. This room housed sixteen metal beds which hugged the walls and were all bolted down to the floor. Each bed had a metal foot locker, also bolted to the floor in front of the beds, military style. When I arrived, a lock and key for one of the trunks was issued to me. Like the day room, this one had a TV on the wall which went off, along with the lights, at exactly 11:00 p.m.

The girls pounced all over me with questions as soon as I walked in. like, "Who came to see you?"

"How could you have a visitor when it isn't Visitor's Day?"

"How come you're getting special privileges?"

"Ladies, take it easy. Let's all sit down and I'll tell you a very brief story. Once Upon a Time, there lived a little 'Princess' who had her very own Godfather and he could make many things happen with his particular brand of magic. End of story. Please excuse me, I've got some very important studying to do before the lights go out." The inmates were stunned and could only utter good night.

The toilets, showers, and dressing area, all made of metal, were behind the right wall of beds. The next morning, after I had showered and dressed, I was walking toward the day room when a feeling came over me that felt like a shadow of some kind. I don't know if that's what made me look up, but when I did, Sherry was hanging from a light fixture with her blanket tied around her neck. I started screaming for help as I tried to hold her weight up. Ideally, the move should have been to push her up from the waist, but I wasn't tall enough to reach it. Julie came running out with nothing but a towel wrapped around her. Maryanne and Gloria arrived at the same time. I was glad that Gloria moved so quickly because she was very tall. They untied her and took her down. She must have just done it. Maybe that was the shadow I saw as she dropped. Thank God she still had a pulse when the ambulance arrived.

Maryanne called all of us into the day room as she had something she wanted to explain to us because we had just witnessed a very disturbing sight, "Ladies, this is the title I will be addressing you by, I'm taking a page from Kiki's playbook because I think she's right. You should keep your dignity. I want all of you to know Sherry has made a suicide attempt once before. We were assured that she was perfectly stable when she arrived here this time. It turned out that Sherry had decided to try it again because she knew when she got released from the hospital, she would get an automatic thirty day stay in the psychiatric ward in the 'Cornerstone.' As strange as it sounds, some inmates believe that it's easy to escape from that place because they lack quality security. It doesn't make sense because, assuming that they survive the suicide attempt, sooner or later they are recaptured and brought back here."

It made me sad to think that she only had to do short time for shoplifting. Now, it was a given that if she came back here, more time would be tacked onto her sentence. She was only twenty years old. Maryanne promised to let us know if Sherry survived just as soon as she got the word.

When Uncle arrived for his afternoon visit, he already knew about the suicide attempt. He promised me that he was going to call my son the next morning and square up my absence to him. He decided to talk to him man to man and tell him the truth and make him swear that he would not tell his Nana.

Uncle returned at 8:00 p.m. to make sure that I was okay and to say good night. Before he left, I told him that the entire day was not a total bust. We did have steaks and baked potatoes for dinner. I thanked him from all the ladies.

I had learned a long time ago that when the hits stop coming, the punches start. We ladies had just finished cleaning up the day room after breakfast. I was placing the pitcher that now held two beautiful roses onto the middle of the table when six of the fourteen inmates from B Block appeared in our day room. They were led by the inmate that I recognized as Casey. I had been given mug shots of each inmate along with the crucial information I had on each one of their immediate family members that had been supplied and paid for by Uncle and then memorized by me.

Maryanne came out of the office and entered our day room. I said, "Please, let us have this room. I have to take care of this myself."

"Kiki, call out my name if you need me."

"Ladies, how can I help you since you broke protocol and etiquette by coming over here uninvited?"

Casey spoke right up and said, "We're not ladies, we are the bitches from B Block who get to take whatever we want."

"Oh really? In case you haven't noticed, you're in A Block where each one of us are 'Ladies.' Be that as it may, what is it that brought you over here?"

"I'm Casey, and I know that you are Kiki, the pretty little girly girl who worked for the mob. I want you to know that I get what I want because I have nothing to lose. I murdered my mother because she wouldn't give me what I wanted. I'm not afraid of anyone so I'm putting you on notice."

"Hey, shit for brains, don't expect me to quake in my boots. You must be the pride of that very expensive law firm of Broderick and Calley that your father hired to represent your dumbass. I do know that you are the spoiled brat daughter of a very high-ranking executive of a pharmaceutical company. I also know that Carley is your twat of choice in here. We all heard your moans last night. By the way, I'm going to ask you to tone it down because I don't want to lose any beauty sleep over you and your sweet thing. Is there anything else you want to say before I tell you to fuck off and go back to where you came from?"

"Just because you worked for the mob in the past, that doesn't buy you a free pass in here from me. I'm going to tell you straight out. I want your pussy and I'm going to make it my mission to get it. When you least expect it, I'll be right behind you. Your ladies, as you call them, can't protect you against my bitches."

"Casey, I've been used to men wanting my pussy for years, but that never applied to a woman. My family knew all about you so I've been prepared for your visit. I'm going to cut to the chase because I'll be sending you back to B Block real fast. I'm going to tell all of you bitches a story.

"A little girl lived in a world of nothing but men. She was loved, revered, and protected by each and every member of the largest and most powerful mob family in New Jersey. She made a ton of money for them. The same way they protected her on the outside is the same way they are protecting her in this jail. I'm afraid I'm going to have to burst your bubble. You will not be able to come anywhere near my pussy because it's reserved for hard bats and soft balls. That means my pussy can only be touched by men and that will be strictly enforced by the family. Let me tell you how this is going to play out.

"First of all, I know who each and every one of you B Block bitches are. More than that, I know where each one of you lives, which people you love, family or otherwise, what kinds of cars they drive and their license plate numbers. In other words, I know when, where, and how they eat, sleep, and shit. I'll prove it.

"Carley, your loved ones live at 232 Cator Road, Pauletta, how about 150 Monticello Street. Earnestine, you've got some people at 213 Fowler Place. Emily, your sweetheart resides at 6 Hunter Court. Jada, your little girl, mother, and father, live at 64 Vista Place. And last but not least, you Casey murdered your mother at 20 Fletcher Avenue. I could go on with this same information that I possess on the rest of the B Block lowlifes, but I think you've gotten the picture. Each one of these homes is already under 24/7 surveillance and will stay that way for the next 27 days and a wake-up that I will have to reside here.

"Casey, you have only one true love in your miserable life and that is your younger brother who has adored his older sister unconditionally. Don't turn away from me when I'm talking to you. I'll continue. His name is Jeffrey and he will probably be the only person to stand by you as you spend the rest of your life in the Big House. Your father will finally turn his back on you. After all, you did murder his wife. I can't say that I blame him. I also know that your brother puts the money in your account. As of today, you have 347 dollars sitting there.

"I'm going to wrap it up now. You have no idea how far my arms can reach. See those two roses on the table? When I walk out of here on February 9th, I will have gotten thirty of them. Every morning I will find one on my breakfast tray. Ladies, please tell Casey what we had for dinner last night."

Julie spoke up and said, "We had steaks and baked potatoes. It was awesome."

"So Casey, you dumb broad, do you see where I'm going with this? I get a very important visitor every afternoon and every evening to make sure that I'm A-Okay. By the way, that money in your account can disappear with the stroke of a pen. Finally, I'm turning the tables on all of you B Block bitches. Don't any of you ever come back over to our side again.

"Look me in the eyes so that you know I'm telling the whole truth. You have insulted me and the rest of the A Block ladies by coming over here uninvited and then by presenting yourself in such an obnoxious way. You're done. It makes no difference to me how many times you stabbed your mother. That deed will pale by comparison to what's in store for Jeffrey. You see, I want something from you and if I don't get it, your brother is going to have a close encounter with a chainsaw while he's still breathing. Then a certain butcher will go down the line with the rest of the B Block bitches and do what has to be done to their loved ones."

Carley became hysterical and started begging Casey, "Don't let her hurt my family, don't let that happen," she screamed. Casey took a deep breath and said, "Kiki, what do you want from me?"

"When you came over here with all of your bluster, you unnerved these ladies. I want you to buy each one of them a carton of cigarettes every week while I'm here."

"What about you Kiki, what kind of cigarettes do you want?"

"Casey, haven't you heard that smoking is bad for your health? I don't smoke anymore."

"Then what do you want?"

"I want a heartfelt genuine apology first. And then, because I am Kiki, I want respect!"

"I humbly apologize to you for my crude behavior and bad mouth. You are obviously unattainable and untouchable. It will not happen again by me or any of the others in B Block. I'll make sure of it. Please forgive me."

"Your apology is accepted, now you can get the fuck out of my face, but know this. One day you will dance with the devil."

Like everything else that ever happened in my life, once it's over, that's it. My life goes forward and I move on. Each day went along smoothly for the next week until one morning right after breakfast Maryanne informed me that two FBI Agents were waiting for me in the visitor's room. As she escorted me to the elevator she said, "Good luck Kiki, the feds seldom ever come here."

"Maryanne, I've been questioned by the feds before. They don't scare me and I'll never give them what they want, but I'm sure going to have a little fun with them since they made the trip here."

"Good morning Miss. Cipo, we are agents Morgan and Visconti. We would like to have a word with you."

"Please call me Kiki, but I will most respectfully refer to you as Agents. How can I help you?"

Agent Morgan spoke first. "Actually, we are here to do something for you. Sometime around 1970, a new law was put in place for the FBI's use. We did not intend to occupy the field of illegal gambling exclusively nor were we to relieve any local enforcement bodies out there of their obligations. We could only get involved in gambling operations of major proportions. The FBI is authorized to intersect wire or oral communications solely on violations involving Organized Crime. Our laboratories are made available to analyze any physical evidence seized and we can be used to support expert testimony at the time of trial."

Then Agent Visconti took over. "We have gone over your 'Jacket' thoroughly and concluded that you don't belong here. We know that you qualified for PTI. If not for an overly aggressive judge, who wanted to make an example out of you, we wouldn't be speaking to you in this jail. We're not even here about gambling. That's the farthest thing on our minds.

"We are here to revisit your past. Your jacket contains information that you divorced Robert Fontana Jr. back in 1969. We want to go back before that and if you cooperate with us, my agency can guarantee that you will walk out of here within a few hours."

I guess it was Agent Morgan's turn to speak, "Kiki, it's obvious to us that you don't have any allegiance to the Fontanas. We want you to tell us what really happened in the disappearance of a man known as 'Brownie.' The FBI has always contended that you covered up for both Senior and Junior that night. As you probably already know, there is no statute of limitations on murder. You would be granted immunity from perjury or prosecution in any court proceedings. That's a bona fide deal and it's on the table."

"Agents Morgan and Visconti, please understand that I never once wavered in what I told the detectives who visited me or the FBI when they came knocking on my door so many years ago. I assure you that my testimony remains the same today. I have nothing more to add to it."

"Kiki, you don't back down, do you? Not even while you sit in jail. Well let's try another tact. We know that you've been around 'Wiseguys' your entire life and we think that you know a lot about certain people. So how about giving us the names of some men who participate in any kind of criminal activity.

That's all it would take to spring you right now. Give us a couple of names and go free."

"Agents, let me get this straight. If I give you the names of let's say, two real criminals, then you guys will get me out of here right away. Do I have your word on that?"

"Absolutely, who do you have for us?"

Without skipping a beat and with a wink of my eye and a smile, I said, "Here's two bad guys for you, Spiro T. Agnew and Richard M. Nixon." I stood up and walked toward the glass window which was right next to the door and tapped on it for the guard to send me back upstairs. As far as I was concerned, this meeting was over so I said to the agents, "You know, I may not stand too tall in stature, but until I take my last breath, I will always 'stand up.' I'm sorry you made a trip here for nothing. Have a nice day, gentlemen."

Then I turned around and never looked back.

Chapter 22

The night before I was scheduled to appear in Judge Moore's courtroom for the reconsideration hearing of my sentencing, Uncle was waiting for me with a dozen peach roses which were beautifully arranged in a vase.

"Sweetheart, I want you to get a good night's sleep because I have everything that I need to make sure you walk out of here tomorrow at exactly 12:00 p.m. Pack up your personal belongings before tonight's lights out. I'll be waiting in the courtroom when you are brought in at 9:45 a.m. I know you were let down by Judge Moore's ruling 29 days ago, but I promise you, it's going to be a whole new ball game tomorrow. Now, I want a big hug before I leave this building for the very last time. By the way, I'm taking the roses with me back to your place because we're going there straight from here at noontime tomorrow."

The next morning unbeknownst to me, Uncle was waiting in his limo two blocks away from the courthouse for a phone call. It came in from a security guard at exactly 8:00 a.m. Uncle had his limo brought around and then he walked right into the building. He flashed his courtesy pass, given to him by his friend, Superior Court Judge Mitch Halpern. When he arrived outside of Judge Moore's courtroom, the security guard greeted him with a warm handshake which just happened to contain an unregistered 32 caliber pistol that he somehow smuggled in.

The Judge's secretary wasn't there yet so Uncle marched in and found him sitting behind his desk in his chambers. He looked up in shock, stood up and said, "Who the hell are you and how did you get in here? I'm going to call security right now."

Uncle brandished the gun and said, "Don't bother. He went on his coffee break. Sit the fuck down and put a lid on it, scumbag. If you open your mouth to speak again, I'm going to put this 32-automatic into it and send your brains to the Promised Land. Some years ago, I heard someone say a line something like that, and I liked it so much I decided to use it on you today.

"You don't remember me. I was in your courtroom right outside that door when you sentenced a beautiful little girl, my little girl, who qualified for PTI to six months in jail. You said you didn't want organized crime to move into your county. So you intended to make an example out of her. I was the man who yelled out to you that organized crime had been in your county since before you were born. You better look me right in the eyes when I'm talking to you, you piece of shit. If you don't, I'll be more than happy to put a bullet right between them.

"The very same mob family that you referred to is the very same one that you stirred up a shitstorm with. You stepped on all the wrong toes. Today, you will have to pay the piper and right the wrong that you did one month ago. I am here on a courtesy pass, given to me from your boss Superior Court Judge Halpern. He just happens to be a personal friend of mine. He never spoke to you about my little princess coming before you because he assumed that as much as you are called 'jail for sure Moore,' it would never apply to Kiki. She is a sweet young mother with a spotless record so you crossed a line with your boss as well. But I'll get back to him in a few minutes.

"You pretended to sentence her because of her affiliation with a certain family, but I'm convinced you doled out prison time for an entirely different reason. You sent her to jail because she is a female, plain and simple.

"You're a pontificating prick. Before I show you these photos, I want you to know that Mitch Halpern has seen every single one of them. Now, you rotten son of a bitch, take your eyes off of me and this pistol and take a good look at these pictures," as he threw them across the desk and hit him in the face with them and said, "Eat these, scumbag."

"There you are, Judge Moore. A degenerate mother-fucker who shows up every Friday night at The Adam and Eve Gentlemen's Club in Union City. Don't you ever eat dinner before you arrive there? You seem so hungry every week because all you ever do is eat pussy all night long. That certainly is your preference. I especially love these pictures of you looking right into the camera. Do you think this is righteous behavior of a man who passes judgement over other people's lives in his courtroom five days a week?"

"How did you get these photos?"

"Well, you lowlife fuck, the very people that you said you wanted to keep out of your county just happen to be the same people who own the Adam and Eve Gentlemen's Club."

"Eating pussy is not against the law."

"Whoa, tough guy judge. You are supposed to be a pillar of the community, besides the fact that you are a married man with children, so let me tell you that while eating pussy may not be against the law, eating the pussy of a fifteen-year-old is."

"What the hell are you talking about? Every employee there is supposed to be eighteen years or older."

"Well, guess what? On the night that these pictures were taken, a certain eighteen-year-old said she was ill so her fifteen-year-old look-a-like sister substituted for her. You know that the club is fairly dark, ergo no one noticed the switch. Your boss is in possession of a sworn affidavit from the fifteen-year-old that she was the one photographed with you, not her sister, and she is willing to testify in court if you are indicted."

"You bastard, you set me up!"

"For a dishonorable judge, you are very astute. When you sentenced Kiki Cipo to six months in jail, just to make a point, you broke the mighty hearts of men that should never be toyed with. Kiki is coming before you today in about one hour for a reconsideration of her sentence hearing.

"I'm going to be waiting in my limo right outside of the jail. If she doesn't walk out of that door at exactly 12:00 p.m., I promise you that at 12:01 p.m. copies of these photos will be delivered to the Jersey Journal, the Newark Star Ledger, the Atlantic City Press, the New York Times, the National Enquirer, and last but not least, to your wife wherever she happens to be at the time since your house is being watched as we speak. We mean business. By the way, one more thing, your boss, Judge Halpern, wants your letter of resignation on his desk no later than 4:15 p.m. today. If he doesn't have it, he told me to tell you that he is personally going to see to it that you are prosecuted to the fullest extent of the law. Lastly, your Dishonor, the very second the Turnkey locked the door behind Kiki Cipo, you sealed your own fate."

Then Uncle slammed his fist down on Judge Moore's desk and said, "Remember, 12:00 p.m., not one second later." He turned his back on him and stormed out.

At exactly 10:00 a.m., the proceedings got underway in Judge Moore's courtroom. They lasted all of about fifteen minutes. Basically, he said that he felt I had probably learned my lesson by serving thirty days and since I did qualify for PTI in the first place, he had no problem with granting my reconsideration of sentence petition. Then he said, "Miss. Cipo, your petition is hereby granted, you are free to go home, this case is dismissed," as he slammed his gavel down. He just about ran out of the courtroom and disappeared into his chambers. After all, he did have to get started writing his letter of resignation.

The jubilation had already spread throughout the courtroom. Uncle gave me a big hug, shook Marvin's hand, and then walked over to a man I had never seen before and shook his hand vigorously. I heard him say, "Thank you for showing up Judge Halpern, I'll be in touch real soon." Nothing was being left to chance this time around, but I didn't know why.

Uncle gave me a kiss on the forehead as he said, "I know you want to say goodbye to the ladies, I'll see you at 12:00 p.m."

By the time I arrived back at the jail, Maryanne had already received the phone call informing her of the Judge's decision. I was swarmed by the four remaining ladies. Fortunately, Sherry had survived the suicide attempt but was still completing the mandatory 30-day evaluation in the psychiatric ward at the Cornerstone. At least she didn't try to escape, therefore she wouldn't be facing additional charges or time.

When I told the ladies the good news, it was bittersweet. On the one hand, they were so happy for me that I got hugs all around. Then, on the other hand, each one had tears in their eyes. It seemed that I had become a sort of big sister figure for them and they didn't want to see me leave. Before I could think about why they felt that way, Gloria spoke up first and said, "Kiki, we're so sorry to see you go and it's not because of all the perks we have received while you've been here, although we have enjoyed them. It's because you referred to all of us as ladies. We think of you as a leader and a very smart lady. How can we keep in touch after you leave us today?"

Then the others chimed in and said, "That's right, Kiki, we want to always remain your friends because from the very beginning you were always a 'teacher,' never a 'preacher.' You made us all believe that we could keep our dignity even in jail."

"Thank you, ladies, let's all gather around the table one last time. I've given a lot of thought about what I'm going to do with the rest of my life, which will be starting in less than an hour. I can tell you positively that I will never break the law again. I will concentrate on becoming a very successful business woman. While I haven't finalized my plans yet, I do know I'm going in that direction.

"With that said, I have a proposition for all five of you."

They looked at me a little strangely.

"That's correct, I said five. Gloria, I'd like to put you in charge of conveying this offer to Sherry when she returns in a day or two. I'd like to think that each one of you can put this part of your life behind you and spin your lives around. None of you have to go back to what you were doing that brought you here, so I have an offer. It will require that all of you go back to school. If you have to work during the day, get a legitimate job and go to school at night. Find any agency out there that will assist you with student loans or any other kind of help for former inmates. These agencies do exist. I will need all of you to study only one thing, 'Business.' Learn as much as you can about management and administration and get certifications because I will have them verified. Only then will I hire you to come and work for my company. Don't look so shocked. Since I won't be staying in New Jersey, I'll expect all of you to relocate to another state. You all have my word and that should be good enough.

"I'll only insist on two things from you. First, that I have your loyalty at all times. You don't ever steal from me and that you always have my back. In other words, integrity above all else. Secondly, that you bring your A game to work every single day. If you're not feeling well, stay home. I worked three hundred and sixty-five days a year for almost thirteen years and I never once brought anything less than my A game to work with me.

"If you ladies will accept these terms, when the time is right, I will find you. I'm not offering you a job; I'm offering you a career. Sometimes, all you need in life to make all the difference is to take a leap of faith. I'm asking you ladies to take a leap of faith with me. Think about my offer and as always, 'I wish you all that Heaven allows.'

"Now ladies, I have just enough time to pack up the rest of my clothes. I'm leaving everything else here for all of you including the money that's in my account. Maryanne will see that it's divided equally and placed into your accounts. Please, don't walk me to the elevator, you see, you're not the only ones carrying a heavy heart at this time."

When we got into the elevator, Maryanne gave me a hug as she said, "Kiki, it was our pleasure to look after you although it didn't take much effort. You did a pretty good job of looking after yourself, you know that don't you?"

"Maryanne, you just reminded me of something. I did stand tall the entire time that I was incarcerated. My father would have been proud, of that I am sure."

"Please thank Milt from the entire staff for overstuffing all of our stockings a few weeks ago at Christmas. He was more than generous. Take care of yourself, and have a wonderful life."

"Please thank the entire staff for me." When the elevator door opened up, Warden Callahan was waiting there to greet me. I had seen him briefly when I was brought in to begin my sentence, but I didn't know him.

He proceeded to take my hand in both of his and said, "Miss. Cipo, I am Warden Callahan and I'm here to escort you out. Please tell Milt that I handled it myself."

"Warden, I won't have to. Uncle assured me that he will be waiting outside this door so he will see it for himself."

"Let's go, we're right on time, Kiki. It's exactly 12:00 p.m."

As the door swung open, Uncle was leaning on his limo looking so elegant, wearing his signature Fedora. He had his hands folded in front of him until he saw me. Then he stood up straight and broke out with a huge smile as the warden said, "Milt, here's your little girl. She's safe and sound." Uncle didn't say a word as he walked toward me, but he did something I had never seen him do before. He saluted him and the warden just nodded in acknowledgment as he went back inside. Uncle lifted me up off the ground. He was having a difficult time containing his joy as he said, "It's over Kiki, let's go home."

When the door to my apartment was opened, I was greeted by Uncle Dom, Gabriel, Salvatore, Uncle Frankie, and Evelyn. One of them had put up a "Welcome Home" banner. Uncle made sure I had thirty dozen roses in an assortment of colors scattered throughout my place. One for each day I was incarcerated. The pink champagne was flowing. There was way too much food laid out on the dining room table, which had been donated by Nardi's Restaurant.

Uncle had wanted to have my family present for my homecoming, but I asked him not to. Since my son already knew about my jail time, he would be calling me as soon as school let out. I wanted to tell Aunt Esther and my mother privately after I returned to Florida. I didn't want them to attend a welcome home party for me when they never knew I had gone away in the first place. Uncle Dom came over to me first, hugged me, and then asked everyone to raise a glass to me.

"Welcome home Kiki, we're so glad to have you back safely." Then I got hugs and kisses from everyone else in the room. "Let's all have a bite to eat sweetheart. Nardi's chefs made an assortment of some of your favorite dishes, I'm sure you're done with the lack of quality Italian food in the jail for the past month. When you are finished, I'd like to talk privately with you in the den, only Milt will sit in with us.

"Now that everyone is gone, I'd like to get started. I don't want to talk about what went wrong now that it's in the past. I do want to tell you about what you have accomplished for the Gallo family. Before I go there, I want you to know just how much your father meant to me.

"Both Milt and I have been in this business for over fifty years and we can say without any hesitation you booked more games that resulted in some of the biggest sport upsets ever recorded. Your Uncle Milt swears it had something to do with a 'magic wand' that the doctor said you were born with. All I can tell you is that you made a tremendous amount of money for the Gallo family. It's uncanny how so many games went our way on your shift. Honey, it goes much deeper than that.

"You went straight to the very top in the world of bookmaking while everyone knows it is run by nothing but men. After I consulted with so many of the top guns in the business, I can now tell you that you have been bestowed with the title 'The Legend.' That's right Kiki, in the world of bookmaking, you are the Legend. You did the unthinkable in a man's world. No woman will ever take your place.

"I'm not finished yet. Over the years, you met or spoke to quite a few heavy D's along the way. You were aware of who some of them were, but not all of them. I have spoken to over a dozen 'Capos' who unanimously said that you are the most 'stand-up lady' in the state of New Jersey. I know you've heard it before. You never gave anyone up in spite of the many times you were questioned by all of the various law enforcement agencies. On top of that, you conducted yourself impeccably every day. I want you to carry that moniker for the rest of your life and use it because you earned it. Besides, if people try to dispute it, they will have to go up against one dozen 'Dons' and that would not be a healthy choice for them.

"I know Milt is chomping at the bit to get started on telling you the entire story that he promised. I have one more piece of family business to take care of and it will become much more valuable than the gift from the Gallo's that Milt will give to you when he is finished.

"Kiki, you started out studying to become an English major. If you didn't have to fulfill your destiny, you would have succeeded. The family wants you to tell your story one day. You can't do it now and not for at least twenty-five years. Think back over your life to the many times Milt told you to memorize all of the details because you could never write anything down. Now, you will find out why he kept telling you that. You were the dutiful daughter and did what was asked of you while abandoning your own dreams. So I'm about to give you a present and Milt must be my witness.

"Please come over here and stand in front of me. Now get this. As I make the sign of the Cross, I'm giving you my blessing to write the book. Without a blessing, the book can never be written. The entire family wants you to do it when the time is right. You are the only woman on this planet that ever went where no other woman has gone before. Only you can tell this story.

"Wherever you decide to go and whatever you decide to do for the next twenty-five years, remember that the Gallo's will always be here for you. When I'm gone Gabriel and Salvatore will take my place. After my boys, their sons will take over. The Gallo family will go on and the name 'Kiki' will always be 'special.' Milt is about to tell you why. Now, give your Uncle Dom a big hug and kiss as I must leave because I have business to take care of. I love you very much Kiki Gallo-Cipo."

"Uncle Dom, I always felt that there was a special bond between my father and you. There always seemed to be an equal amount of respect given to each other from such an important man and a humble bartender. That says a lot about your character." Both Uncles shot each other an unusual look, which surprised me. It looked like an alarm had gone off, but I continued on, "Your sons have always been wonderful to me and my son. I know what it takes to be a 'Gallo.' Whatever I decide to do with the next chapter of my life, I promise to do the family proud. I will always bring my A game to work every day as I am determined to become very successful. If I ever need advice this lady knows where to go for it. I will always be led back to the best and that is to my beloved 'Uncles.' Now, I'm going to say it. I will give you my word as the most stand-up lady in New Jersey that when the time is right, I will tell the story the way it should be, so help me God. I love you very much Uncle Dom, and thank you for everything you've done for me."

Uncle Milt walked Dom to the door. They hugged each other and Dom whispered something into Uncle Milt's ear and then he just nodded his head.

"Kiki, I'll call Yolanda and tell her to come down here to tidy up because I've got a story to tell."

Just as Uncle and I were about to sit down, the phone rang. "Mother, welcome home. I can't wait to see you."

"Thank you R.F. It's good to be home. Uncle and I have some business to take care of so I'll be busy for a few days, but I promise to come down there as soon as possible. Son, I'll talk to you in the morning."

"Dom and I will be long gone when you write your novel. I'm positive that you are going to be asked these same five questions for the rest of your life once you are published. I'm going to ask you all five right now because I want to hear the answers while I'm still alive, so here it goes:

"1. What really happened to Brownie?"

"Brownie who?"

"2. If you could have been allowed to have one favorite professional athlete, who would it have been and why?"

"Uncle, while I was sitting in jail with nothing but time on my hands, I thought about that same question often. There were so many phenomenal athletes in all of the professional sports that I booked for all those years. Most of them are legends today, will be tomorrow, and probably forever. In the end and after much consideration, I had to go with the one man that I believe had the most God-given natural ability, the one and the only Broadway Joe Namath a.k.a., the Gunslinger. I understand that he was a very good basketball player, could have been a professional baseball player, and was the only player that the 'Legendary Coach Bear Bryant' said was 'the best player he has ever seen.' My guess is that he is probably a good pool shooter and a better than average golfer as well. Years ago, I knew someone and saw firsthand what a 'phenom' looked like and Broadway was so much better. I will stand by my humble and unbiased opinion forever."

"3. As you are the most undisputed stand-up lady in the state of New Jersey, who would you say is the most stand-up man? You must have thought about that from time to time."

"I have thought about it many times, Uncle. I have met many people from Newark over the years. Every one that I have ever spoken to concurs that Newark's very own son, Frankie Valli did pay off all of Tommy DeVito's debt. I could never find one person to contradict that story. The bottom line is that he assumed the debt, and 'stood up' by paying every penny back. It is my belief that he earned the title and I'll always stand by it."

"4. Knowing now that going to jail would become the ultimate price you would have to pay, would you do it all over again?"

"Uncle, absolutely in a New Jersey minute."

"5. Lastly, could you have given the order to Mr. Z to come out of the office, proceed to carve up Marco Polo, piece by piece while he was still alive, right in front of your eyes?"

"I would have to insist that the person asking the question must be the same one who answers it because I never will. People must think what they want. You raised me right alongside of my father so I suspect that you alone are the one person who knows the answer."

"Kiki, of course I do and I will take it to the grave with me just as I know that's exactly what you are going to do.

Chapter 23

"Come on, I'm about to fulfill a promise I made to Hemmy a long time ago. I can't be certain where to begin so I think I'll go back to your great grandfather, Gabriel Gallo or, as he was always called G.G. He was already the Godfather of the largest and most powerful mob family in all of northern New Jersey, and ultimately the entire state, before Prohibition. You know that your father had a speakeasy during that time. He had a lot of connections because his mother was the Godfather's daughter, and her younger brother, Dominick, was the Godfather's son.

"I'm going to fast forward to 1941 when your father and Uncle Frankie joined the army together right after the attack on Pearl Harbor. After they completed their basic training, they were separated. Soon after, your father met a man who was twelve years younger than him. His name was Leonardo Patane and he was from Brooklyn. Hemmy saw something in him that he hadn't seen since he met Frankie Daily on the day he walked into his speakeasy looking for a job.

"Your father was made platoon leader very quickly. He always had leadership qualities. All of the men respected him. Leo was no different. He grew to love Hemmy like a big brother. Your father wrote to me weekly before he went into combat. He told me that when the two of them returned from overseas, he was going to bring Leo and his family to New Jersey because he wanted to keep him close by. I'll never forget the letter your father wrote to me which said that Leo had asked him to be his son's godfather when they returned home. When Leo joined the army, he didn't know that his wife was pregnant. He had never met his son and had only seen him in the pictures that his wife sent to him. Obviously, the Baptism had been put off for the remainder of his service.

"By 1943, the war was raging on. Hemmy told me this story in graphic detail when he returned. His platoon had orders to advance to a certain point and then take out a bridge. As they pushed forward though a wooded area, they were stopped by the constant barrage coming from a machine gun turret besides the presence of a large number of German soldiers. Some of his platoon were picked off and the others were basically pinned down so Hemmy decided to pass the word to the others that he wanted to try something. He asked his Lieutenant if he could get as much cover as possible while he zig-zagged through the woods to get close enough so he could lob enough grenades to take the turret out. Your father still had a good amount of speed in his legs as much as he still had fast hands so his Lieutenant Okayed the plan. But Leo didn't like the idea that Hemmy would be taking all of the risk himself. When he yelled 'I'm ready,' Leo ran out with him. About half way to the turret Leo stepped out blasting away which bought your father the precious seconds he needed to hit the ground so he could crawl to get within striking distance of the target. Unfortunately for Leo, he took a bullet in the head and died instantly.

"When Hemmy got close enough he lobbed two grenades at the machine gun and blew it to smithereens. With the turret taken out, the platoon started running forward and caught up with Hemmy. He wanted to know where Leo was and one of the men told him that his friend had taken a bullet to the head. He became so enraged that he just started running. Somewhere along the way he surprised three German soldiers and put a bullet right into the first one's head. Before the other two could react, he slit their throats with his M3 fighting knife which had a blade that was a double edge stiletto. His platoon lost a total of sixteen men while taking out at least seventy-five Germans and the bridge.

"Later that night, the lieutenant told your father that he was going to put in a recommendation that he be awarded the CMH (Congressional Medal of Honor). Your father turned him down flat by telling him he would never accept it. You know how much your father hated the limelight and he had a very good reason for being that way. I'll talk about that later. Hemmy believed to himself that Leo had taken a bullet for him intentionally as it was his duty to do so. Your father wanted Leo's widow to be the recipient of the medal posthumously. The lieutenant didn't have a clue and therefore didn't see it that way, so the entire C.M.H conversation ended right there.

"Soon after your father returned home, I relocated Leo's widow and son from Brooklyn to an apartment that I found for them in Bayonne."

"Uncle, excuse me, I'd like to interrupt for a moment. How come I never met her or her son? My father never mentioned her name. I don't understand that."

"Sweetheart, I'll answer that later. You once asked your father why he encouraged you to marry Bobby J. Now, I will answer for him. It seemed that G.G. and the Godfather of another family made a pact that one day a suitable marriage would be made between the two families and your father honored it. Long before you were introduced to Bobby J, I started putting a file together on the entire Fontana family. You saw a small portion of that file on the day you confronted your soon to be ex in my office.

"I'm going to skip around a little bit because I think my story must be told in a certain way. There hadn't been a mafia war for almost thirty years but I can tell you that on the day you were held hostage in Newark, the Godfather was so enraged that he was ready to go to all-out war. He was a lethal man, but he was also a fair man. He felt that the two men who held you and Mario hostage had crossed a line by insulting the Gallo family. It didn't matter to him that they didn't know that you were a Gallo-Cipo, they only knew you as Kiki Fontana. He wanted me to put all of the family on notice. 'We're going to war,' he roared. I seized the opportunity to calm him down by telling him that I didn't think the timing was right. I will tell you why my feelings ran so deeply against an all-out war at the end of my story. I satisfied his thirst for revenge by coming up with a bright idea for you to use in the future. Then we calmly sat down together and mapped out the plan that you eventually very successfully carried out.

"Do you remember saying to Mario, 'Someone had better answer for this one day.' You said a mouthful that day without even knowing it. I'm going to take you back to the first two weekends you started working for me. I gave you a long list of college basketball games to bet for me with The Sandman and The Skull. You made a very unusual statement that first evening and my heart skipped a beat when you said, 'Uncle, one of those voices sounds familiar to me but I just can't place it.'

"Well, you hit the nail on the head. We didn't want you to know then what I'm about to reveal to you right now.

"The restaurant that you and Mario were held hostage in was a front for a large bookmaking operation and it was owned by The Sandman and The Skull.

"By the second weekend that you were on the job when I won 21 out of 22 games, on top of the beating they took the previous weekend, they didn't have the money to pay me so they were given the ultimatum that they could give me their homes or they would disappear for good. When my real estate company took possession of their two homes, they were immediately and very unceremoniously thrown out on the street so to speak. They were forced to move in with relatives. On top of that, they lost their bookmaking business because they couldn't pay their bettors anymore and subsequently, they had to close their restaurant. Their lives were completely ruined. You busted them out. Mission accomplished and the reason that the mafia war was averted had finally been avenged.

"Kiki, I want you to know about something I did on purpose those first two Saturdays when you gave my bets to those bastards in Newark. It was the only time I ever gave out a tainted line and it was only given out to those two low-life hostage takers. I moved the line up or down on the games I had selected for you to get me down on. No other games were involved. The truth be told when all the scores were in, I didn't need the help. Each game was won by a lot more than the one-point change that I made. You see, I made a promise to a certain someone that you would be the one to carry the creeps out. That's why I wanted to make sure that an edge was put in place for you. You know I toned the language down for you, but I assure you that the Don and I used completely different adjectives to describe those two dirt bags."

"Excuse me, I never heard you refer to Uncle Dom as anything other than the Godfather. Never 'the man at the top' or 'the Don.' What's going on?"

"As I continue, I must use those references for this part of the story so please bear with me. Your father knew so many people and made an enormous number of contacts over the many years he was in business including the Prohibition years. But it is still going to come as a shock to you as I now tell you that it was Hemmy who sent Evelyn into the Fontana and Sons store looking for a job the year before you were introduced to Bobby J. Some of Big D's customers knew your father as well. He learned everything he could about Big D from them, including the fact that he always had women on the side and that he liked them full figured like Marilyn Monroe. Evelyn was a close brunette version of her. As soon as she walked into the store, Big D was a goner. He hired her on the spot. The 'shill' or another word for it, 'the plant' was put in place on that day.

"Remember the night Big D was stabbed right before you walked into the store to deliver his dinner? Evelyn was crying as she rushed out past you. She begged you not to go in there and get yourself involved. Later that evening you asked me how I always seemed to know everything that went on in that store so quickly. Now I can tell you. Evelyn called your father and told him every single word that was ever said in there as well as everything that went on inside that building. She was on your father's payroll long before she ever became the shill. She purposely learned to care for Big D and allowed herself to become his mistress. After all, he was a charming, good-looking man, but her loyalty always belonged to Hemmy first. She loved him like a big brother because Evelyn was the lady we brought over from Brooklyn with her little boy when your father returned from the war.

"You see, Kiki, Evelyn is Leonardo Patane's widow. Your father asked her to go back to using her maiden name, St. John. He had his reasons. Put two and two together right now and you will understand why she was allowed to view your father's body right behind the family. You asked me who she was and why she took Hemmy's death so badly. Everyone knew her as Big D's girlfriend only. And now you have it. Your father trusted her as much as he had trusted her husband Leonardo. He took care of her and her son for all those years. Of course, her son is a grown man now, but the Gallo family still keeps her on the payroll."

"Hold up a minute Uncle, why would the family do that. It doesn't make sense?"

"It will very shortly sweetheart. Your father couldn't have asked for a better shill to keep an eye on the Fontana men and once she became Big D's squeeze, nobody could have done it more effectively. Another piece of the puzzle has just been added. What are you thinking?"

"I had no idea who she was. That's why I asked you 'what's up with her?' because she took my father's death so hard. Now, it makes perfect sense and it explains something Evelyn said to me after my father was buried. She said, 'I love you like a daughter.' It's beginning to fit together."

"I told you that nothing was left to chance when it came to you. It was Evelyn who deliberately left the front door unlocked when she arrived at the store on Valentine's Day. Her son is the one who got the word to the young thief Leroy that the door would be left open so he would steal the coats. It was a set-up from start to finish which ended with his death in the cell. I will tell you that it was not a suicide. I'll say no more. That chapter of my story is closed forever.

"I'm going to move on to October the 20th, 1973. It was the first time I ever told you to go 'bet the farm.' Even though you were asked to do it several more times after that, this one remains my all-time favorite. I asked you to take the Chicago Bulls over the New York Knicks even though they were playing in the Garden. Do you remember telling me the next day that it was as if the New York Knicks didn't bother to show up for the game as they went down in flames? I said to you 'you're close, but no cigar,' and promised to tell you one day just how that happened. And now, you shall have it. You know I paid for information wherever I could find it.

"My secretary took a call from a concierge of a well-known hotel which was located near my office. It appeared that a certain acclaimed and extremely talented professional basketball player had checked into the hotel. After he settled in, he called the concierge and asked him to send up a fine bottle of Cognac because he said he had a very bad cold and wanted to sweat it out.

"I seized the opportunity immediately and made a phone call. Because the man felt so poorly, I thought it was my civic duty to help him out. It behooved me to send in three nurses to look after him. A good friend's agency furnished a blonde, a brunette, and a redhead. He described them as 'bombshells.' I paid fifteen hundred dollars apiece for them. It was well worth it as you know. The next day, my friend told me that the patient proceeded to take their temperatures with his thermometer all night long. We heard that he neglected to call his team manager and tell him that he was too ill to show up for the game. I'm sure he got handed a heavy fine, but it's a good bet he didn't give a damn and now you know how all of that got put into motion.

"Yolanda, please bring us some snacks and open up a bottle of Dom."

"I'm going in a completely different direction with this part of the story. I purchased a warehouse for the Godfather in 1950. He told the parents of three young boys that one day he would come for them. About five years later, the boys spent every Saturday at the warehouse. A Karate Master was waiting there to instruct them. The boys were about seven, eight, and twelve years old at the time. Within two years, the now fourteen-year-old was so good at the martial arts, the Godfather decided it was time to bring in a man who honed his craft as a butcher from New York City. He brought in a cow's carcass which was already hanging in place from hooks every Sunday afternoon when the young man arrived to begin his lesson. He was taught how to carve up an entire cow, limb by limb, piece by piece. In less than a year, he could do it with his eyes closed.

"You are very astute. I can tell by the look on your face that you are beginning to connect the dots once again. You know I'm talking about Mr.'s X, Y, and Z. You've met X and Y, but you didn't get to meet Mr. Z because you never had to call him out of the office in the Butcher Shop that fateful night. I didn't want to revisit the most horrific night of your life, but I had no choice because it's important to the story.

"I named one of my real estate businesses after the three young men because they really are successful, licensed real estate agents. The Godfather sent them to school just like he had them taught their other skills. I have more to say about them. They are also the painters in the warehouse. They take turns painting a five-foot square area so that the smell of that industrial strength paint permeates the building at all times. You've been in there so you know what the butcher shop is occasionally used for. When a human body is carved up, the mixture of blood, bone, body fluids, and muscle leaves a terrible stench. That paint helps mask that smell whenever it is necessary. You know Marco Polo was the only man to ever leave there alive. I'll tell you more about him later on.

"It's time for me to reveal who X, Y, and Z really are. Mr.'s X and Y are Uncle Frankie's sons, and Mr. Z, 'The Butcher,' is Kenny Patane, or St. John. He is Evelyn and Leonardo's son. That same little boy that Hemmy brought over from Brooklyn. And yes, they were the three young men who stood at your father's casket so respectfully. They have faithfully worked for the family all these years. Because they were so highly skilled and trusted, they were given the most important assignment of all. That was to guard your life every week wherever you met your clients for as long as you were in my world. On the day that I had to send you to the stacks, the next two phone calls I made were to Mr.'s X and Y. They high tailed it to the office and were very busy dealing with real estate business when the law came sniffing around. At the same time, Mr. Z was showing a house to a client. I know that you have a lot to process, so I suggest that we make it an early night. You have had a very busy day sweetheart, get a good night's sleep. Come up tomorrow morning and have breakfast. I'll answer any questions that you might have and then I'll continue with the rest of the story."

"That's a good idea Uncle, I'm very tired. I'll come up tomorrow morning just as soon as I take my son's phone call. Thank you for getting my sentence terminated and for arranging my welcome home party. And most of all, I thank you for telling me the truth. I love you Uncle, goodnight."

After he went upstairs, I donned my PJs and hunkered down under the covers in my own bed for the first time in twenty-nine nights. Before I fell into a deep sleep, I went over every part of the shocking story that Uncle had finally started to reveal to me after all these years. I was trying to process who this man Leonardo was and the how and why he seemed to have taken a bullet for my father, then to find out that he had been married to Evelyn and that their son, Kenny, became the clean-up man for the family. I shook my head as I thought that I had known Evelyn all these years and never suspected that she was anything other than Big D's girlfriend. And I certainly never would have guessed in a million years that she was put in place at the store as a plant. Next, it was difficult for me to comprehend that a mafia war had been averted and that I had been instrumental in helping the family seek revenge all because I had been held hostage in a restaurant. Finally, I got such a kick at the way Uncle sent in the nurses which made it possible for me to go out and 'bet the farm' for the family.

Wow, I thought, that's one hell of a story. As I felt my eyelids getting heavy, I told myself that tomorrow wouldn't get here fast enough for me as I couldn't wait to hear the rest of it.

When I went up to the penthouse, I told Uncle that I hoped everything would be wrapped up by the weekend because I had just promised my son that I would try and shoot for it. After I finished my breakfast Uncle said, "It's that time, Kiki. I'm about to finish telling you what you have the right to know. At the time of your split with Bobby J, I made it very clear that you could never have contact with him or his family ever again nor could the Fontana name ever be repeated. Today, I'm going to change that decision because I now want you to know exactly what became of them before you move on with your life.

"Big D died of Pancreatic Cancer about two years after your divorce. In what seemed like no time, the store went under and Rose had a meltdown. Bobby J and Mario got busted for selling swag and did some time. None of the other siblings ever amounted to anything. When Bobby J got released from the Slam, he opened up a small store on his own and continues to hustle every day. It turned out to be a very sad ending for a bunch of spoiled wrongos.

"By the way, the young woman who caused the mistrial for Senior and Junior received a very lavish all-expense paid two-week honeymoon to Tahiti.

"On the one-year anniversary of the night Marco Polo put his hands on you, he committed suicide by putting a pistol in his mouth and blew his brains out. Turned out to be a very odd coincidence."

"Wait a minute Uncle, time out. You told me so many times that my father and you never believed in any such thing as a coincidence."

"You're correct, we did say that often. Oh well!"

"Understood Uncle, say no more."

"I'll move on to the one and only time you drove up to Harlem all by yourself to meet The Silver Fox. Mr. Z arrived before you and was parked right around the corner as he watched out for you. As you know an accommodation was reached that day so that you never had to return there.

"Next, I want to go back and tie up one last piece of the story that has to do with the business. The only place that you ever settled up in that wasn't sanctioned by the family was Mr. Whisper's Restaurant. The family couldn't allow that so we intervened and made sure that a special someone was put in there to watch over you on the night that you had to meet with the owner.

"One night, Judge Halpern and the Mayor were enjoying a sumptuous meal on the house. Mr. Whisper joined them at their table to thank them for frequenting his place of business. He told them how honored he was to have them. They seized the opportunity to do what they had been sent in there to do. The Mayor proceeded to tell him about a bartender who had glowing qualifications by the name of Deimos who was in need of a night job. They asked if he could be counted on to help them out by hiring their friend. He just about tripped over his feet to accommodate these two very influential gentlemen, if you get my meaning. Deimos started bartending there on the very next evening. You never told me about the events of the night that you went upstairs with Mr. Whisper. I wouldn't expect anything less from you. That's part of what makes you so stand-up. Of course, you didn't know that we placed Deimos in there to keep an eye on you. On the evening in question, he was listening on the other side of the door to the apartment while holding a 45 pistol in his hand. If Whisper had laid one hand on you, he would have busted in and put a bullet in his head. No one was ever going to put their hands on you again. He was ordered to protect you from any harm every time you went in that building. That about wraps up three quarters of the story. What do you think so far?"

"Well, this story has shock value beyond my wildest imagination. First of all, nobody is who I thought they were. I can maybe understand why I was trusted with so much of the family's money, after all, you owned that world. What I cannot comprehend is why I was protected and guarded by everyone my entire life as if I was made of gold or something. I'm not even Uncle Dom's niece, I'm his great niece and the daughter of a humble bartender. Uncle, please don't tell me that's it's because you were the biggest oddsmaker in this country. It just doesn't add up. There's a major piece to this story that is missing here. It's time you tell your little girl what's been going on for her entire life."

"Kiki, when your father was dying, he told you that I would have to be the one to tell you everything one day. He wanted to do that himself, but he knew that was never going to happen, so he left it up to me. It will all make perfect sense as soon as you take a deep breath so I can continue with the rest of 'the story.'

"On the day your baby brother died, your fate was sealed. The entire family did everything collectively to ensure that you would have a normal, happy, and protected life as you had become 'the golden child' on that day. I can't even try to remember how many times over the years I told you that nothing ever happened by chance in your entire life and now I'm about to tell you why Ms. Kiki Gallo-Cipo. It's because you are, and always have been, the Godfather's daughter."

"What did you just say? I'm not Hemmy's daughter? Don't you dare go there. I'm not Uncle Dom's daughter. This is crazy talk."

"Calm down, you've got it all backward. Uncle Dom was never the Godfather, your father was up until the day he died. I know you're having a tough time believing what I just said. I'm taking a five-minute break so you can get your bearings.

"Yolanda, crack open the bottle of Crystal that I've kept chilled for this special moment. I'm going to be the first person to raise a glass to the Godfather's daughter, to Kiki Cipo."

"Oh no that's not so. I'm the bartender's daughter."

"Oh yes, Kiki, you are the Godfather's daughter as well as the bartender's daughter. Sweetheart, Dominick was never the Don, not until your father passed away. He was made to pretend to be him at your father's insistence. It was so easy to pull it off because he was G.G.'s son so everyone automatically believed he took over as head of the Gallo family when the original Godfather died. Your father became the Don at only 26 years old during Prohibition. Before G.G. died, he called for a meeting and made it very clear that he was passing over his son in favor of his grandson because Hemmy was older and more mature. It was not a surprise move to Dominick as his father had already discussed it with him the year before.

"G.G. always knew that Hemmy was a much better leader and was more intelligent. He also had an exceptional way with people. Dom knew it also and agreed that it was in the best interest of the family. He was never opposed to it, offended by it or jealous of it. In fact, Dom and his sons worshipped your father. By now, you should be able to see clearly why you have been overly protected your entire life. G.G. was considered to be a great Don, but in the end, your father was said to have been even better.

"Hemmy chose to remain just a bartender because that's what he loved to do and it afforded him the perfect cover so that he could run his family under the radar of the law. He conducted all of the family business at his bar, first The Tioga and then at Cipo's. The story about Hemmy going back to the restaurant every night to count the till was nothing but bull. Hell, he could have done that the next morning. He went back every evening to preside over the Gallo family business. Only the Gallo's and his most trusted members were privy to the truth. All of the beef's were settled there and then his orders were dispensed by him from behind the bar. That is precisely why he couldn't accept the C.M.H. as too much publicity is attached to it.

"Your father discussed the transition of power with Dom after he received his cancer diagnoses. All of his plans for you and Angela were carefully spelled out. It was the family who bought Cipo's from your mother under the name of one of my many companies so that they could continue to conduct all of the family business at Hemmy's bar to this day. That was part of your father's plan. Hemmy was so good at masking his identity, that is probably why he never took one pinch in all those years.

"I guess you can now understand why we were all so destroyed when you were sentenced by Judge Moore. That was never supposed to happen. The thought that Hemmy's little girl had to go to jail in light of the fact that he never served one single day of jail time made us even more aware that we had failed him big time."

"It makes sense now. As the Godfather's daughter, I understand why everyone seemed to be protecting me as if they were my Guardian Angels. I guess that would explain why you practically insisted that I take care of Marco Polo myself. I'm going to move forward now. I'd like to ask some questions before you continue. You're the only person left whose true identity hasn't been revealed. My logic dictates that since I now know who my father was, then you must have always been his Consigliere. Am I correct Uncle?"

"Of course, Kiki. I was Hemmy's advisor and confidant long before he became the Godfather and I have continued in the same position for Dominick. As I can never completely retire from the family, when I make my home in Florida, my permanent home, I will always only be a paid phone call away from Dom and his sons should they ever need me. Sweetheart, do you have any other questions before I begin to wrap up the story?"

"Yes...who else knew that my father was The Godfather outside of the men in his family?"

"Evelyn knew for sure. If Leonardo had lived, he would have been a Capo right alongside of Frankie. He certainly knew who Hemmy was and as any good Capo would do, he wanted to protect him with his life which is exactly what he did when he took the bullet. That explains the close bond between Evelyn and the family for all these years. Aunt Esther has always known the truth. I would never keep that from my wife and my best friend knew it."

"Well Uncle, that leaves only one other person. Did my mother know who her husband was up until the time of his death?"

"Sweetheart that is probably the only question that I truly cannot answer. I asked your father if he was going to tell Angela right before they got married. He told me that he wanted to think long and hard about it. When he never brought the subject up again, I knew better than to ask. He kept that private. Angela has never uttered a single word about it one way or the other. Kiki, don't ever ask her, because if she doesn't know, you would open up a can of worms. If she does know, I'm sure she will tell you when she thinks the time is right. On the other hand, I suggest that it's in everyone's best interest if you go on as before and just pretend to be the 'bartender's daughter.'

"I want to end this story by using a line that I'm happy to say Hemmy stayed away from for most of his reign as the Godfather. The last time he had said it was in 1959, but that was on a smaller scale.

"I'm going back to 1938. Prohibition was over, so there was no money to be made in illegal booze. A certain 'family' was trying to take control of the waterfront which belonged to the Gallo's. Things were heating up.

"One day, while Dominick was at the tailor shop being fitted for a new suit, a Coca-Cola truck was coming up the street to make a delivery. Suddenly, the driver swerved to avoid hitting a little boy who had gotten away from his mother and ran into the street. Instead of hitting the child, the truck driver crashed into Dom's 1938 Cadillac V-16 Formal Town Car which exploded on impact with such force that some pieces of that big, heavy car were found a block away. Unfortunately, Dom's chauffeur, the truck driver, the little boy, and his mother were all killed by the blast. It's a good thing that Dom and the tailor were in the back room when the car exploded because all of the storefront windows on that side of the street were blown out.

"Within a few hours Hemmy got the word, it was determined that a bomb had been rigged underneath Dom's car. When the truck rammed into it, the bomb was set off ahead of schedule. Your father went ballistic and said to me, 'Have every one of my family Capos at my bar at midnight. It's not a request. Make sure they're not followed and tell them to come packing heavy.' After everyone was assembled, Hemmy started, 'Dom, those motherfuckers would have killed you if not for a freak accident. On top of that, they're trying to muscle in on our waterfront. It's just a matter of time before they come for each and every one of you. This bullshit ends now.'

"'I'm coming out from behind the bar, and you all know what that means. We are going to Mafia War. I want them all dead. Hunt them down and find them. We move tomorrow. Dom, I want you to tell all of my soldiers that you will consider fast tracking any of them that makes a hit, to become a made man. Then tell them that you will open up the books after the war is over. Frankie, I want you to personally take care of the Don, that scumbag, and make sure you leave the body where it will be found. I'm sending a message to the rest of the families.'

"I guess you could say that they were properly motivated because over forty bodies were found and quite a few others disappeared forever. When their godfather's body appeared floating in the Hudson River with a bullet in the back of his head, the war was over. It took less than a month.

"On the day that your son was born, which should have been one of the happiest days of Hemmy's life, all hell broke loose. Bobby left the hospital without even knowing that you had been rushed into emergency surgery and went straight to Caesar's Lounge where he cozied up to his redhead. Within five minutes of his arrival, Frankie took a call from the bartender at Caesar's informing him that Bobby had just arrived. Of course, your mother and father were at the hospital, along with Aunt Esther and me. Frankie sent one of the waiters over to the hospital with the update. When Hemmy was told, he became even more enraged because Bobby didn't stay at the hospital where he should have been. He roared that the level of disrespect shown to his little girl and the entire family would no longer be tolerated. He told me that he was going to 'come out from behind the bar' once more. He wanted the Fontana men and their family members who had put your marriage together in the first place, dead. Kiki, your father was the owner of Caesar's Lounge. That's how he always knew when your husband was there, but this was the last straw for him. I managed to hijack his rage, so to speak because I realized how stressed out he was while you were being operated on. So, I told him that I was positive that you would not want the father and grandfather of your newborn son to disappear. So he calmed down and decided not to do it. I've stood by that decision all these years, but now I want you to tell me if I did the right thing."

"Yes, you did. In spite of all the aggravation that those crazy Fontanas put me through, the fact remains, Bobby J gave me the only treasure that I will ever be able to have, and that counts for something."

"I think that covers the entire story, but before I ask you if you have any questions for me, I have one question for you that I've been curious about for thirteen years.

"On the day that I brought you into my world, I told you to find a safe hiding place for your work. Now I'd like to know where you hid it for all those years?"

"Well Uncle, when I was getting ready for bed that first night, as I looked down underneath the sink, there it was, a box on Tampax. I hid my work in the bottom of the box, underneath them. It made sense to me. After all, no man would ever go there. Hell, no man would ever mention the word, much less touch the box. I figured that it was the safest place in the entire apartment."

Uncle was laughing as he said, "Only a lady who possesses a magic wand would think like that, outside of the box. What a brilliant idea. That's my girl. Now, do you have any questions for me?"

"No, I've pretty much connected all of the dots now that I know who I was for all those years. You have told me quite a tale and I promise you and Uncle Dom that someday I will write a novel about the Gallo world and I will do it the way it should be done. It occurred to me that over the years I have been questioned by every law enforcement agency out there except for the K.G.B., M.I.6., and the C.I.A. If I have earned the moniker 'the most stand-up lady in New Jersey,' it's because you and my father are the men who took me there and opened the door for me to become 'the Legend in a world of nothing but men.' Isn't it ironic that on March 20th, 1931, the very first legal gambling license issued in the state of Nevada was given to the owner of the Northern Club located at 15 E Fremont Street, who just happened to be a woman named Mayme Stocker. Maybe it was pre-destined for both of us."

"Kiki every once in a lifetime, a bright shooting star flashes across the sky. You are that star and you did it all on your own. So much happened on your shift that cannot be explained. It usually happened on your lucky #3 where you laid -2.5 and took +3.5 and caught the middle to win both ways. To see that once or twice would be the norm, but seven or eight times, no way. It worked out just fine for the family. There really must have been some magic in the room on the day that you were born."

Uncle was smiling as he walked over to me, kissed me on the top of my head and said, "I would caution everyone who ever meets you, 'handle with care, contents priceless!'

"Take this suitcase, it contains the $3,000,000.00 that Dom and I put up to 'keep you out of jail' and then to 'get you out.' We replaced anything that we used. Now, it's time. We want you to get on with the exciting business of living. You've earned it. Well done, Kiki. Well done!"

The End

"Broadway" Joe Namath and Tootsie

www.ingramcontent.com/pod-product-compliance
Ingram Content Group UK Ltd.
Pitfield, Milton Keynes, MK11 3LW, UK
UKHW022228230426
12048UKWH00016BA/1123